# Praise for *East*

"She writes with the clarity and delicacy of butterfly wings. Most of these enthralling stories are located in India, a country and people that Catherine loves and knows with the deepest understanding"
**– Roshan Seth, Actor**

"Rich and gripping, superbly written– and moving"
**– Muzaffar Chishti,
New York University Center on Immigration**

"Authentic, insightful, and informative"
**– Chip Beck, author of *The Alamo Conspiracy***

"Truly gifted"

**– Patricia Gaul, Actress**

"A great storyteller …highly insightful and impartial … unique, wonderfully written and enchanting. Not only worth reading, but reading again and reading aloud to others"
**– Ravi Ravindra, Ph.D, author of *The Bhagavad Gita:
A Guide to Navigating the Battle of Life***

"Memorable stories …so different from each other in theme and characters –yet each located in that place in the heart where east and west meet. Beautifully transporting and evocative"

**– Betty Sue Flowers, Ph.D., editor,
Joseph Campbell's *The Power of Myth***

"In the best tradition of storytelling in India. A modern classic. Seemingly covering the entirety of Indian culture, values, current events, and philosophy, the fifteen stories in this collection will long be treasured.  Catherine Ann Joness' dharma is storytelling"
> – R.E.Mark Lee, author, *World Teacher:*
> *The Life and Teachings of J. Krishnamurti*

"Shows how how deeply Catherine Ann Jones understands our Indian ways and cultural heritage. ... visceral experience ... emotions captured and expressed ... beautifully nuanced, with a deep understanding of the human psyche. These delightful stories are like a fresh-water shower"
> – Meena Kaushik, Ph.D. and CEO of Quantum
> Consumer Solutions,  Bangalore, India

"Exceptional stories of India, gently spun.... A trip to India on a quiet afternoon..."
> – Arthur Kornhaber, M. D., author of
> *Spirit: Mind, Body, and the Will to Existence*

"Heart wrenching, beautifully told, and tragically based in truth"
> – Kitty Winn, Actress

"Tranquility, peace, and kindness – though suspense, grief and reality too. When I finished reading *East & West*, I sat motionless for several moments, feeling the

wisdom and beauty of the portrayal. Excellent stories of India. A memorable work of art"
                                        **– Dianne Skafte, Ph.D., author,**
                                        *Listening to the Oracle*

"Beautiful settings and poignant descriptions of all that is perceived – both inner and outer; the known and the unknown; duality and non–duality; Neti Neti and Tat Tvam Asi. Interweaves history and culture with the story – making India a character in itself. Powerful and intimate. Beautiful. An unflinching portrayal of western influences on India's culture, reflected through the lives of her fictional characters. A must read"
                                        **– Dana Macy, author of**
                                        *Fragments of a Fragmented Life*

"Brilliant! In these fifteen short stories, the eminent writer and global teacher Catherine Ann Jones takes us on a sentient journey into the diverse past and present soul of India - from tea plantations in Assam, devout chaos on the banks of the Ganges, cosmopolitan Delhi, to the humid, traditional South. All come alive in this fine collection, leaving us wanting more"
                                        **– Robert Walker, London, England**

# Other Books by Catherine Ann Jones

*The Way of Story: The Craft & Soul of Writing*
*Heal Your Self with Writing*
*What Story Are You Living?*
*Freud's Oracle*
*True Fables: Stories from Childhood*
*Buddha and the Dancing Girl: A Creative Life*
*Remarkable Women: Four Plays*

# Plays & Screenplays by Catherine Ann Jones

## TELEVISION
*Child of Destiny* (Last Queen of Hawaii)
*It's Only Women* (The Dalkon Shield Scandal) NBC
*Death of an Innocent Child* (starring Ellen Burstyn)
*Summertime* (Hallmark Hall of Fame)
*Touched by an Angel* (series episodes)

## FILM & CABLE
*The Pact*
*Sammy and Son* (Universal feature)
*Wolfbride*
*Poe: The Dark Angel*
*The Christmas Wife* (starring Jason Robards, Julie Harris) – HBO, 4 Emmy Nominations
*Unlikely Angel* (starring Dolly Parton) – CBS
*Angel Passing* (co-writer), (starring Hume Cronyn, Calista Flockhart) – 15 Awards

## PLAYS
*Freud's Oracle*
*Calamity Jane*
*Calamity Jane the Musical* (Best Production 2015)
*The Women of Cedar Creek* (NY Drama League Award, Beverly Hills Th. Guild Award)
*The Myth of Annie Beckman*
*On the Edge: The Final Years of Virginia Woolf* (NEA Award)
*Somewhere-in-Between*
*Difficult Friends*
*The Hill*
*The Friend*
*A Fairytale for Adults*
*Always a Tomorrow*

# EAST & WEST
## Stories of India

# CATHERINE ANN JONES

*Introduction by* DIANNE SKAFTE

**Pippa Rann**
books & media

**Pippa Rann**
books & media

*An imprint of*
Salt Desert Media Group Limited,
7 Mulgrave Chambers, 26 Mulgrave Rd,
Sutton SM2 6LE, England, UK.
Email: publisher@pipparannbooks.com
Website: www.pipparannbooks.com

ISBN 978-1-913738-88-4

Designed and typeset by raghavdesign.com

Printed and bound at Replika Press Pvt. Ltd, India

MIX
Paper from
responsible sources
FSC® C016779

*The whole of life can be a meditation – even writing.*

SRI ADWAYANANDA

*Fiction is the lie through which we tell the truth.*
ALBERT CAMUS

# Contents

# Introduction
by Dianne Skafte

$\mathcal{S}$hortly after my 13th birthday, I summoned my courage and walked into a travel agency. I couldn't have done it without the support of my best friend, who shared the enchantment that claimed me. We must have looked peculiar to the man behind the counter. Our hair was pulled back into long braids, we wore improvised saris that only approximated the real thing, and the lipstick *tikkas* adorning our foreheads were starting to melt.

"How can I get a ticket to India?" I asked in a quavering voice.

"Where in India?" He was trying not to smile.

"Anywhere!" My friend and I breathed the word in unison, at which the agent lost control and burst out laughing.

I look back on this moment with amusement yet also with wonder. What is it about India that captures our imaginations so powerfully? Yes, the region offers countless treasures of history, culture, and beauty, but other countries of the world can claim these merits. I believe that India possesses a rare quality I call, "archetypal shine." Archetypes are psychological motifs shared by all human beings in one form or another. Coming of age, learning from a teacher, falling in love, standing up to tyranny--these templates of experience (and countless others) give meaning to our existence. They elevate the events of daily life into stories with universal significance.

India's mosaic of archetypal symbols is so varied and multi-splendored that its light dazzles the mind. One suddenly believes that anything is possible. In the creative collision of ideas, old structures crumble and new realities are born. Innovations arise that change the course of human history. As the scholar and philologist Max Muller said, "If I were asked under what sky the human mind has most fully developed some of its choicest gifts, has most deeply pondered on the greatest problems of life, and has found solutions...I should point to India."

Against the backdrop of my romance with India's myth and mystery, I received an unexpected surprise. Catherine Ann Jones asked me to read her newly-completed book of short stories of India. I had long been a fan of the author's books, stage plays, movie scripts, and seminars. So, I looked forward to enjoying her latest work. I knew I would find the rich interweaving of psychological insight, spirituality, and great storytelling that characterizes all of Jones's writing.

But I also looked forward to this experience for a more personal reason. This author had forged an intimate relationship with the country I loved from afar. Every winter for over 30 years, she returned to her second home in South India to meditate and study with a revered spiritual master. At the age of nineteen, she had fallen in love with and married Raja Rao, a renowned Indian novelist born in Karnataka. They later had a son and lived fascinating lives on two continents. "Here is someone who knows India from the inside as well as the outside," I thought to myself. "Here is someone who can deepen our understanding of this land and its people."

My own study of oracle traditions around the world attuned me to a feature of these stories that has special meaning. The word "oracle" derives from the Latin *orare,* meaning "to speak." To receive an oracle is to be spoken to by a sacred agency that offers guidance or illumination. Signs, prayers, dreams, and the arts of divination have, from the earliest times, given us inspiration to surmount obstacles. They whisper assurance that we are never alone, for Something Greater knows who we are and can show us the way forward.

In a similar manner, the *Stories of India* take place on multiple levels of reality. Themes from ancient mythology are woven into worldly events. Forces of destiny thwart one's desire then open splendid new gateways. Ardent love from a past incarnation reaches across the centuries and heals a wound of the heart. Uncanny dreams warn of danger ahead. For me, following these stories was like watching a drama unfold on the stage, then looking up at a higher platform and seeing the gods enacting a play of their own.

This collection of short stories vividly reveals facets of Indian life that range from sublime mystical encounters to the vilest acts of human depravity. They introduce us to characters we would never encounter during a casual visit to the country, such as the homeless orphan girl who possesses a profound connection to Divine Presence, and the lowly plantation worker who carries heartbreaking secrets as she mirrors the plight of countless other victims today. Stereotypes about monastic life fall away when we encounter Threptin Choden, a young Tibetan monk with a surprising destiny awaiting him. And what would it be like to step off a bus on an ordinary afternoon and suddenly find yourself in another dimension of reality, where deities from Hindu mythology come alive? All is revealed as "The Hill" takes us on an extraordinary adventure. Never again could I picture Indian life in flat storybook colors, for Catherine Ann Jones had shown me complex portraits of humanity ribboned with strands of dark and light.

Yet India is more than its people. One must experience sights, sounds, and feelings to experience a land. Reading these stories, I could hear mosquitoes droning in tropical Kerala and feel the crisp ice air of the alpine Himalayas. I appreciated the way Jones often mentions the food her characters enjoyed in their daily lives. "I ate a hearty breakfast of roti and potato curry with hot coffee mixed with buffalo milk and sugar," one woman mentions casually. It was interesting to learn about green gram, idly, coconut chutney, bhindi, and other foods that were little known to me.

I found special delight in the sensory complexity that Jones brings to her description of locales. For instance, in "The Ashram", a young American woman visits Varanasi, where Hindu pilgrims come to die or have their ashes scattered in the sacred Ganges River. We can well understand Kayla's feelings of tremulous awe as she encounters a universe of "layers behind layers confusedly blended into One."

I walked with intimidation in the streets, the sounds of temple drums, cymbals, and chanting of Sanskrit *slokas* mingled with the smell of lit camphor, incense, and spices sold in the crowded markets. Near the Ghats where people bathed in the holy Ganga, purifying their souls, I noticed colorful graffiti murals on the walls: Shiva, standing on the demon of ignorance, dancing the dance of life and death, and another large, overpowering mural of a naked sadhu (one who has renounced worldly life) standing, holding a skull in his hands, with raised arms reaching to heaven. Another reminder that death comes to us all.

One reads fiction not only to absorb experiences, but to expand one's knowledge. I had hoped that *Stories of India* would enrich me with glimpses into India's rich cultural heritage, and this wish was generously fulfilled. "My Life as a Devadasi" presents fascinating historical details about the devadasi tradition in which young girls were dedicated to the temple and worshipped The Divine (Deva) all of their lives by playing classical music, performing traditional dances, and sometimes serving as "sacred prostitutes" for noble patrons of the temple. In the story of "Tea with Mrs. Gandhi", I learned about the inspiring and sometimes grim political realities of India while Indra Gandhi was prime minister. "The Philosopher" includes rich descriptions of the Ajanta Caves and legends associated with them. Jones' description of an ancient *Theyyam* ritual dance performance is so vivid that one feels transported thousands of years back in time.

After reading Catherine Ann Jones's book, I sat in silence and reflected on what I had gained from her fifteen diverse stories of India. I became aware of how my understanding had increased in depth and breadth. Not only did I make the acquaintance of characters worth knowing, I absorbed rich details about Indian history, mythology, and experiences of daily life. Seeing India's contrasts of dark and light that only increased the brilliance of its timeless 'archetypal shine'.

I recalled again that teenage girl standing at the ticket counter with a smudged *tikka* on her forehead, reaching for a mystery beyond her understanding. She knew few details about the land she longed for, but perhaps her instincts were right after all. India's soul contains stories within stories, a million layers deep. Strange and familiar, ancient and contemporary, human and divine, they beckon us to know them so that we may better know ourselves. *Stories of India* opens a gateway to wonders we will long remember.

Dianne Skafte, Ph.D., is the author of *Listening to the Oracle* (Harper, San Francisco, 1997.)

# Preface

*The world is made up of stories – not atoms.*

Muriel Rukeyser

Stories orient the life of a people through time, establishing the reality of their world. Thus, meaning and purpose are given to people's life. Without stories, we do not exist. They are how we discover who we are.

This particular collection of stories is imagined though sometimes inspired by fact. They came about because of a marriage that carried me away to far-off India, which, in time, became my spiritual home. India is a vast and complex country and one that can change a life, containing the highest mystical experiences side by side with the lowest dregs of humanity. From my own experience of living many years in India, the sublime mythology of this incredible and complex culture so permeates the personal that myth often becomes reality – and reality, myth.

> Ancient countries and people are brought in, ideas from all climes and epochs mingle; myth, romance, and realism make up a single whole. For here the state is the human mind of all times.
>
> Sri Aurobindo, *Collected Poems and Plays*

The aim of these stories is to serve as a kind of portal into the daily lives and emotional realities that reflect the rich depth and humanity that is India.

Catherine Ann Jones
Ojai, California

~ 1 ~

# The Cat Who Would Not Die

*I love cats because I enjoy my home;*
*and little by little they become its visible soul.*

Jean Cocteau

Gurgaon District near Delhi lies on the Sahibi River, a tributary of Yamuna. In India's great epic *Mahabharata*, Gurgaon is described as the village of Guru Dronacharya, the revered teacher of the Kauravas and the Pandavas who fought the great war. So it was that Gurgaon is even today known as 'the village of the guru'. However, modern times have changed much. After the major American company, General Electric, in 1997, other large corporations followed, such as Coca-Cola, Pepsi, and BMW. Now, giant shopping malls sprawl the land where one and a half million privileged residents have settled and shopped.

It is July in Gurgaon, hot and humid with a temperature of 40 degrees C. Everyone impatiently awaits the coming monsoon. Kamala lives alone in her fine house after long years of marriage and a nasty divorce. Her children have grown up and away, busy with their own lives – some with children of their own. They all live in New Delhi which is more exciting for them. Though traditionally not the Indian way, Kamala was surprised to discover that she did not mind living alone. She enjoyed the peace and quiet and being able at last to do whatever she wanted to do and at the time she wanted to do it. She could eat when she was hungry, and no longer have to think of what others needed. It was a simple life. A good life, mostly. Though late at night, her thoughts would sometimes roam, thinking of the husband who had found solace in a younger woman. At first, she had tried to be angry – even jealous – but she failed, for she could only feel the loneliness that sometimes prowled around her in the night as a silent tiger seeking its prey.

One day Kamala sat in her garden with her favorite breakfast of soft, pillowy steamed iddlies and coconut chutney. In the *Indian Express* she read about a clothes designer from Delhi who had retired and built a sprawling refuge for abandoned cats. The woman would go out and find feral cats living on the streets, and collect them ensuring they were well and had the necessary shots for people to adopt them. Curious, Kamala decided to visit the cat refuge and see if it was as interesting as the newspaper said it was. A small lizard startled her as it scampered near the food tray. "Oh," she cried, "Let's see what you will do when there's a cat around."

It was a short drive from her home in Gurgaon district to the small village just outside Delhi. There were eighty plus cats living in the refuge. To keep them safe from predators such as circling hawks, various cat residences had been built high up in the air. An enclosed runway connected them so that the cats could walk or run and visit other cat lodgings. It was indeed an interesting place, a cat village unto itself with tall fishtail and coconut palm trees providing some shade for the shelters and a sense of calm protection. It reminded Kamala of how her father had loved cats and would sit on the floor eating his lunch on a fresh green banana leaf carefully making balls of rice and yogurt, then tossing them to two unnamed pet cats who waited patiently for their treat. Her father was three years gone now. He had died as quietly as he had lived, simply going to sleep and not waking up. How like Appa not to cause any bother to anyone. Somehow this morning, it seemed that his devotion to cats had lingered and lived on in his daughter, for Kamala too, had always loved cats. Her husband's asthma had prohibited having pets, and after some time, she had put them out of her mind.

Nini, the former clothes designer with short hair and simple attire first warned her that she didn't let just anyone adopt her cats, but felt instinctively that Kamala would be a suitable guardian. Kamala smiled, and then Nini showed her a female calico cat who had given birth four weeks earlier to a litter found in the street – born wild. As the kittens were too young to be separated from their mother, Kamala was told that she could have the first pick of the litter yet could not take the kitten for another two weeks as they were too young to be separated from their mother. Kamala took her time watching the mother cat and her five kittens. They were all quite different from one another and she learned that they had had different fathers. It seems that cats and dogs can have different fathers in the same litter. Only after several minutes did Kamala make her choice. He was the most beautiful of the kittens, and looked a pure Russian Blue breed, exactly as his father must have been. Soft light grey short hair with striking green eyes, his manner was shy, cautious. Having made her choice and paid a reasonable fee, which covered neutering and vaccinations, she left with the understanding to return in two weeks to collect her new pet.

With a clear purpose now, Kamala shopped for a cat bowl, water distributor, litter box, and even an adorable toy mouse with bells. Paying for her purchases, she went next door and ordered a mango lassi. Surprising herself, she told the proprietor that she had just adopted a kitten, though it was not like Kamala to talk to strangers like that.

Two weeks later, after thanking Nini, she carried the kitten home. She called him Sasha, as he was a Russian Blue.  At first, Sasha would hide under the bed and stay there for hours. Kamala had all the time to be patient and talk softly to her new companion. Slowly, Sasha would crawl out from under the bed and find his water bowl and Kibble waiting for him in an adjacent stainless-steel bowl. Gradually Kamala and Sasha became used to one another and one day, surprisingly, Sasha jumped into Kamala's lap as she sat reading the newspaper. Soon after, one night, Sasha decided to sleep on the bed next to his new mistress and continued to do so from then on.

Kamala found herself eager to return home after shopping in order to share whatever she saw or heard that day with Sasha. He would sit very still and look directly into her eyes, listening to every word, so it was easy to believe that he understood all that she said. When her children invited her to visit them in Delhi, she would say, "Oh, dear, I would but I cannot leave Sasha." So, after a while, they stopped inviting her, explaining how they or their children were so busy in Delhi that driving over to her was not a choice. Kamala understood and didn't really mind.

Three years passed quietly and contentedly for both Kamala and Sasha, until one hot summer day, she noticed that Sasha's eyes were dull and he was lying down more than usual. Even when she opened a can of sardines and called him to come, he still would not stir.

"Sasha, dear, what is wrong?" He raised his head and looked at her then – as if it were too heavy for him – rested his head on his paws again. Kamala gently gathered the cat into her arms, placed him in a small cat carrier and drove to the vet. Dr Karma told her that it was stomach cancer and it would be best to put Sasha down. Kamala couldn't speak at first then drawing her shoulders back, she said, "Thank you, Dr. Karma, but we shall seek a second opinion."

Three days later, as Sasha could no longer eat, drink, or walk, and after seeking a second opinion, Kamala reluctantly agreed to end his suffering. Returning to the original vet, she stood next to Sasha at the end, holding him as the cat never took his eyes from his mistress. The ever-patient Dr. Karma administered the fatal injection as Kamala wept more than she had even for her late father. Later Gopal, the gardener, helped her bury him in the back garden in front of a small statue of Krishna. She had Gopal plant white jasmine vines on the fence behind the Krishna statue.

Two nights after Sasha died as Kamala lay in bed in the dark, she distinctly felt a cat walk across her legs as Sasha had done so many times before. This clearly felt like him, the same weight and gentle, hesitant steps. However, she rationally thought, "Oh, it's probably a bold mouse, or some other creature." Kamala turned on the light, and could find nothing in the room anywhere. The same occurrence happened several times in the following weeks. There was no doubt in her mind that it was Sasha's spirit. Sasha, whose love was stronger even than death.

Kamala would now have her tea in the back garden near the Krishna statue where Sasha lay buried. The jasmines were blooming, and their seductive aroma filled the air. The lizards had returned as there was no longer any threat. She continued to talk to Sasha every day and felt he heard her. The memory of him had become as strong as his actual presence had once been.

One day, Kamala smiled as she put down her tea cup, and as tears ran down her cheek, she said, "Dear Sasha, you will never leave me. I know that husbands and children may leave, but you will never leave me." Somehow, the silence that followed reassured her and though alone again, she did not mind as her heart was full. Though it occurred less often now, on some dark nights, Kamala would be awakened by a small body walking hesitantly across her feet, as she lay in bed. This occurrence no longer frightened her, for she knew beyond doubt that it was her own dear Sasha – and that not even death could keep him away from his mistress.

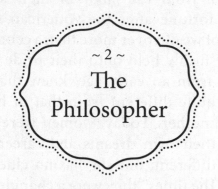

~ 2 ~

# The Philosopher

*We never stay the same person.*
*We change as we grow old.*
*The things that happen to us make us different*
*people. It's part of the story of our life.*

William Boyd, *Any Human Heart*

ℒeila was nineteen and a seeker. Having left organized religion the year before, she now voraciously read both western and eastern philosophies, inherently believing that there were answers to those universal questions somewhere, somehow. "Who am I? What has meaning? Where is my purpose?" Born in New Orleans, she was a southern girl from aristocratic ancestors who had grown rich from the labor of their slaves then lost their fortune after the American Civil War. Deprived of wealth over more than a century before, the family firmly held onto their pride of lineage. Yet Leila, from an early age, knew that her path would be quite different from that of her mother and grandmother. Today, women were beginning to follow their own dreams and careers. Her life would be different, but she has no clue what that might be. The times "they were a changin'," and the young were in revolt, distrusting government, and hungry for answers born of the raging tumult they felt within.

One afternoon on campus, Leila now in her junior year, noticed a poster near the Student Union with a striking photograph of a philosopher from India speaking that evening on Buddhism and Hinduism. Four hours later, she sat at the back of a large classroom overflowing with other students, desperate for alternative solutions. The speaker had a powerful presence, and though he spoke softly, the silence was profound as the crowd listened with their hearts as well as their questioning minds. Leila had noticed the young man, who sat at the back of the room near her, and how disturbed he seemed. At one point, the disheveled young man stood up and shouted, "Tell me this. Why shouldn't I commit suicide?" A hush filled the room as the audience held their breath, waiting for what the philosopher would say. The pause was long. Then patiently, the Philosopher looked up and gently yet firmly responded, "Yes, that's exactly what I want you to do – but not the body. Kill the ego." It transformed the young man on the spot and his face seemed to glow from within. Others began to cry as they breathed a sigh of relief. Something was happening in America, in this very room, and though none could name it, all present knew without knowing that something real was happening. It was the first of ten lectures the visiting philosopher would offer and Leila came each week, always sitting at the back of the room, seriously taking notes yet never venturing to ask a single question.

The day after the tenth lecture, Leila was at the local public television station on campus where she performed in a children's show each week, portraying a little girl in an enchanted forest. As she was leaving, she noticed that a man was interviewing the Indian philosopher, in the adjoining studio, so she stepped into the studio control booth and watched the interview. When it ended, she quietly slipped away. Leila was surprised when the Philosopher called out to her, "Pardon me, but didn't I see you at my lectures?" Shyly, Leila nodded. The Philosopher then said, "Tonight, there will to be a dinner for me as I leave tomorrow. My friends and I would be happy if you would come." Thereupon, without waiting for her response, he wrote down the address and time." Leila thanked him and hastily departed, wondering if she dared go.

Later in her apartment, at the last minute, she dressed and ordered a taxi to attend the farewell dinner, at an address that turned out to be only a fifteen-minute drive from campus. Up a steep hill and set back from the road was a modest house with a large wooden deck at the back, overlooking the west hills. Several students and a few professors mingled on the deck as the sun was setting. She met an Englishman born in Calcutta who taught art at the University and his welcoming Swiss -German wife who were hosting the dinner, they had met the Philosopher some years earlier in England. The Philosopher waved to her to come and sit next to him. He was smiling and now, seeing him close up, Leila noticed that though he was much older, he was quite handsome, with thick black hair covering more than half his neck, and magnetic eyes, the dark pupils encircled by a silver-bluish ring. He was about her height, slender, and wore a black Nehru jacket, white western shirt, and black trousers. Leila also noted that though seemingly modest, the Philosopher had a distinct air of confidence as one could only achieve from discovering who he was.

"I have seen you at each of the ten lectures sitting at the back of the room and taking notes yet not once did you ask a question. So, do you have any questions for me now?"

Hesitantly, in a shy voice, Leila answered, "Yes sir, I have seventeen questions." The Philosopher erupted into spontaneous laughter, "Seventeen questions. Seventeen questions!" And so, the dialogue between seeker and master began. Leila learned that the Philosopher was born a Brahmin in south India, and on a scholarship, studied at Oxford University in England then had lived abroad for many years. He spoke of the philosophy behind Hinduism called Advaita Vedanta. Advaita meant 'non-dual' so all is one – not two. It believes that any god is subordinate to the impersonal Pure Consciousness that pervades everything. He said, with humor, "It's all right to be born in a temple as long as you don't die there. In other words, religion is the stepping stone to a higher philosophy." Leila sighed and could not speak. She felt deeply that at long last, she had come home. Here were the answers she had sought for years and years. The other guests had discreetly withdrawn, and gone inside, leaving the two in deep communion. Time passed unnoticed. Much later, the guests began to leave, and the Philosopher told Leila to come the next morning to the Faculty Club where he was staying.

The next day, skipping class, Leila walked briskly across campus to the Faculty Club to his room. The English professor and his Swiss wife were there and gave no impression of surprise that Leila would be included. The Philosopher was wearing a bright purple sweater hand-knitted in England. The bright color made his brown skin shine. Two suitcases lay open: one with a few clothes, all identical black trousers and jacket, white cotton shirts, and the second full of manuscripts and books. It was all so natural being there that Leila felt it was not the beginning of a relationship but rather a continuation of an existing union from long ago. She wondered if the Philosopher might feel the same, but she dared not ask.

Leila did not see the Indian philosopher for a year. She experienced her first trip to Europe, studying there for two months. Yet from time to time, she would think of the Philosopher, of the blue-white rings around his black pupils, and wonder if he would ever return.

She was often invited to the home of the English professor and his wife in the hills west of town, for they had become for her a family away from home. Once on her birthday, they had invited her to celebrate, and the Swiss wife had chosen a flowering peach tree planted next to their home, a tree which they named the Leila tree. Later during dinner, the Philosopher called from Europe and when told she was present, asked to speak with her. He said he would be coming to lecture in the spring and hoped to see her.

And so, the Philosopher returned the following spring of her senior year, and called her, inviting her to dinners where they engaged in long discussions. He told her that her name was also an Indian name though spelled differently. In Sanskrit, *Leela* means a divine play. They shared the sensation of having always known the other and basked in a silent understanding of what may have happened between them. Leela – a divine play. So, a few weeks later when he asked her to marry him, there was really no decision, no doubt. It was as though their union was already in place as an unstoppable river. One only had to embrace the flow. The lives of seekers seldom travel in straight lines. Their paths often diverge on what may become a precarious yet exciting adventure.

At her graduation, she invited her parents to meet the Philosopher over dinner. Later, after returning home, when Leila informed her Southern Protestant family that she would marry the Philosopher, they were stunned. "He is too old." "He is not a Christian." "His skin is dark" Even her sweet grandmother told her, "Leila, you must know if you ever had a child, you could never bring a black child home." Racism can enter even the sweetest of hearts. It was useless when Leila tried to explain that east Indians were not Black but an ancient Aryan race. Seeing that Leila was resolute, both her mother and grandmother wept. Leila told them, "You may be right in that the marriage will not last. All I know is that it is true now, and if I don't act on what is true at each moment then my whole life is a lie." How simple everything seems at twenty!

Leila left the following day, flying to New York, where her future husband awaited her. They flew to Europe and were wed. Leila became pregnant the first week of the honeymoon and gave birth to a son when she had turned twenty-one. It would be a year after their marriage before she learned that the Philosopher had no money, and in fact, the first job in his life was lecturing at the American university where they had met. Fortunately, the university had invited him to be a full professor in philosophy. Returning to the south, her family met their first grandchild and great grandchild, a boy, and they softened toward their dark-skinned son-in-law. Love had triumphed after all.

The early years of her son's life were magical as Leila had effortlessly put aside her ambition to have a career as a writer. Her pride and fulfillment now lay in her husband and their son. The Philosopher won accolades for his books on philosophy and was in demand to lecture at various universities. His classes would overflow with other, younger seekers. Leila's happiness rested in doing her *dharma*, a concept she had learned from the Philosopher. Dharma is not only duty but the law of one's existence. As said in India, "It's better to be a good wife than a bad king."

He also told her that, "For a woman, surrender is the path to bliss." She wondered at this, yet the desire to plunge deeply into this love overcame any hesitation.

In time, Leila gradually ceased to exist as a separate individual. She had become one with her beloved. These next few years were indeed pure bliss. That is, until she grew up.

The Philosopher's classes were always full and students flocked afterward to his office. Leila was left alone more and more, then slowly discovered that her dear husband was distracted by younger women. At first, she could not believe it until one day she found that her friend, Celia, was pregnant. The Philosopher attempted to persuade her friend to get rid of the baby, and when she refused, he announced that he would have nothing to do with the child. Celia kept apart, bore the child – a boy - and never married.

In this way, Leila learned that even great men have their shadow side. At this time, Leila began to travel and pursue her ambition to write. Strangely, at first, the separations seemed to make their bond stronger. The Philosopher now encouraged her to find her way and though she had to earn her living, she did. They began a commuting marriage when her career carried her to New York, and they often met in Europe or India at various conferences where the now-famous philosopher was invited. Years passed and though still fond of one another, each found temporary solace in the arms of others. Leila's maturity made her more realistic as now she had learned that sometimes love is not enough – that you can love another yet not live with them. She delayed the inevitable for a few years until their son was older.

On one of her many visits to India, Leila met a Sage in southern India who lived a simple, reclusive life with his wife and children. He was called the Householder Sage as he did not renounce family life. He did not seek fame or fortune yet his modest light shined so bright that seekers would be drawn to him.

Leila, too, had heard of him and one afternoon found her way to his village home. From the first moment she saw him, she knew her search had ended. Before he uttered a word, his very presence quelled her longing. His words were imbued with the power of this presence as when he said, "Do not talk to me about past and future – they exist only in your mind." Leila experienced a clarity she had never before known. Though her philosopher husband had said many similar and wise words to her, they had failed to carry the power she experienced now. She realized that it was not the philosophy or the words alone that held the power to transform, but rather the one who spoke those words. It was the presence of the Sage that had made the experience complete. Leila stayed on for several months and learned to open and listen with her whole being.

"You ask what is Truth, but you cannot see it because you look too far away from yourself.

Truth is not outside; it is your innermost being. Once experienced, you will find it in all places and at all times."

Leila listened and listened until there were no more questions. She listened until the missing piece so long sought was found. She listened until she had returned to herself.

Leila continued to return each year to south India, often with her son, to visit the Householder Sage. Her son, now seventeen, had begun himself to ask questions of the Sage.

On this particular return, Leila had an unusual experience while standing near a holy river in Kerala. The Sage had told her the story, and it had become one of her favorites. Lord Shiva had given Ravana in his previous life a choice. "You may return as a good man and then must live another ten lives. Or you may return as a ten-headed monster in order to be defeated by the god-king, Rama, and show his victory over evil. Only then will you be freed from rebirth. By the grace of Lord Shiva, you will attain moksha (liberation). Ravana at once accepted the role of the evil ten-headed monster as his duty to attain liberation – for dharma demands that all beings must play their role in the great Leela of life.

Immersed in the humidity and sensuality of tropical south India, which is in itself a living dream, Leila was not surprised when two five-foot- long cobras slowly approached each other. Standing about six feet away, Leila watched them for over an hour, as the serpents danced the ancient mating game. Their tails intertwined while the upper bodies, facing each other, swayed to the hidden music of Eastern erotica. It was no less than the cosmic dance of Shiva – enticing and sublime.

Two village girls excitedly and fearfully gestured that Leila should come away quickly and go inside the house. She listened as they told her a remarkable story. Five years before in nearby Arunmula, a five-year-old boy playing near the ancient Arunmula Temple also came upon two cobras mating. The little boy threw stones at them when suddenly the male cobra reared its head and stared straight at the boy in a piercing manner. The little boy laughed while the cobras returned to their mating dance and the child ran away and thought little of it afterward. However, late that very night, as the young village boy lay in a one room hut with his family, all sleeping in the same room, that same male cobra found the boy, bit him, and killed him. Understandably, Leila was urged not to disturb the cobras and to keep her distance. She slowly returned to the scene though not so close this time and stood quietly, lest she disturb the poisonous serpents.

Mesmerized, the time flew. Later, after two hours of sexual delight, the two serpents shot upward in rocket orgasm, then slowly, slowly uncoiled, slithering away in opposite directions!

Leila took this as a sign of questioning her marriage that she had been struggling with for several months. The answer was now clear: what is sublime and true may reach its purpose, and afterward, those, once bound, may —as in nature — unbind and go their separate paths. Let each moment be sufficient unto itself. And when over, allow the simple act of going one's own separate way, without judgment or regret. Such can be true of marriage, where sex and bliss, positive and negative residues reside, sometimes giving birth to a new life.

Though they would never know how they changed her life, Leila vowed that she would be forever grateful to those two wonderful cobras! She understood now that divorce need not mean that the marriage was a failure, only that it was time to go separate ways, as did those amazing serpents under the swaying coconut trees in south India.

Returning to New York, Leila's son, now having turned eighteen, was soon off to university. At exactly the right time, Leila asked for a divorce as she had found love again, and the man, who was of her own generation, wished to marry. It was he who insisted she divorce while her philosopher husband resisted. The Philosopher knew that his marriage to Leila now conveniently suited his lifestyle. In other words, he could 'play' without the burden of commitment.

Leila flew to the university where her husband still taught. As they had for many years, she and the

Philosopher took a long walk across campus. After walking by the university library, Leila told her husband that she would always care for him despite the heartbreak, and she was never, ever bored being with him. This fanned his vanity, and he finally agreed to the divorce. Leila returned to New York and her fiancé, and hired an attorney. The legal action was swift with no demands from either side.

Yet before long, Leila awoke one morning and knew beyond doubt that she no longer wanted to marry her fiancé – or indeed anyone. Devotion to the Sage had become a portal to a love far greater than any she had ever experienced – one that transcended even the love for a husband or a child. India had awakened her to an unconditional love asking nothing in return. Leila was born with a question mark in her soul, always wanting to know, only to discover – through the grace of the Sage – that "Love is knowing with one's whole being."

Her life was full. She had made good friends and had focused on her career, gaining recognition and success. Invited to teach at a university, she enjoyed being with the students. Her son was doing well at university and returned to her for holidays and summers.

Not surprisingly, the Philosopher had married again – a younger woman, who now devoted her life to caring for him. And Leila was pleased that he had found a suitable wife. They lived together for twenty years. Despite the Philosopher's later dementia, he lived well into his late nineties devotedly cared for by his wife.

Leila had begun a new life, content in the discovery that though she had enjoyed being a wife and mother, there was so much more to learn and do. As other women had done before her, Leila had discovered herself as a separate yet whole individual, and had found, too, the strength that rested within that knowledge. The following years confirmed all that she had learned from her past, so that now she only looked ahead to the next adventure. She had told the Philosopher that she would always be grateful as her journey began with meeting him, and being taken to India, where she had met her Teacher.

Having met the Householder Sage, India had changed her life and would remain her spiritual home – without claiming all that she had now become. Leila would continue to visit there each year – often with her son. As those two mating cobras had shown her, those, once bound, may — as in nature — unbind and go their separate paths. And when over, allow the simple act of going one's individual way – without judgment or regret.

~ 3 ~

# The Song of the Hill

*Each friend represents a world in us,*
*a world possibly not born until they arrive,*
*and it is only by this meeting that a new world is born.*

Anais Nin

He was a stranger to India. Business brought him from his home in New York to a world unlike any he had known before. When he returned from India, friends and family said that he had changed, that he was different. It was true though he could never explain why, mainly because he did not know why. That is, until the time came to explain – if only to himself – how that change had taken place. He took leave from his company, disappeared to a cabin in the woods outside New York and turned within, to relive his stay in India. He kept a diary, and with its help, he attempted to remember what exactly had happened in that faraway place.

"Two years ago, my software company sent me to India where I had never been before. I was twenty-eight, not married – not even a steady girlfriend. My life was work and I did it well." Reading what he had written caused him to ponder and he determined to find the answer to the definite change in himself – since India.

I didn't even know what was missing in my life until early one morning when I was on a train bound from Mumbai for Bangalore in south India, a most unusual thing happened. It stopped. Now, that's not unusual, of course, that a train stops. The train stopped at a small village that I had neither seen nor heard of before and whose name I have now forgotten. Nevertheless, as the train pulled into the crowded station, I grabbed my bag and jumped off, without a thought in my head. Just like that. One jump. Fate or foolishness, I cannot say – only that that jump would change my life forever.

It sounds crazy, but I felt something pull me off the train that morning. Something invisible like a... a – what is it called – like a magnet. Yes, something invisible like a magnet pulled my feet and bade me leave the train. Stranger still, I felt as though I had been there before. But when? How?

I had never been to the country before that week. Or had I? I remember feeling as though I'd walked among those very stones before. There was a small mountain, a hill, really. I looked up at it and that was when my voice changed. The next moment I heard myself speak in a voice that was not mine: "I have observed with my own eyes the birth of the sun." Did I say that? Amazing. Amazing. People would think I'd gone bonkers. I'm not sure that I'm the type of man to go bonkers. That's for sure. And then my voice changed again: "This is the eighth time we have met together. In five creations has the earth come and gone. Twelve times has the ocean of milk churned. Of all these I was a direct witness. I have observed with my own eyes the birth of the sun." There I go again. I haven't gone bonkers, have I? Is it this place? Perhaps the tropical sun as well as this place. Something very strange about this hill.

I read somewhere that the earth is four and a half billion years old. Four and a half billion years. Just think how many birthday parties that would be! Geologists think this land may be among the oldest on earth. My mind falls backward as I feel the pulse of India.

"What time has brought about, time will take away."

Did I say that? How did I say that? As I touch a rock, a little head appears then disappears, followed by a boy's laughter. What was that? It sounded like a small animal. There! There it is again! A tiger? Wolf? Jackal? Then the sound of children laughing. I don't know any animal but the two-legged kind that laughs like that. Still, one can't be too careful in a foreign country. It might well be some dangerous animal. I creep around the large rock and spot two boys, Veenu and Gopal.

Aha! You two up to mischief again. I know you.

The two boys scramble then shout, "What is your name? What is your name?"

"You two tried to carry my bag at the station. I know you."

"What is your name? What is your name", they repeat, gleefully, without remorse.

"Now off you go before I -."

I raise my hand as if to strike them.

"Shoo! Shoo!"

The boys race off, laughing.

"Where was I? I should say, "Where am I?

Oh, yes, this morning, perplexed at my situation, I sat down to think. I always make it a point to sit down and think when I get myself into a situation. Something that happens to you that you can't readily explain. So, I sat down on a rock at the base of the hill. Soon I came to this conclusion. You see, the good thing about thinking is that sooner or later, you're bound to come to some kind of conclusion. As the urge to get off the train was so overpowering, there surely must be some reason for it. Yes, that sounds logical, I told myself. Therefore, there is some reason for my impulsive action. I promised myself that I would not leave this place until I discovered why. All right I say to myself, that makes good sense and one must always try to make sense, right? But now what do I do?

As my thinking had been pretty good so far, I told myself that perhaps I should think some more. That is precisely what I did. Just like knowing I've been here before ... even though I have never been here before. Is not life full of countless mysteries and magical wonderings? Unexplained wonderings. That is, if you dare to feel them. This hill is just a hill, you might say, so why all the fuss. Yet I am certain there's more to it than that.

"Why is that?" you might ask.

Then I should have to answer, if I'm honest - - and I think it is best to be as honest in one's thinking as one can. Well, I should have to answer that I don't really know. I don't know. And that exactly is where all my thinking this morning has led: not knowing. I don't know and yet I know this place. Some invisible tug deep inside tells me that it is so.

"I have observed with my own eyes the birth of the sun." There, I've said it again. Or something inside me said it again.

As I walked among the village today, I heard many stories about the hill – some credible, others fantastic. Perhaps they are only village tales but then again, maybe – just maybe – these stories may provide a clue to my reasonable, unreasonable behavior. Maybe, if I can solve the mystery of the hill, I can find out why I jumped off that train to Bangalore this morning. So, I soldier on.

The sound of sticks hitting sticks as the Stranger looks and spies the same two village boys peering out from behind a rock. Veenu, the leader of the two, whispers, "Is he gone?"

Gopal answers, "Who?"

"Who do you think? The Stranger. The Stranger. Is he gone?"

"Oh, him. Yes, he's gone, Veenu."

In turn, Veenu pokes Gopal with a long stick.

"Hey, Veenu, watch it. Stop! Stop!"

The boys begin to fight with long sticks resembling Kalaripat, a martial art found in Kerala. As the young warriors are engaged in battle, a third boy the same age appears and slowly climbs up to a second level of the hill to shyly observe. It is Madhu.

"Oh, no, you don't. Take this and this and this!".

"Too late, Gopal." Gopal is backed into a rock, then Veenu viciously knocks the stick out of his hand.

"Aio! I am killed. I die."

Gopal feigns death dramatically while Veenu poses as the victor.

"Get up, Gopal. Let's start again. Gopal shakes his head. Come on, Gopal. Let's do it."

"You always win. I always die. I've died a hundred times."

"Then what will we do, man?"

"Something else, eh, Veenu?"

"What?"

"I don't know.   Why don't you suggest something?"

"How should I know?"

"I'm hungry."

"You're always hungry."

"I can't help it, Veenu. We could climb up the hill, no?"

"You know we're not allowed. Besides, it's too far."

"Hmm?"

"Too far. We could cut a banana branch, strip away the leaves, make a boat, and sail it on the river."

"Too much work. I'm hungry."

"You're always hungry."

"What can we do? We could ask Madhu."

"That idiot. That cloud boy. What can he know? Anyway, he's not here."

"Oh, yes, he is."

"Where?" Gopal points to Madhu who is uphill from them, cloud gazing.

"Hey, Cloud Boy, what can we do? Madhu. Madhu. Hey, Gopal, tell him he can play with us if he thinks of something."

"Hey, Madhu. Madhu"

"Why bother with him. He's cracked."

Both boys shout, "MADHU!"

Madhu turns as if from a dream and says, "Hmm? Yes?"

"What can we do? A game or something."

But suddenly Madhu is distracted as he sees a radiant young girl drift softly, sadly nearby. She appears not to see them at all and seems to float by as if in a trance. The Stranger turns just in time to catch a glimpse of her and is struck by her other worldly beauty. He speaks to her, "Hello. Don't go." Like a bird in flight, she has gone.

The boys turn to flee.

"Oh, boys, wait. No, please don't go. I won't hurt you. Tell me, who is that young girl? Is she all right?"

Veenu spits out, "What girl?"

"There. There on the hill above us. She seemed so sad.:

Gopal and Venue shake their heads, having seen nothing.

"Didn't you see her?"

Veenu again, "There's no one there, Mister, except Madhu. He's cracked, but he's no girl."

The two boys laugh at this.

"But I saw her," as Madhu slowly approaches the boys, shyly holding out a small red ball. Veenu starts to grab the ball. "Give it to me. Here." Then Gopal jumps in, "No, give it to me, Madhu. Me." Veenu tosses the ball to Gopal, and soon they are lost in play yet continue to shout to one another.

Gopal speaks, "My father told me never to play on this hill."

"Mine, too," laughs Veenu, "We are very naughty."

"Yes, very, very naughty," the boys laugh.

Madhu makes a small attempt to join in, "Amma will beat me if she knows I'm here."

Veenu responds "Except you're always up here. And by yourself, mostly. That's dumb. Don't you know there are spirits here, and they can eat you."

"I don't much like it here."

"Then you feel it, too, Gopal?" says Madhu.

"Feel what?" snaps Veenu.

"This place is different from other places."

Gopal chimes in, "Looks the same to me."

"Me, too," confirms Veenu, tossing the ball to Madhu who fumbles it. "Hey, watch it, stupid."

"Sorry," says Madhu.

Veenu gives Gopal a look. He nods. Then walk in a sort of circle around Madhu.

"Hey, Madhu, want your ball?"

"Hey, Cloud Boy, here it is. Here. Here. Come get it."

With a loud yell, Veenu pushes Madhu over Gopal who is on all fours on the ground. Veenu, wildly grabs a stick, yelling like a banshee, and runs to attack the stone. Madhu gets up, brushes himself off then speaks urgently to Veenu.

"No, No, No. You mustn't do that, Veenu. You know what Pandit says about the stones on this hill."

Gopal adds, "I heard the teacher, too, Veenu. Wait, maybe he's right."

"That old beard. I'm not afraid of him," says Veenu, who strikes even harder. "There and there!"

Madhu says softly, "Maybe it feels the blow just as we do."

Veenu laughs, "Stupid. Then it would be alive just as we are. Hey, stone are you alive?"

Gopal follows his lead, says, "If you are, Mr. Stone, please speak to us, won't you?"

"Good afternoon. What is your name?"

Madhu speaks up, "Maybe it can speak. Just because you've never heard it speak doesn't mean it can't." The other boys mockingly laugh as Veenu says, "He's crazy."

Suddenly the sound of a single wooden flute descends, heard by all. Gopal stops laughing, "Did you hear something?" Veenu stops hitting the stone and listens.

Hey, Veenu, what was it, do you think?

Madhu suddenly smiles, "It must be the Hill's Song just like Pundit said."

Veenu drops his stick, saying, "I …I … I think we go home now. Don't you think, Gopal?"

Gopal, speechless, nods. "Then what are we waiting for. Ayee!" Gopal drops his stick and runs after Veenu.

Madhu does not move, "It's beautiful. So beautiful." The Stranger approaches Madhu as they eye each other cautiously before Madhu starts to run away.

"Wait, please don't go yet. What was that strange sound?"

"Then you heard it, sir?"

"Heard what, Madhu?"

Madhu remains silent.

"Do you like peanuts? Here, have some. Go on. Go on, they're quite good."

As Madhu hesitates, the Stranger takes his hand and fills it with peanuts.

"You come here a lot, don't you?"

Madhu slowly eats one peanut at a time. "Yes sir, I do. Please don't tell Amma. She will beat me. She will beat me for sure."

"I won't tell. Promise."

"I didn't want to come here – at least, at first. But I couldn't help coming back."

"Why is that?"

"I don't know, sir. Something pulls me here. I can't explain. The others, they laugh at me."

"They think you've gone bonkers."

"What, sir?"

"Bonkers. Never mind. I won't laugh. I think I understand. Something pulling you. Some invisible tug deep within?"

"I am happy here. Sir?"

"Yes, Madhu?"

"You heard it, too, yes?"

"I heard something. Sounded like a shepherd's flute and bells."

"There are no shepherds on the hill, sir."

"Well, I heard a flute and bells. I'm certain of it."

"It was the Hill. The Hill's Song. It spoke to us. Not all hear it in the same way. Some never hear. Gopal and Veenu are afraid of it. And my Amma, she doesn't hear anything. Grownups can't hear it – except for Pundit. But you heard it, sir? You are blessed. Is it not beautiful? Is it not, sir?"

"No. No, it is not. The boys are right. It is a fearful sound. Who plays this frightening sound?"

"Nobody knows. Some say the gods, some the wind."

"The Hill's Song."

"That's it, sir. That's it." They remain silent for a time.

"And that girl. You saw her, too, didn't you?"

Madhu nods.

"Perhaps she makes the music?"

"Mayadevi? No, Mayadevi doesn't make the music, but she's part of it."

"Maya. That means illusion, doesn't it?"

Madhu nods, saying, "Mayadevi is like a goddess."

"She has no family?"

"You are right, sir."

"About what?"

"About the nuts. They are very tasty."

The Stranger smiles, handing him the bag of nuts. "Here you are. What of her family?"

"I go now, or Amma will be angry"

"Madhu, wait. What does Madhu mean?"

"It's a name for one of our gods. For Krishna, the cloud-colored one."

"Cloud Boy," the Stranger mutters to himself.

A voice from afar is heard calling, "Madhu. Madhu. Madhu."

"Oh, that's Amma. I go quickly."

"Wait, please. Madhu, uh, what do you want to be when you grow up?"

"Want to be?"

"Sure. A cowboy? Doctor? Lawyer? Engineer?"

"Oh. I guess I want to be like Pundit. He is my teacher. I want to be like Pundit and follow in the footsteps of the ancients."

"Madhu! Madhu! Madhu"!

"She will beat me for sure this time," Madhu says as he runs away.

"Cloud boy," the Stranger says to no one in particular

Three village women walk up the hill carrying baskets and a clay water jug, gracefully balanced on their heads held by one hand. Jayamani leads the way, dragging Madhu by the ear. "Didn't you hear me calling? What are you doing here?"

"I heard the hill sing, Amma. It was so beautiful."

"So now the hills speak, do they?"

"It says what cannot be told, Amma. Truly."

"And a beautiful beating you get if you don't stop such nonsense."

Madhu ducks her blow, "If only you could hear the Hill, Amma. There's such happiness in her song."

"You bring us sorrow. Why can't you be like the other boys? Go. Look to the rice fields as your father does. To eat we must work."

Madhu stands, reluctant to leave.

"Try to be like Veenu and Gopal."

"But I don't wish to be like Veenu and Gopal."

"Go now or I'll –." As Jayamani raises her hand to strike the boy, Madhu runs away. She is embarrassed that the other women have heard but they are not listening, occupied with the Stranger. Giggling, Meenakshi beckons to Jayamani to join them as they plot in whispers.

Shanta, a few years younger than the other women, cannot stop blushing and laughing.

Meenakshi scolds her, "Hush now, Shanta, don't be a silly goose. What will your husband say if you carry on so? Jayamani, come, come." The women form a half-circle around the Stranger.

"Mangoes?" offers Meenakshi.

"Flowers?" adds Shanta.

"Why, thank you, they're lovely," the Stranger says.

"One rupee," Shanta adds shyly.

"Oh, yes, here." Shanta takes the rupee, smiling, and says, "To give is good karma. May you prosper a hundred lives."

"Mangoes. Nice, ripe mangoes," announces Meenakshi, in her loud voice.

"No, no thank you."

"Only four rupees," insists Meenakshi.

"No, really."

Jayamani, not to be left out, "You give me a sari?"

"English? American? Rich American?" squawks Meenakshi, sounding more like a crow.

"I just want to talk with you."

"Married? How many children?"

"No, none. No children. I –"

"Why? What's wrong with your wife that she does not bear fruit?" Jayamani says sadly.

A confused Stranger responds, "There's nothing wrong with her. I mean, I'm not married. No wife."

Jayamani, surprised, "No wife?"

Laughing, the Stranger says, "Not yet anyway."

Shanta steps forward, "The true wife thinks not of God when she rises in the morning. She offers her devotion to the husband."

Meenakshi adds roughly, "Hmm, some pray to be free of them."

Jayamani, not wishing to miss an opportunity, "I have one daughter, not married. You like?"

"No. No wife, thank you."

"He who leads his life in this world as he should

is like the gods in heaven."

Shanta adds, "All men should marry. It is the law."

"What about sannyasins?" says Jayamani.

"Sannyasins. They are your priests, aren't they?"

Meenakshi, exasperated, "Who wants them? They renounce the world for God, but does God fill their empty bellies? No, we do. Always, always begging for food. All they do is eat and pray, pray and eat. Good for nothing."

"Meenakshi," cries Shanta, "What are you saying? The gods will hear you and punish us."

Jayamani, thoughtful now, says, "I fear my Madhu will become a sannyasin. Then who will tend the rice paddies when we are old?" She pours water from her clay jug into a clay cup then drinks water without touching the cup to her lips. Tilting her head back, Jayamani pours water into her mouth. The Stranger looks on as the other two women drink in the same fashion.

Meenakshi quips, "You want mangoes, Mister?"

"First, I'd like some water, if I may? Very hot today."

Shanta laughs shyly, "Very hot today." Then hands cup of water to the Stranger.

"From my father's well. Very cool. Good water." The women laugh as he tries unsuccessfully to drink Indian fashion, spilling water down his shirt.

"Guess I'll have to practice."

"You want mangoes, Mister?" says the persistent Meenakshi.

"Yes, all right. Talk to me first then I'll buy some mangoes."

"How many you want? Our village tree very good mangoes. Ripe. Juicy. See the color."

"First talk and then –"

"Two dozen, nine rupees. Three dozen?

"Later. I want to ask you about this hill."

Suddenly no one is speaking. Then Shanta softly says, "You know about it then?"

Meenakshi interrupts, "Hush, silly goose. He is a stranger."

"I mean no harm. There is something special about this place. I mean no harm. And I will buy your mangoes."

Shanta adds, "Lakshmi, the goddess of prosperity, will bless you with a hundred sons."

The Stranger laughs, "I hope not."

Meenakshi, down to business, "What you wish to know, Mister?"

"Well, to begin with, why are you here?"

"We live here," says Jayamani.

"But why here? Why come up here to the hill?"

Shanta responds, "To gather herbs. Some for cooking. Some to bless the house, to bring us good fortune. For Lakshmi to smile."

"Money," says Meenakshi.

"Children," adds Jayamani.

"The herbs found on the hill are blessed by the gods," says Shanta.

"And the stones here? Are they ordinary stones?"

Shanta continues, "Pundit says that some can look at each stone and tell you, its story."

Jayamani adds, "It is said each stone has a soul. My grandfather told me that the great lord, Brahma -."

"Who is Brahma?"

Meenakshi says, "Brahma is the Creator, of course."

"The lord Brahma was born in water."

"No, he wasn't, Shanta. The lord Brahma was born in an egg," Jayamani smiles.

Meenakshi, "Humph, in an egg? What is he then, a chicken?"

Young Shanta stands, and gracefully as a dancer makes a lotus flower with her hands, "The great Lord Brahma was born in water inside a lotus. He rose like bubbles in the air on the surface of the great ocean. Then He set to work creating the universe. He stopped for a moment to rest and look around at all He had done. He looked up and down and all around and saw that the world was not yet beautiful and He wept because of this. As the tears of Brahma fell to earth, they became these stones. Later He made the flowers and the trees."

Jayamani, shaking her head, "No. Not like that. My father told it like this. All the gods fashioned this hill for themselves. You see, they needed a meeting place for they enjoyed gathering every evening at Sandhya."

"Sandh ya?"

"The special time of day when it is no longer day and not yet dark. When the sun begins to sleep and night not yet come," Shanta added with sweeping gestures.

Jayamani continued, "So the gods heaved a sigh and blew down toward the earth. Such was the power of their breath that sand and dirt and stones came together and made the hill."

Meenakshi shrugged, "What does your father know, Jayamani. My grandfather learned it from his grandfather and his grandfather from his grandfather."

Jayamani," My father knows everything."

"Anyway," continued Shanta, "the gods would come gather as the sun set every evening."

Jayamani joined it, "Sometimes they were late."

Meenakshi, "Only when they wanted to be late."

"They would stop the sun and have it held in the sky waiting for their pleasure."

"Jayamani, please let me. They would gather and tell of their creations, battles – and loves."

"That's the part, Shanta likes best. Love." Meenakshi adds, causing the women to laugh.

"And the wind hearing the stories of the gods would draw them on the stones so they would not be forgotten," Jayamani said, clearly enjoying herself in the telling.

"But not everyone can see the drawings on the stones," adds Shanta.

In unison, the women nod.

"That's not the way my grandfather told it. Want your mangoes now? Very ripe."

"Soon. Soon. Any of you see the drawings?"

Shanta responds, "Once Pundit said each stone is the soul of a sensitive one who has left the body in death and come to dwell on the hill. That they are alive and in meditation here waiting."

The Stranger, enthralled, "Waiting for what?"

Jayamani "Their next birth."

The stranger chuckles, "And just how many births do you think we have?"

"Hundreds."

"Thousands," corrects Jayamani.

"Too many if you ask me," pipes Meenakshi.

"Shanta, I never heard Pundit tell it like that," puzzled Jayamani.

"He told it to me."

Jayamani shook her head," He never told it like that, Shanta."

The Stranger, disappointed, "I'm afraid all I see are a pile of rocks." Suddenly, his voice changed, "I have observed with my own eyes the origin of the sun." Then, out of nowhere, the Stranger hears the sound of a wooden flute again and he becomes completely still. Time stops.

Mayadevi appears higher up the hill and this time, the Stranger sees her at once and is struck again by her great beauty. "Who is she? Tell me please, who is she?"

Meenakshi offers "Bad luck. The gods will punish us with bad crops as long as she lives on the hill."

"No, Meenakshi, she is as harmless as the footprints of a cow," Jayamani says.

Shanta, frightened, "She is not from the village, sir."

"But who is she?"

Jayamani adds, "No one knows for certain where she is from, just that she is not one of us."

"Has she been here for long?"

"Maya Devi is as permanent on this hill as a tree or stone," says Shanta, softly, then begins to chant or sing:

Dark girl of dark hair
For you the moon your lover has risen in the
    east
For you the moon your lover has risen in the
    east
Clearing the dark
For he has sown the stars
The clouds are come to hide them
Then comes a girl as silent as the wind to
    drive them off

Her bangles jingle and the bird-clouds fly by
The birds as clouds fly beyond the Hill.

Meenakshi stands up and points a crooked finger
to the girl, as she chants a warning:

Maya. She is black as a crow.
Oh, sisters, I don't want this Maya.
Her teeth like fingers on a jackfruit
And her head is full of lice.
Oh, sisters, I don't want this Maya.
Where are her father and mother?
If they don't want her,
Let them send her packing in a boat and rid
    us of such rubbish.
Oh, sisters, I don't want this Maya.

Meenakshi picks up small pebbles and throws
them at Maya Devi, saying, "Go away, evil one.
Go away and leave us alone." Shanta restrains
Meenakshi, "Meenakshi, no. She is harmless. What
has she done?"

Jayamani joins Shanta in holding Meenakshi
back, "No, Meenakshi, she is a woman like us."

"No, she is not one of us," as she picks up another
stone to throw, "She is not one of us."

Jayamani chants or sings as Maya Devi begins to
sway and dance above them:

Did she leave the heavens
To light on the good earth?
And to reach the earth
Did she descend in a golden chariot?
Wherefore has she come
To dance in the rice fields
And bring seeds into being?
Are there such women in this world?
Has she perchance fallen from heaven?
Or from the earth sprung up like Sita?
What can we say of such a creature?
She is like to the jasmine flower in bloom on
     the hill,
Like the sapling of the mango tree shooting
     its leaves,
Or like the hue of the tender palm leaf.
Are there such women as this in the world?

Maya ends her dance then disappears into the hill. The Stranger's face has changed so that he can barely speak. Haltingly, he says, "But she must live somewhere."

Shanta wipes a tear from her eye, "On the hill. She's always here. Says it brings her closer to him."

"Him? Who?"

"A strange one that one. No good will come of it. Mark my words," Meenakshi gruffly says.

Jayamani, moved, adds, "Pundit told my husband once. She had a lover before this life and then she left him to be born again. And he was left behind."

"I don't understand. Left?"

Jayamani continues, "Left the body. To be born into the next life."

"Died," adds Meenakshi.

"Oh, I see. But I don't understand."

Shanta, as if caught in a dream, "I heard it told once that she roamed everywhere looking for him and he was nowhere. She cried and cried all the time and would have none but he."

Meenakshi, "I know. I heard it. That she came here and found the hill. And was told."

"Told? Told what?"

Jayamani adds, "Told that she must suffer because her lover has not yet come.

Meenakshi explains, "Not yet been born."

Jayamani concludes, "That she'll never find happiness apart from him and that they will never meet in this life." Shanta begins to weep, "It's so sad, so very sad."

"But why?" protests the Stranger, "Why must they never meet?"

Laughing, Meenakshi mocks, "Why, why, why?"

Jayamani, holding Shanta who still weeps, "Because he won't come until she leaves."

Shanta dries her tears with the end of her sari, "That's what Pundit told my husband. Until she dies, he won't be born."

"Why?" is all the Stranger can say.

"You hold too many whys in your head, American," quips Meenakshi.

Jayamani stands up from holding Shanta and arranges her sari, "That is her karma, her fate."

"Karma? Fate? asks the Stranger.

Jayamani steps in, "Our fate is decided by what we do before. In the past."

Shanta adds, "From good, good will come."

Meenakshi, "From bad, bad."

The Stranger asks, "But why here? Why does she remain on the hill?"

Meenakshi in a raised voice, "Makes no sense. Like mating a virgin in the waking state with a husband in the dream state. Makes no sense."

Shanta, "I heard it said that she sees his face in the clouds and hears his voice in the hill's song."

"Do you hear the music?"

"It frightens me."

"Ugly it is, ugly," says Meenakshi.

"Some say that it is beautiful," says the Stranger.

"That's what my Madhu says."

"What becomes of the one she loves and waits for? What happens when he comes again?"

The women, baffled, for the moment have no answer until Shanta adds. "It begins all over again. When her suffering ends, his begins.

"You mean he will search for her not finding her?"

Shanta is crying, "So sad. So sad. And she is so

beautiful."

Meenakshi looks up, "It is late. Time to light the lamp. Shanta. Jayamani. We must go.

Here are your mangoes, Mister. Six rupees."

The other two women try hard not to smile.

The Stranger warily says, "You said four rupees before."

"That was long ago. They are more ripe now."

Shanta giggles as the Stranger smiles, "Very well, here you are."

A large owl flies over with a screech as the women hastily gather their belongings.

"Please sir, if you see my Madhu, send him home. Yes?"

The Stranger turns around just in time to catch a glimpse of Maya Devi.

"Yes, yes. I will." However, his attention is on Maya Devi. He ducks down behind a rock so as not to frighten her away. Maya Devi comes closer after the women leave and chants or sings:

> Till I come back
> Wait ... wait for me
> Why do you cry, my dear one?
> I am not going to die
> I shall come very soon
> Wait ... oh, wait for me.

He will come, oh yes, my beloved will come
Like melted gold
Like the rising sun in the east
And the setting moon in the west.

I will tie my waist girdle around his waist
Like the jasmine creeper entwines the mango
    tree
So that where he goes, I will go
And where he lies, I will lie
Then we shall never part,
Then we shall never part.

The hill's music accompanies her as she dances closer and closer to the Stranger, not seeing him. Cautiously, he approaches then, seeing him, Maya Devi bolts like a startled deer. Yet she doesn't go far away as she sees him lay the mangoes at her feet. She looks long at him then accepts the mangoes. Silently, Maya Devi gazes at the Stranger without emotion. It is as if the sound of the flute and the girl are one. She smiles softly at the Stranger. Together they listen and sway to the Hill's Song. Then, without warning, Maya Devi turns away – as if called. She pauses, looks quizzically at the Stranger, and gathers the mangoes. She stands, smiles at him, then disappears silently up the Hill – as the flute plays. The Stranger is at a loss, something has happened to him.

Then he sees Madhu sitting quietly just above on the hill.

"Madhu! Thank heavens." The Stranger climbs up and sits beside the boy.

"Madhu, she would not talk to me."

"Maya has no need to speak."

"Well, that is rude."

"Rude?" Madhu laughs.

"Why do you laugh?"

"Maya does not care what others think. She does not live in the world of others, sir."

"Nonsense. We all live in the same world. Madhu rises but does not leave."

"Why do you come, Madhu? Why do you come back again and again?"

"It calls me. I am happy here."

"Well, it called me, but I am not happy here."

"I know."

"How could you know, son?"

"Pundit told me."

"Told you? Told you what?"

"That you are not happy."

"Madhu, your teacher has never seen me. We have never met."

"Pundit is very old and very wise, sir."

"That may be, but how can he know what he hasn't seen?"

"It is so."

"Did he say why I am not happy?"

"Yes sir."

"Well? Tell me. Please."

"Pundit says the Stranger is not happy because he does not know what he is. He thinks he is only what he sees and this makes him unhappy."

"And if I am not what I see, then what am I?"

"Pundit says that is why you crossed the ocean. To know what cannot be seen."

"This is all very confusing, Madhu. It just doesn't make any sense. I came to India on a business trip." Silence. Then the Stranger continues, "How? How to know?"

Madhu turns and points up to the Hill.

"The Hill? Always the Hill. I don't know any more now than when I got off the train this morning. I think your mother is right to keep you away from this place. It's giving you crazy ideas."

"Are you going to tell Amma I am here, sir?"

"That depends. I won't tell her if you'll tell me about the Hill. Something. Anything."

"What can I know, sir? I'm only a boy."

Suddenly angry, the Stranger, "Something. You can tell me something. Maybe something your teacher said?"

"Once Pundit came to our house. I was supposed to be asleep, but I stayed awake to hear. He said that there are birds on the hill."

"Madhu, there are birds on every hill."

"Not like these. These are rare and lovely birds,

Pundit said, with all the colors of the rainbow. They are not weighed down with thoughts like men but have much heart. They fly very high and are seen nowhere but on the Hill. Sometimes someone tries to bring one down into the village."

"Have they ever caught one of these birds?"

"Oh, they can catch them easy enough, but they cannot keep them."

"They fly away, you mean."

"No sir. They die. Pundit said as soon as they leave the hill, they die. He says they cannot live away from this place. I think Maya Devi is like that bird. I think she cannot live away from the hill. This hill is the only home she knows."

"Madhu, why don't the others in the village hear what you and Maya hear? Veenu and Gopal, your mother, the other mothers, why don't they hear?"

"I must go home now, sir."

"Tell me, Madhu. I want to know. What is the hill's secret?"

Madhu remains silent, looking down at his feet. The Stranger growing impatient, "Tell me what the hill says to you?" After a pause, the Stranger insists "Madhu."

"I cannot, sir."

"Why? I won't laugh or tell anyone. I promise."

"It isn't that, sir."

"Well, then? Well, then?"

"It's just that it cannot be told."

"Nonsense. "

"It's true, sir. It not in words that the Hill speaks."

"Is that why Maya didn't answer me?"

As if in a trance, Madhu replies, "I have observed with my own eyes the birth of the sun. There exists an ancient link maintained through many lives."

"What does it mean? Is it a riddle?"

The flute music builds as a soft tabla drum beats, growing slowly louder. Hearing the Hill's Song, Madhu smiles, nods his head, and slowly climbs to the upper level where Maya Devi is seen again. The Stranger becomes more and more disturbed by the music.

"Is it a riddle? Madhu? Maya? It's very rude not to speak when you're spoken to. Madhu. Where are you going? Madhu! All right then. Go on. Go on. I'm glad to be rid of you. All of you. As for your stories about the hill, I don't believe them. Do you hear me? I don't believe any of them. Myths. I think this whole damn country is a myth. Who knows? Maybe I'm still on the train and never got off at all. Maybe I'm still on my way to Bangalore, fast asleep, dreaming. Dreaming this whole idiotic story. The hill, the boys, the village women, you, and Maya are no more than creatures of my dream. What about that? I don't know. I can't think very clearly ... that music ... that music. I won't listen anymore."

As the music builds, the Stranger, frightened, holds his hands tightly over his ears.

"No, no. I won't listen. I don't believe any of it. Do you hear me? Madhu. Cloud boy. Gods. Being born life after life. Birds of Paradise. Oh, oh, I can't think. I can't think. I know nothing."

Suddenly from the top of the hill, a beautiful bird with all the colors of the rainbow flies in an aerial dance to the music of the flute. Behind the bird, trail two thin tails that float up and down as streamers waved by the gods. The Stranger sees the Bird of Paradise and can no longer doubt. Something speaks within that is more than himself.

"Keep your mind silent and you shall discover."

What? There. There. It does exist. And it's so beautiful. And the music … the music …

The Stranger is transformed from some deep inner core. Silence reigns.  The Stranger is on his knees, his head bowed. Tears stream down his face as he raises his head to the sky and places one hand over his heart, "I understand. I can hear the Song of the Hill. Maya's song. "My heart is full."

As the Stranger looks up, he sees Madhu and Maya Devi standing near each other as the flute music with the drum gradually becoming louder and louder.

"Yes," the Stranger exclaims in a joyous cry, "Wait. Wait for me." The Stranger walks slowly up the hill as the flute music softens so that it is hardly heard at all. The persistent beat of the tabla lessens, sounding more like the soft beat of one human heart.

And then, Silence.

The Stranger remembered nothing more until he found himself at the train station with young Madhu beside him. They looked at each other – no words were needed. And when the train stopped, the Stranger calmly stepped aboard, and looking back, saw Madhu waving.

~ 4 ~

# The Body
# in the Well

*Samsara from Sanskrit means
'the ever-turning wheel of life'*

Manikkal is a small south Indian village like hundreds of other villages in India. As they have for hundreds of years, villagers live in thatched huts under coconut palms that sway to the soundless exotic music of south India. Ripe banana trees flourish in this tropical world as well as over a hundred species of colorful birds from geese and ducks to egrets and herons as well as green hanging parrots and multi-colored river kingfishers. The life of the village has remained remarkably unchanged for the past centuries – so much so that seeing a black Ambassador taxi drive up was an anomaly

– indeed an aberration – causing a stir among the overly curious inhabitants. That was the day Susan Edwards arrived to rent a small white-washed house with a slanted red-tiled roof, the traditional style of Kerala homes.

Susan just turned twenty-three and a graduate of the University of Michigan had decided to take a year off before considering a steady job or career. She had come to India in order to study Kalari, the ancient martial art of Kerala. Most American girls who come to India study music or dance, but though Susan Edwards looked like a typical American girl, she was not. Her Scandinavian ancestors had bequeathed her rich blonde hair and sky-blue eyes, yet Susan was not typical of her mid-western American family. She had so deeply embraced the Hindu culture that she preferred living in a village near Trivandrum, the center for her study of Kalari, a martial art that centuries later, still exists today.

Susan had purchased a motor scooter, putting her life at risk in Indian traffic, commuting daily to East Fort in Trivandrum. The state capital of Kerala had recently been officially re-named Thiruvananthapuram in an attempt to remove the reminders of British rule in India. Other examples were Mumbai instead of Bombay, Chennai instead of Madras. Even so, change is sluggish here, so most natives still said 'Trivandrum' – so much easier for all.

Classes began early morning due to the tropical heat. Locking her scooter, Susan arrived with ample time to gather herself for her first lesson. She was privileged to study with Govindan Kutty, a descendent of one of the great Kalari warriors. Kalari drew students from all over the globe. Though she was the only western woman in the class, her enthusiasm was contagious, and with her outgoing, pleasant nature, Susan was soon accepted by all.

Only one mile from the Kalaripat where Kalari is taught, Rama Pillai was leaving his family home to go to work. Rama always felt a certain pressure about his work. His grandfather had written the police manual for the state and his father had been a DSP (Detective Superintendent of Police). And though Ram Pillai had graduated with honors from an American university and had considered law school, he had returned home to Kerala, and followed in the footsteps of his father and grandfather. Now twenty-nine, he had become a policeman, living at home, unmarried. His mother worried about that. "Plenty of good girls here. Why wait? I want grandchildren, son. Do your duty." So, the pressure of duty was as fierce at home as at work, causing Ram to wonder if he had made the right choice in coming home. He had felt so free in America and had learned a great deal though there had remained a continual and inevitable pull to return home to India. And, too, he was the only son with two unmarried sisters, his mother a widow now as well, so responsibility hung heavily on his young shoulders. It seemed to him that family responsibility was felt more keenly by Indians than by most American young men who would fly away to chase whatever ambitions or dreams they had, regardless of who was left behind.

Susan was so fascinated by the history of Kalari that she had read everything in English she could find. The myth was that Kalaripayattu was first introduced by Lord Parasurama, the sixth incarnation of Lord Vishnu, after he reclaimed the land of Kerala from the Arabian Sea. Historians could never agree about Kalari's origins. The best they could offer was that the time of its birth was anywhere between 200 BC and 600 AD. During the fourteenth and sixteenth century, Kalari's popularity was high. What has not varied is the wonder with which chroniclers and poets throughout the centuries have recorded the liquid beauty and complexity of the moves demonstrated by the practitioners of Kalaripayattu.

Kalaris were invariably found living near Devi temples, and the master used to be called "Kuruppu" or "Gurukkal". In olden times, those who could not wield the sword were considered lacking in masculinity and hence deserved to live like slaves. Susan was delighted to discover references to women warriors who could match their male counterparts in all aspects of the martial art. And she intended to do just that.

Ram Pillai had rapidly risen in rank to Inspector in the Trivandrum Police Unit though he wondered if it was partially due to his distinguished lineage rather than his abilities. Most police matters were simple – drunkards, minor thieves, and occasional domestic abuse. He was thorough in his duties and reports, and while there was no cause for complaints, he felt that something was missing in his life – especially since his return from America seven years ago.

Though Susan loved her parents and brothers, she was surprised how little she missed them – or America. In fact, since her very first day in India, she felt completely at home – as though she had lived here before. Awakening each morning with an eagerness to attend her Kalari classes, she admired not only the superb skill of the Master, but his devotion to the seven gods, and his natural humility to one and all. Susan sat enthralled her first morning as the Master demonstrated the forms of Kalari to perspective students.

Traditionally, there was a rectangular pit with a dirt floor. A few feet above and before the pit was a long bench where students could sit and observe. Master Kutty entered the pit along with his son, Joshi, now in his late twenties and well-trained since the age of nine. Kalari is often referred to as an art as it more resembles a dance – though it was unlike any Susan had seen before. At one moment, the Master had crouched low like a panther and the next moment had jumped high into the air several feet above his opponent. The amazing part was not only the height of the leap, but that he seemed to remain halted in mid-air before returning to earth. Susan had read of the Russian ballet genius, Nijinsky, who could do such a feat, but she had never seen it before now. Later Kutty and his son fought with long sticks, then with metal daggers and swords. Susan did not move and hardly took a breath for one hour as she watched and learned how all parts of the body could be utilized as a weapon – even the forehead. The steps, jumps, and stances were to be mastered in order to gain total control over one's body.

For his mother's sake yet against his instincts, Ram had already encountered two young, suitable women in meetings arranged by his mother and her well-meaning friends. Arranged marriages were still a regular happening in India. He was polite as they sat having tea and biscuits and was thoroughly bored with the whole process which inevitably led to nothing.

"What is wrong with this one, Rama? She is from a good family and has an M.A. from university. I do not understand you."

After being accepted as a student, Susan and four other beginning students, were taught seven steps after which they bowed before seven lit oil lamps honoring the seven immortals who protect the earth. Only then were they ready for their first lesson.

Along with the daily physical training, the students were also schooled in the healing arts of oil massage, herbs, and bone setting. Traditionally the early warriors studied the healing arts of herbs and oils and bone-setting as they lived a nomadic existence, going where they were hired to fight or guard. Susan embraced the science of healing as well. She took to this easily and thoroughly enjoyed receiving her first massage with sesame oil mixed with various herbs. Master Kutty himself gave the massage after lighting a small lamp on an altar near the massage table. Before the massage was over, Susan became so relaxed that she had fallen into a profound sleep. She dreamed of living in India centuries before as a man and learning the martial art. In her dream, she travelled much, defending those she was asked to serve. When she awoke and told Master Kutty of the dream, he simply nodded his head sideways, saying, "It is no surprise."

Ram liked to have lunch in town on his own, combining solitude with good food at the Hotel Annapoorna not far from the station yet far enough not to attract other policemen. In this way, undisturbed, Ram could review his case notes and consider his personal life.

It was a Thursday and Susan, hungrier than usual, desired a full Indian meal. She had heard that Hotel Annapoorna was one of the best places to go for a lunch buffet so decided to treat herself. The hotel was situated between East Fort where Kalaripat was and the Scree Padmanabha Swamy Temple which she had not yet visited. She noticed on the sign that the hotel's restaurant was mostly vegetarian, but included fish. Though she still ate fish and sometimes chicken, she loved Indian vegetarian food as well.

Entering the restaurant, she smelled the rich and subtle south Indian spices and eagerly found a table before going through the varied buffet. Fish tikka, sag paneer, basmati rice, poppadums – and other favorites tempted her as she filled her plate. Locating a small table near the wall, she sat and began to enjoy the sumptuous meal. After a few moments, she looked up and noticed an attractive young man looking at her. Aware that she was greedily eating, she smiled, and Ram returned the smile, wondering what part of the United States she was from. Probably a tourist, he thought. His time was up so he rose and went to wash his hands. As he walked toward the exit, something made him turn and look at the young girl again who was oblivious to anything except what she was eating. However, it so happened that as soon as he turned his back, she looked up to see him leave.

Susan chided herself for eating so heavily as she found it difficult to do the afternoon class and made a vow not to do so again. Driving home in late afternoon traffic, she found herself a bit drowsy and made a mental note to eat light until supper from now on.

Ram found himself thinking of the young fair-headed girl he had seen at Hotel Annapoorna. He smiled remembering the relish she showed toward good Indian food and wondered if she might return.

Exhausted, Susan reached her village home. She noticed that fires were lit and meals being prepared as the villagers still lived by the rising and setting of the sun. She could smell the dal and rice cooking as well as those Indian chilies and spices which fire the belly and the blood.

After carefully locking her scooter, she went indoors to change her clothes. Needing a bath after the soot and dust from the road, she went to the well for a bucket of water. It was near sunset or *Sandhya*, symbolizing the space between two thoughts. No longer day and not yet night. After dropping the bucket, she heard a dull thud and worried that the well might have gone dry. Suddenly a large black crow made its harsh crackle as it sat atop the well as if taunting her. Indian crows are so much larger and more fearless than those she had seen in America. The sudden sound and sight of it caused shivers to run up her spine.

Kapil, the teenage son of her neighbor, always kind and helpful, asked, "Everything ok, Miss?"

"I don't know, Kapil, when the bucket drops there is no sound of water. Has it dried up?"

"No, Missy, not at this time. Let me try." Kapil wound the bucket then dropped it resulting once again in the sound of a thud. "Wait here. I get my torch (flashlight). Sometimes a small animal may fall in and drown. We will see, ok?"

Susan thanked the boy and sighed, longing for a good wash. She heard Kapil's Amma calling him to supper, but he came quickly back to the well with his flashlight. He then proceeded to bend way over shining the light to the bottom of the well.

"Careful, Kapil, don't fall."

"No, Miss … Aio!", he suddenly cried out.

"Kapil? Son? What is happening?" shouted his mother.

Soon three or four neighbors came out, hearing the boy's cry. Thinking some animal had fallen into the well, blocking the water pail, the men began to work. Susan breathed a sigh and returned to her house, thinking, "Well, if I can't bathe, at least, I can eat." Several minutes later, hearing raised voices, Susan reappeared to see what was up.

"Police. Get the police."

"Why the police?" Susan queried.

Kapil's mother turned briskly to her, exclaiming, as if to accuse, "Because there's a dead body in your well!"

Without answering, Susan walked directly to the well as the villagers backed away to let her through. Looking down as others shined their flashlights, she saw for herself that there was indeed a body in the well.

"We don't even know who it is. Bring it up. Bring it up!"

"No," said Susan. "No, we must wait for the police. Don't touch anything. Wait for the police."

The villages seemed unconvinced until young Kapil spoke up, "Miss is right. We must wait."

Kapil's mother grabbed his arm and pulled him inside their thatched hut. Susan walked back to her small house, called the police, then made a cup of tea. Later, she sat on her porch shocked at this unexpected death, drinking tea, and waiting for the police.

The siren was heard by everyone in the village who peered out or brazenly walked out to see who had died. The police car abruptly stopped, scattering chickens here and there, and Ram Pillai got out along with Pradip, his sub-inspector. Though a couple of years older than his boss, Pradip had great respect for him. "This way, sir. This way."

With the support of two of the men from the village, the body was hoisted up and laid upon the ground next to the well. The two men identified the dead man as Ayyappa, a road worker who lived nearby. Ayyappa was known to drink toddy and beat his wife. They had no children. He was about forty years old and his wife was in her mid- twenties. She was called Shanti.

Susan watched from her porch as Ram looked up and noticed her as the young woman that he had seen that very day lunching at Hotel Annapoorna.

"Good evening, ma'am. I am DSP Ram Pillai. And you are?"

"Susan. Susan Edwards."

"American, yes?"

Susan nodded.

"And may I ask why you are here in this village?"

"I live here. That is, I am visiting India and renting this house. And that is my well."

"May I trouble you to come in and make a statement?"

Ram told Pradip to stay with the body and wait for forensics to come. Then he followed Susan into her house, removing his hat.

"Would you like some tea, Inspector?"

"Yes, please."

Ram settled himself at the wooden table and took out his notebook and pencil.

"Did you know the deceased?"

"No. No, I did not. I have only recently come."

"What are you doing in Kerala?"

"Studying. Studying at Kalaripat in Trivandrum."

Ram, looked up, trying to mask his surprise.

Susan noticed it at once. "I know. Not what you would expect from an American girl, right?"

"You said it was your well?"

"Yes. I last took water from the well yesterday about 5 p.m."

Hearing a car arrive, Ram got up to ascertain that it was the forensic team who after their analysis would take the body to the morgue for further tests. Nodding to them from the porch, Ram went back inside, and the team continued to do what they were trained to do.

Before asking the next question, he simply stared at Susan who now recognized him from lunchtime earlier.

"Yes, Inspector, I was lunching today at the Hotel Annapoorna and saw you there."

"Correct, Miss Edwards. I remember. I'd like to ask you to come to the station tomorrow at your convenience to sign a statement. When would suit?"

"I finish my classes tomorrow at 4pm. Would that work?"

"Certainly. Here is the address. It is not far from the Kalaripat," handing her his card.

"Thank you, Inspector."

Ram continued to stare at her before nodding and turning to leave. Susan watched as he joined his team outside, but decided not to invest more time in what how now become a murder mystery. She must eat something then sleep or she won't be much good for her strenuous classes the next day. Yet just before she went to sleep, she asked herself, "Why my well?"

Ram went early the next morning to the morgue to ask Dr. Thomas about her findings. Dr. Adele –

short for Adelaide – Thomas was respected by the entire police force for her intelligence and ethical values. She came from an old Kerala Christian family named after Thomas, one of the twelve disciples of Christ who came to south India to spread the Christian message. Thomas was martyred in Madras (Chennai), and his bones lie in a Christian church there. One finds these Christian doctors and nurses all over the world, respected for their abilities and excellent care. As usual, Dr. Thomas was prepared for Ram's early call.

"Good morning, Inspector. I should begin by saying that this was not an accidental death."

"No?"

"No, Inspector. He was bludgeoned to death, hit five times on the head. I would say a frenzied attack."

"Time of death, Adele?"

"I may need more time to be exact."

"But?"

"But my guess would be sometime night before last between 10 and midnight."

"Thanks, Adele. How is your father?"

"Better, thank you."

Susan was grateful to be able to focus on the strenuous Kalari classes and mostly forget about the unexpected death in the village. She had carried a light lunch of chapati and dahl with her. Hurriedly, after her last class, she hurried to the police station, arriving exactly at 4pm.

Ram thanked her for being so prompt and had prepared a statement from her notes of the last evening. After reading the statement, she signed the document then prepared to leave.

"May I ask you, Miss Edwards, if you knew the deceased. His name was Ayyappa."

"No, no, I did not. But, as I told you, I have not been here very long."

"Why your well, then?"

"No idea. Your English pronunciation is very good, Inspector."

"I was four and a half years in America. University of Michigan, actually."

"Oh. As it happens, I also graduated from there, but grew up in Wisconsin. Next door, you might say."

"Why martial arts?

"Why not?"

"Good answer. I'll be driving out to your village now. Could I give you a lift?"

"No thanks. I have my scooter."

"Well, perhaps I'll see you there later."

"Any idea what happened? Did he fall?"

"No, Miss Edwards. He was murdered and thrown into your well."

"Oh, dear." Susan walked to the door then turned back and gazed at Ram, but could think of nothing to say.

Stopping briefly to purchase a few groceries, she

drove home, wondering what might happen next in what was once a peaceful village.

More than usual, the villagers were talking to one another, gathered in small groups here and there, trying to find out if their neighbors knew more than they did. Susan soon learned that Ayyappa was not liked in the village as he beat his wife and made no friends. He also was known to hang out with ruffians who were often drunk on toddy. In talking with the neighbors, Ram learned that Ayyappa was also a toddy tapper. Toddy was a cheap liquor made from climbing to the top of a coconut tree and tapping the palms. Ayyappa could earn more from the toddy business than being an ordinary road worker elsewhere. The problem was the workers would usually be found drunk by nightfall. Ayyappa was no exception.

Ram found Ayyappa's home and interviewed the wife – now widow – who was called Meena. A slight young woman in her mid-twenties, she dabbed her eyes with the end of her sari. Bowing to the policeman, she backed up respectively as he entered her modest home. Ram saw that there were many reddish clap pots on the ground and the recognizable smell of toddy filled the room. Further inspection revealed a large square-shaped knife with a wooden handle used to cut and tap the toddy on the top of the coconut palm. Closer inspection showed bits of hair and blood on the knife. Ram turned and leaning outside the house, called for Pradip who came at once.

"Pradip, bag that knife then take it to Dr. Thomas."

"Yes sir."

Ram then turned to look at Meena whose head was bowed as she continued to cry. Ram also noticed that her face was cut and badly bruised.

"Meena, I think you had better come with me to the station to make a statement."

Meena's eyes, widening as a frightened deer caught in the headlights of a speeding car, slowly shook her head no.

"Come now, no one will hurt you. Come."

Meena backed up and appeared to shrink in front of his eyes.

There was a commotion among the villagers, their voices raised as they encircled the toddy tapper's hut. Hearing them, Susan appeared from her house, remaining quietly on the porch. Concerned, Susan watched as Ram escorted the frightened young widow to the police car. As Ram closed the back door of his car, he turned and saw Susan. Without thinking, Ram slowly nodded to her before getting in the front seat and driving off. The sound of crows created a cacophony like some Greek chorus, heralding tragic events.

Susan looked up just in time to see a large, graceful black bird with two long white feathers flowing from its tail, resembling streamers at a football game. It seemed more like a sky ballet. She had read somewhere that this bird was known to be a good omen, and was called the bird of paradise. She thought it odd how this terrible event could be a good omen.

After classes the next day, Susan walked over to the Police Precinct. She shyly asked to see Inspector Pillai. After a few moments, he appeared, surprised yet not displeased.

"Miss Edwards?"

"Yes. I wondered if I might ask about the case -, if that's all right, that is."

"Do you have time for a cup of tea?"

Susan nodded.

"Let's go out. Fresh air helps the thinking."

Susan followed Ram to the Hotel Annapoorna where they found a secluded table at the back of the hotel's restaurant. They were silent at first, remembering that this was where they had first glimpsed the other.

"I'm not sure why I came, but I keep thinking of that poor woman. Surely, it was an accident?"

"Hit over the head then falling into the well? I rather doubt that, don't you?"

"Was he already dead before?"

"Oh, yes, it was a fatal blow. It may have been self-defense as his wife was beaten, and I'm told it was not for the first time, either."

Susan sat silent, taking it in. "Does she have any

family to visit her?"

"Not that we know. She is not from these parts. It was an arranged marriage."

"I wonder, might I see her?"

"Does she know you?"

"No. I don't know her, Inspector, but I'd like to help her, if I can."

"Why, when you don't know her?"

"Because she has no one else."

Ram looked at Susan in a new way, thinking, "This is a good woman."

"She's a rather small woman, wouldn't you say?""

"Yes."

"And thin?"

"Yes."

"And her husband was much taller and very strong to do the work he did, don't you think?"

"I suppose. What are you saying, Miss Edwards?"

"Well, Inspector, I was just wondering how such a slight woman could have managed to give such a blow as to kill a man then carry him to the well and throw him in?"

"I'm not sure it's a good idea, but yes, you can see her. She's very upset."

A few minutes later after Susan signed some papers, she was admitted to Meena's cell.

Meena lay crumpled up on a plank which also served as a bed. Susan approached and gently touched her shoulder, "Meena? Meena?"

Meena turned, recognizing the woman as the one who lived in her village. Her eyes grew large as she dabbed them with her already wet tail of her sari.

"Is there anything I can do for you? Are you hungry?"

Meena shook her head, saying, "What can anyone do now? It's too late. I have done the greatest sin."

"Your husband, he beat you, yes? Badly? Often?"

Meena lowered her head as if to say yes and feel the shame of it.

"Then what you did was done to protect yourself, isn't that right?"

"No, Miss."

"No?"

"Not me. Not for me." Then Meena unwrapped the top of her sari to reveal the child she was carrying.

"Oh, you are going to have a baby. You were protecting your baby."

"Yes, Miss. "

When Susan came out of the cell, she learned that the Inspector had already left for the day, so she returned to the village, deep in thought about what she might do to help this young widow and her baby. Arriving home, she made a cup of strong tea, sat down, and wrote down word for word everything that was said in the cell. Tomorrow before her first class, she would leave her notes with the Inspector. Susan began to prepare a light supper of green gram and chapatis when there was a knock on her door.

"Kapil? Is everything all right?"

"Yes, Miss. I was wondering if you heard anything about Meena?"

"Come in. It's all right. Come in. I'm just making some supper. Have you eaten?"

As they sat there, Susan saw that Kapil cared about the young widow so she shared what she knew and her determination to help her.

"That is good, Miss. Meena is not a bad person. She was very kind to me."

"Did you know her husband, too?"

"He was a very bad man. He beat her all the time. He would drink too much toddy then beat her. "

"How old are you, Kapil?"

"Fourteen, Miss."

"You look very strong for your age."

"Miss?"

Susan stood up and Kapil did the same. "You best go home now, Kapil. Don't say anything to anyone, ok? I promise to let you know of any developments."

"Thank you, Miss. Thank you," he said, as he bowed and quickly left.

The following day, Susan was in the middle of her class, jousting with a long stick with the Master's son, Joshi. The heat was such that she had to work hard to focus on the task. When they finished, she was told she did well and that someone had left a note for her. It was from the Inspector, asking her to stop by when she could.

Ram sat in his office, having hung up his jacket. He stood up as Susan entered.

"Please, sit down. Would you like some tea?"

"Yes, please."

Ram nodded to his aide who quickly left, returning soon with two cups of tea and a plate of digestive biscuits. Susan helped herself, hungry from the jousting.

"I read your notes. I did not know of her condition."

"I think I may know something more, but I don't want to get anyone into trouble."

"Well, I guess you'll have to trust me then, won't you?"

"Kapil is a young boy, only fourteen, a good lad. He came by to see me last evening, concerned about your prisoner. He confirmed what others say, that her husband was drunk all the time and beat her often and badly."

Susan stopped talking as if deciding to continue.

"There's more you want to tell me? What is it?"

"Yes, that is, I'm not sure. It's only an assumption. I have no proof."

"But?"

"But I'm guessing that Kapil may have helped her."

"Helped her how?"

"Carry the body."

"Hmm. Possible. Possible. I think perhaps,

Miss Meadows, you would make a very good police woman."

Susan smiled, almost blushing. Ram noticed what a nice smile she had.

"It's time for supper. Would you allow me to invite you to dine with me? And we can talk some more."

Hesitant, Susan looked directly at him across his desk, and intuitively knew that she could indeed trust this man.

"Yes, thank you. I'd like that. Has Meena eaten anything? She must, for the baby."

"I'll make sure matron sees to it. Shall we?"

Ram assured her that he would share her discoveries with the barrister who would be defending her and suggesting it be called self-defense. Dinner went longer than either thought as they ventured into other topics, discovering that they had more in common than the body in the well. As he paid the bill, as if an afterthought, Ram invited her to a Kathakali Performance Friday evening since she had yet to see the well-known dance-drama that originated in Kerala a few hundred years ago.

"I should warn you that these performances last for hours, but we need not see it all."

"It will be in classical Malayalam, won't it? Since my Malayalam is more the everyday Malayalam, perhaps you could tell me the story."

"Of course. As a matter of fact, the word

Kathakali means 'story play'. It began in the seventeenth century in Kerala as a courtly dance drama enacting mythic stories of the Hindu gods and goddesses."

"I'm intrigued, Inspector."

"The name is Ram."

"And mine is Susan", as she raised a cup of sweet milky tea to her lips.

After Susan brought Meena some of her clothes and toiletries, she met her defense lawyer or barrister and ascertained if he was well-informed as Ram had promised. He was. The hearing would be the following Monday, and Susan agreed to be a witness for the defense. The police guard seemed attentive and made sure she had all she needed. She felt better, knowing that Meena was in a better state and eating well for both herself and the baby. Leaving the station, she met Kapil who handed her some sweets.

"Hello, Miss. She likes these. Could you?"

"All right, Kapil. Wait here."

She let Kapil ride behind her as they returned to the village. Kapil smiled when he got off the scooter, saying, "One day, I will have a scooter like this. I will work hard."

"First finish your schooling. Then you'll get a good job."

"Yes, Miss. I will do so."

Two hours later, Ram arrived to drive them to the outdoor area to see the Kathakali. A huge crowd gathered, and luckily, Ram had arranged for some chairs to be roped off near the stage. He gave her a Limca soda pop, and Susan smiled thinking, "This is a real date!" The actors were stunning as were the colorful costumes influenced by the seventeenth century Portuguese. Amazing how much travel to India had occurred centuries before.

The story was from the great epic, *Ramayana* – Ram's namesake. Sri Rama was an incarnation or avatar of Vishnu as an example of a noble and courageous king who was also spiritual. When the ten-headed monster, Ravana, kidnapped Rama's wife, Sita, Rama went to Sri Lanka (Ceylon) battled Ravana and carried Sita home. Re-united, Rama and Sita pay homage to the gods for their safety and happiness, and his subjects rejoice knowing that the Good will always win over evil.

It is so Indian to see story as destiny in action – where the good triumphs in the end. She could not help but wonder if Meena's life would triumph in the end.

It was Monday and the heat was relentless as it usually was before the rains came. Susan alerted Master Kutty's son that she had to miss class to attend the court hearing.

She visited Meena who did not want to attend. She had already accepted the total blame for her action. Her passive surrender aggravated Susan. How could this woman not fight for her life and that of her child? Clearly the fault was not entirely hers. Susan promised to sit with her throughout so, in the end, Meena agreed to go. The defense attorney was young, probably just out of law school, with no experience. But he was earnest. Meena insisted she plead guilty and the young attorney added, "My client pleads guilty out of self-defense." The judge set the trial date for two weeks ahead and, as it was a murder trial, bail was denied.

Susan came daily to bring Meena what she might need, and always stayed a few minutes to sit with her. Meena told her that her husband was not a bad man. Not his fault. It was the toddy. The drink made him mad. He never beat me except on nights when he would drink. Susan told Meena that she would have to admit that her husband beat her every night and that you feared for the life of your child. Meena trusted the American lady so she bowed to her instruction.

As she visited the police precinct daily, she would always have a few words with Ram. Sometimes they would share a meal near the station before she drove back to the village. She knew that Ram would do all he could for Meena so that they shared a common cause which seemed to bring them closer together.

His mother tried to arrange another tea date for her son and suitable bride but he put her off, saying, "Not now, Amma. The trial is soon."

The trial date arrived and Meena was shy and frightened to appear, so once again, Susan promised to stay with her throughout. She was disappointed to miss her classes but felt that sometimes a warrior must fight in different ways. The judge was in his late fifties and had a kind face. There were no witnesses for the prosecution except the Police Inspector who mentioned that he had learned that the deceased had the habit of beating his young wife daily.

Susan was the only witness for the defense and echoed what the Inspector had said, adding that, "Meena had never resisted his beatings before now. But knowing she was pregnant, Meena instinctively knew she must defend her baby. She blames herself and suffers because of what she has done. Surely, her suffering is justice enough?"

Meena took the stand and was sworn in. She averted her eyes from the judge. The Prosecutor tried to shame her, resulting in more tears, so that she could not say a word. The Defense gently asked her questions and she answered as prompted by Susan. It was obvious to all in the courtroom that Meena deeply regretted her action.

Meena and Susan had tea in a nearby room while they waited for the judgment of the court. After one hour, Meena's attorney came and said, "It is time."

The paper from the jury was handed to the judge who asked the defendant to stand. Meena stood with her attorney facing the judge. She was trembling and trying hard to stop her tears. Susan crossed her fingers and said a prayer.

"The jury has found the defendant not guilty."

Susan put her arm around Meena, "It's over, Meena, it's all over. You are free."

Meena looked up at Susan, not believing. "It's true, Miss Susan?" Susan nodded then turned around and smiled at Ram, grateful that he had no small influence on this decision.

Meena returned to the village only to pack and leave as one of the police officers from the station had in the past weeks fallen in love with her. They would marry and the soon to be born baby girl would be fathered by a good man. Susan promised to come to the wedding to be held at a local temple.

Ram and Susan continued to see each other and Ram's mother continued to organize teas with suitable girls. In one month, Susan's student visa would end as would her Kalari training with the Master. Decisions would be thrust upon both of them. Ram was torn between family duty and his growing attachment to Susan. And it was the same with her though neither would say anything about it. Ram had suffered from indecision all his life. No wonder *Hamlet* was his favorite of Shakespeare's plays.

Late afternoon on Friday, they drove to Kovalam Beach not far from the city. Susan took off her shoes and walked in the sand with waves from the Arabian

Sea. They had enjoyed fresh seafood from an outdoor café, and now it was *Sandhya*, the setting of the sun – between light and darkness. Silence stood between them like an impregnable wall.

Susan was watching the cormorant birds diving into the sea for their supper. She remembered seeing the beautiful bird of paradise at the time the body in the well was discovered and how she wondered why such a good omen appeared then. Now she knew that as terrible as a death was, it had brought them together.

Ram stopped walking while Susan slowly strode ahead a few steps before realizing he was not beside her. She turned and gazed at him, and at that very moment made up her mind. As a determined Kalari warrior, she walked back and without a word, kissed him for the first time, fully on the lips. "I cannot leave you, Ram. I cannot."

Ram paused, weighing all the considerations, yet logic failed him. Susan stood her ground, waiting. After a lengthy pause, Ram spoke.

"No, and I cannot let you leave. If you did, I would follow you to America."

After a long pause, Ram added, "Samsara"

"What?"

"Samsara. It means the ever-turning wheel of life. The endless cycle of birth and death. Life. Love. Come here, Miss Edwards."

"Yes, Inspector," said Susan, softly laughing.

Ram, confused, said, "What's the joke?"

"The joke, my dear love, is that it all began with the body in the well."

~ 5 ~

# The Bus Home

*Live as though you were to die tomorrow.*
*Learn as if you are going to live forever.*

Gandhi

From the start, the day had been both hot and humid. Geeta awoke later than usual, hearing the radio weather report, and hurried to heat the porridge for her mother. In her mid-twenties, she already knew she was not beautiful and might never attract a good match. However, she was not unattractive either. Geeta washed and dressed quickly, because she had somewhere special to go today.

Originally from a small village over two hours from Delhi, Geeta had grown up in old Delhi since age six and had loved the four years of schooling she had before her father died. He had driven an auto rikshaw, worked hard seven days a week, and died young. There was only her mother and herself, and Amma could no longer work, rarely now even leaving the flat.

One day each week after selling spices in Palika Bazaar, Geeta would treat herself to seeing a new film. She was aware that though Amma did not like to be alone at night, she understood that her daughter had to have some special treat at least once a week, even if it meant her returning late. Today was Geeta's special day.

"I must hurry, Amma, or I'll be late for work."

"Go. Go, my child. Don't forget the Digestive Biscuits – the ones with Plain Chocolate."

"No, Amma, I won't."

Geeta always enjoyed the bus as it was a time to rest and dream. She usually sat near the back of the bus, and by a window if she was lucky enough to find a seat. Unlike most young women, Geeta did not dream of marriage, but of returning to school. There was so much she wanted to learn, such as the philosophy of *The Mahabharata*, India's great epic.  Yes, to learn and to travel. Travel! That was something she had yet to experience. She read books from a free library she had discovered a year ago, mostly history and travel books. That was how she knew where she would like to visit once she was free to do so. Varanasi (Benares) was on top of her list, and she would often imagine going to the temple pujas and bathing in the sacred Ganga to be blessed by the gods. She had cut out pictures from magazines and Sunday papers and had pasted them on her bedroom wall. So, the images danced in her daily life, becoming so real, it was as if she had already travelled and experienced their wonders.

But for now, Geeta knew her duty and that was to care for her aging mother, whose arthritis was so advanced that even walking was a daily challenge.

As she peered out the window of the bus, seeing well-dressed women in colorful saris and gold bangles, she thought, "But at least we have each other." Geeta had learned from an early age 'to expect little but to dream big'. After all, dreams cost no rupees. This made her laugh and then blush when a man in tie and suit turned around to see who was laughing.

"Connaught Place" shouted the bus driver. Geeta quickly rose and barely made it to the rear exit in time to get off. From here, it was a short walk to Palika Bazaar, the sprawling underground market that provided her livelihood. Near the entrance, she spotted a large poster advertising the latest Hindi film starring her favorite actor, Akshay Kumar. Excitedly, she smiled before descending the stairs to sell spices. How long this day seemed before she could shop for Amma and then get to the cinema. Bollywood had thrived, providing dreams for all castes and classes, producing more movies than Hollywood. And everyone needs their dreams.

For lunch, Amma had packed some rice and dal with mango pickle. Geeta enjoyed watching the multitudes of all kinds of folk pass by. She smiled when they stopped at her stall. Sometimes tourists would ask her questions and she would respond, smiling, educating them on such matters as which spice was best suited to cook what. "Turmeric, mustard seed, and cumin, along with chilies are the basic ingredients for Indian dishes – and good for your health as well." They liked that -especially the Americans.

The day seemed long, but at last, it was time to close up the stall and shop for Amma. She was careful to remember to buy the Digestive Biscuits with Plain Chocolate as these were Amma's favorites. As she walked up the steps to ground level, she saw that, in contrast to the brightness of the morning, clouds now covered the sky. By the time she reached Connaught Place, she could see that the darkness had overtaken the light. Due to the increasing downtown traffic, waiting for buses took longer each day, but eventually the bus arrived. It was night, yet the bus was nearly full. Still, Geeta was able to go to the rear of the bus to a window seat where she could sit, rest, and dream her dreams.

Though she had never seen the Taj Mahal, she knew the beautiful story about the Mughal emperor in the seventeenth century who had built the mausoleum for his dead wife, Mumtaz. And it was said to be the most beautiful and perfect building in the world. She had seen a movie about the Taj and read the story in a book from the free library. "One day, I will take the bus to Agra and see it for myself." The anticipation alone excited her.

She left the bus, carefully holding her groceries, and walked two blocks to the Cinema House. The movie had been on for five minutes, so she hurriedly found a seat in the crowded hall. The film was called *Kesari,* a story about a battle at Saragarhi in 1897, when twenty-one Sikhs had stood out against an army of ten thousand Afghans. Geeta was enthralled, because the film was tremendously entertaining and was also history. She could learn something she never knew before. She slowly unwrapped a menthol sweet she had kept in her purse – until now. Her modest pleasure was complete as she slowly sucked the sweet and watched Akshay Kumar portray the hero of the story.

So absorbed in the film, Geeta did not notice the three boys who sat behind her, laughing and watching her. After three hours, the Bollywood extravaganza ended, causing Geeta to wipe her tears, reluctantly get up and walk out of the cinema. Her bus station was only two blocks away, and it was nearing midnight now, so she looked neither left nor right and focused only on going home. Twenty minutes passed before the bus came and she was happy to find it almost empty due to the late hour. As she paid her fare, Geeta could smell the alcohol on the driver, who quickly turned his face away. She walked to the rear, which she had all to herself, and found a window seat.

Gazing out the window into the darkness, she could still envision the historical drama unfold: the battle scenes and the courageous exploits of the hero. She clearly remembered every scene in the long film re-enacted now as if the outer darkness itself became a cinema screen just for her. She considered the horror of wars and why men must always kill one another. She remembered a book she had read from the Free Library about the *Mahabharata* when Satyavati, mother of Vyasa – who wrote the *Mahabharata* – implores her son to rewrite this terrible epic of violence. She begs him to rewrite the story – erase all hatred, and save the world. Vyasa sadly responded to his mother, "I cannot invent the story. I am only the channel. The story invented itself, as it has invented you and me."

Not having had supper, she considered unwrapping the digestive biscuits. "No," she thought, "Amma likes to unwrap them to eat. I will wait and have one with her."

As she carefully returned the wrapped biscuits into the plastic bag, she looked up to see three rough-looking hooligans in their twenties coming towards her. They were dark-skinned laborers wearing white tee-shirts stained with red beetle-juice, and worn, loud-colored lungies wrapped around their waists, pulled up to show their legs. Instinct had told her not to make eye contact and look away, which she did at once.

It was then she heard their guttural laughter and looking around, noticed that the bus was empty except for the surly, drunk driver, herself, and these rough boys. She got up to move closer to the front to be near the driver, reaching up to take hold of the shoulder strap, when one of the boys pushed her backward, causing her to fall. Geeta struggled, causing the bag of groceries to spill. When she tried to scream, another boy who had trampled over her fallen body now held her down and quickly placed a soiled sweat-stained cloth in her mouth.

The boys were upon her now and she smelled the cheap toddy they had drunk mixed with their day's sweat causing her to recoil from disgust as well as fear. They were young, but they were strong as one now held her from behind while another raised her cotton sari and petticoat over her head, making it difficult for her to breathe. Sheer terror caused her to stop struggling and freeze, unable to move. Then one by one, the boys had their way with her, ripping her private virginal parts as they did so. The pain was unbearable. She could hardly breathe which meant it was no longer possible to scream. She thought, "I'll not fight and when they are done with me, they will run away. At least, I will live. I must live."

Such were Geeta's terrifying thoughts as she tried to summon the cinema's hero to come and rescue her. When no one came, she called for Amma. The rough boys all took turns a second time, quieter now but with clear purpose. She felt cold liquid streaming down her legs. Was it blood? Or from the boys? "If only I could breathe!" was Geeta's last thought before she lost consciousness. When they had finished, they mumbled quietly among themselves before making their decision. Together they pulled her bloody sari, drawing it more tightly across her face then pressing hard until they were sure there was no breath left.

The inebriated and indifferent driver stopped, routinely glancing over his shoulder to see if anyone wanted to get off. The boys bolted as fast as they could – the leader grabbing the unopened digestive biscuit packet that had fallen to the floor – as he kept pace with his cohorts – jumping down from the bus then running, running as if chased by demons, while a young girl at the back of the bus lay completely unmoving. Both the girl and her dreams together had come to an end.

~ 6 ~

# The Men's Club

*Friends are the family we choose.*

𝒜deep was the first to arrive, as always. He wiped his forehead, carefully replacing his pocket handkerchief, and walked into the India International Center. A handsome man with thick wavy black hair and light skin, he smiled and nodded at all the staff. Unusually tired after teaching his graduate history class at Delhi University, he made his way to the upstairs dining room, chose a table in the back with a view of the garden, then all but collapsed into the chair.

Looking down as the workers prepared for Diwali, Adeep was comforted. No matter how much new money moved into Lodhi Gardens, the IIC never seemed to change. Founded in the 1960s as a venue for vigorous intellectual and cultural debate, the debate remained fresh, the food excellent and reasonably priced. Some called IIC a "geriatric club," and indeed there was a cadre of formerly prominent men who came to have tea, nod to each other, and to hold court.

Adeep's cell rang, and he looked down to see if it needed answering. After a moment, Adeep got up and went to the verandah to answer. It is late October, the day before the Festival of Lights. Lamps already placed down the long driveway leading up to the sprawling building. It is hot, nearly 80 degrees. In a month it will be much cooler.

"Yes, Bhavani, I am already here, waiting. Don't wait for dinner. I may be late. Remember that today is the anniversary. Good bye, my dear."

As Adeep returned to the table, Amaan walked up. Amaan's hair was shorter, and thinning, but otherwise he looked the same as he had last week, last year, last decade. Amaan's jacket needed ironing, but he never noticed such trifling details. The first time Adeep saw Amaan, at St. Stephen's college in Delhi thirty years earlier, Amaan had that same sense of purpose and rumpled jacket. Adeep felt tired remembering how young and bold they once were, how they believed then that anything was possible.

Amaan looked at Adeep with genuine affection,

as a reminder that there was still hope for the world, hope for India. As Amaan slumped into his chair, he noticed that though Adeep looked tired, he was nattily dressed, with perfect hair and perfect posture, just like that first day in the canteen at St. Stephen's. "Come, sit," Adeep had unexpectedly said that day, noticing that Amaan had a tray of food but literally could not find a place to fit in. It took a moment that day, long ago, for Amaan to believe that this ideal Brahmin in his perfect suit would so easily break bread with a poor, brash Muslim who could barely put on a tie properly. Without Adeep's naive kindness, Amaan wondered if he ever would have had the courage to even stand for Parliament. There were countless times at St. Stephen's, later in politics, and even in his neighborhood, where Amaan keenly felt that he was 'the other'. But never, not once, at Adeep's table.

Amaan smiled and said "You, man. You're always the first here." Adeep chuckled with amusement, and with no hint of judgment. As Amaan knew, Adeep preferred to arrive early and wait. It gave him time to collect his thoughts.

"And, of course, Nathan will be last," said Adeep.

"He may be in surgery."

"No doubt. No doubt." Amaan looks out at the workers in the garden.

Adeep says, "They're preparing the garden for Diwali tomorrow."

"So that Lakshmi may smile and bring us good fortune."

"Well, yes, that, too. But remember that on Diwali, Rama rescues his wife, after slaying Ravana. He is enthroned as a king, but also as a god, pure and good for all beings."

Amaan usually loved to hear Adeep's naïve recitation of Hindu myth, the same stories over and over. But today Amaan was irked for some reason. Amaan put down his menu, and challenged Adeep. "I cannot but wonder, Professor, if that was ever so. A leader who is pure and good for all. Today, if you are not a Hindu, it's bad luck all around."

Adeep nods, "No better for us, Amaan. I'd say it is bad luck for all of India today."

Amaan shakes his head, "What is happening to our modern, secular democracy, Adeep? The British are long gone, Nehru's vision already forgotten, and the lines of caste and religion run even deeper. Just look where we are today."

Adeep smiles, "You should still be in Parliament, Amaan – where you could make a difference."

Amaan scoffed. "How could a Muslim make a difference today in this Hindu nation? Corruption knows no bounds. The Justice system - and not only the lower courts but even the Supreme Court toes the populist line."

"I know. I know. The government claims to move forwards by walking backwards. India seems to want the light of dawn yet embraces a never-ending night."

"And you, my old friend, are a poet, wasted in teaching those college kids." Amaan poured a glass of water and drank it all in one long gulp before continuing, "Remember College? Remember Morning Assembly? Tagore's prayer, envisioning India's "tireless striving, stretching its arms towards perfection."

Adeep, ever the professor, absent-mindedly added: "From Tagore's *Gitanjali,* "Where the Mind is Without Fear."

Amaan continues, unabated "Yes, well, now everything has changed. Joining the government was once a badge of honor, and I think a quarter of our college became civil servants. Today, the smart kids are avoiding government and running to multi-national corporations. I see it with my students. The corporate mentality has usurped 'Ask what you can do for your country.'

"And you, Amaan, were the brightest of the smart kids. And you can still make a difference, to make this country what it should be."

Amaan could not be cross with his old friend's undue optimism. He pondered that if Rama himself came tomorrow and India made a throne for the god -king, Adeep would not even be surprised. It was almost as if sometimes he was so pure that he could not imagine impurity – not in his friends, not in his country.

Amaan changed the subject. "I'm starved. Where's Nathan?"

"Saving lives as every good surgeon's vow commands."

"Well, at least one of us is making a difference."

Adeep points across the room, "Speak of the devil."

Nathan hurriedly makes his way to the table. "Sorry. Tricky procedure."

"And the result?" enquires Adeep.

"Oh, he'll live."

Amaan retorts, "But I may not unless we eat soon." The others chuckle as they pick up their menus. Deciding between English, Chinese, or Indian food, the three order the Indian Thalli: basmati rice, three hot curries, mango pickle, and raita – a yogurt dish designed to cool the palate. Adeep, the vegetarian Thalli, Amaan and Nathan, the non-veg.

Nathan notices the flutter of workers hurriedly preparing the garden for tomorrow's festivities. "Diwali?" His friends nod while starting on their meal. Conversation waits until coffee and they face the decision to order dessert or not.

"Hmm, well, no contest for me. It's the caramel custard pudding. Better than the ones I had in England, actually," says Nathan, looking again like the young student he once was at the University of

London. The others submit to his enthusiasm and order the same.

Nathan looks at his friends and says, "Can you believe that we graduated thirty years ago and here we are, still friends. Still meeting here at the IIC every Saturday."

Adeep with kind mischief, chirps, "Sounds like we're in a rut."

Amaan looks across the room at an empty table against the wall, "Many years ago, I was taken to lunch here by my father, and you'll never guess who was sitting across the room. Mrs. John F. Kennedy and her son, John."

"No way," said Nathan.

"True." Later we learned that the boy studied Indian history at Delhi University for a year and stayed here at the IIC.

"There was such a love for America at that time. Many students did their graduate work here instead of Oxford or Cambridge. Years later we even created our own Silicon Valley in Bangalore," Amaan commented.

Nathan added, "From my point of view, the sad thing was that Indians more and more incorporated the worst traits of America. Importance of money without consideration of ethics or morality."

"You said it, brother, and here we are today," added Adeep.

"Amaan, did you meet them?" asked Adeep.

"Who?"

"The Kennedys when they were having lunch here."

Amaan shakes his head, modestly, "No, no, I did not wish to intrude. Besides, it was thrilling just to see them take an interest in India."

At this time, the custard pudding arrived and was given due attention along with the steaming coffee. Whether they spoke or not, an effortless camaraderie was apparent as with any who have sustained a friendship for over thirty years. After a sizeable pause, Nathan said, "Once I attended a concert in the auditorium downstairs. I had time and did not even inquire as to what the program was. Imagine my surprise when a lovely Irish woman stepped out on the stage with a small harp and was introduced as the granddaughter of W. B. Yeats. She sang Celtic songs as she strummed the harp. Imagine, the spirit of W. B. Yeats in New Delhi!"

"Yes, one never knows what will turn up here. International in every sense," said Adeep, continuing. "Thirty years ago, we graduated from St. Stephens College which everyone considered an ivory tower of knowledge. Well, ignorance is bliss and all that. Were they our happiest years, do you think?"

Nathan looks at Amaan who smiles, "Well, Adeep, I for one cannot say those were my happiest years.

"No?"

"Nor I" adds Amaan. You forget that Nathan and I, as a Christian and a Muslim, were then as today, minorities in both college and country. What say you, Dr?"

Nathan puts down his coffee to answer. "St. Stephens was a very snobbish place. Not only were the majority Hindu such as yourself, Adeep, but the aristocrats of the country were there. Sons of maharajas and so on. Cliques based on pedigree. Don't get me wrong. I grew a lot there. Surrounded by wolves in a jungle, something rubs off on you, and to survive, you grow. I gained confidence along with a first-rate education, so I have to say I am grateful for that experience."

A surprised Adeep responds, "But we were friends. We were all friends."

Amaan smiles, "You, Adeep, were the exception to the rule." Perhaps you don't recall the ragging that went on. Being stripped naked and sent to your room. Sometimes kept up all night running errands for the upper classmen. 'Fresher, come here. Do this. Do that.' Some had breakdowns and left college. And if you complained about a senior, well your life would be a misery for the next three years. But the real danger was later on becoming like them, behaving just like them."

Nathan adds, "Humiliation was simply part of the initiation. They ragged you then introduced themselves, then sometime you passed muster for a while and they could not rag you unless you forgot their names. Seniors would choose two or three freshers and it was down on all fours while they stood on you as if you were a donkey."

Adeep protests, "But we were all ragged like that for a while."

Amaan: "Perhaps, Adeep, but if you were a minority, like Nathan and I, it was harsher."

Adeep shakes his head, "So much for Nehru's vision of secularism. Nonetheless, I remember college as a time of hope and expectation. The distinct feeling that we could achieve anything."

Amaan says, "Yes, yes, of course, that, too. But have we?"

Adeep adds, "Well, Nathan has. He's the best heart surgeon in India."

Nathan modestly raises his hand in protest, "Fortunately Ruth and the children know no such thing."

The friends smile and sit quietly for a time while Amaan stares out the window as if mesmerized by a gardener burning leaves. The fire soars upward toward the sky, retrieving an old memory. His friends notice a change and lean forward.

Nathan speaks first, "Amaan? Amaan? What is it?"

Amaan slowly turns back to his friends, "Hmm? Oh, strangest thing. Watching that bonfire below, I remembered something. Something I thought forgotten long ago."

Adeep signals for more coffee and the waiter obliges. No one speaks until the cups are full.

Nathan pours milk into his cup, stirs then inquires, "So, what memory?"

Amaan almost blushes, "Oh, it's a trifle, nothing, nothing at all."

Adeep: "Not by the look on your face, it isn't."

After a pause, reluctantly, Amaan replies, "O.K., as you know, my mother died when I was eight. She was everything to me. She had given me a stuffed animal, a little horse, for my fifth birthday and I took the horse with me everywhere, slept with it every night. The night after Ma died, my father got drunk. He never drank at all until the night after she died. But that night, he did. At first, he just kept looking at my mother's photograph and continued to drink the whiskey. Then he saw me clutching my horse and suddenly became angry. He shouted, "Why do you cling to that toy? You must be a man now." I had never seen him so angry. I couldn't speak. Then he abruptly stood up, grabbed my horse, walked outside and threw it into the trash can. "No, Papa, no." I tried to get it, but my father held my shoulders from behind, and shouted, "No. You must be a man now." Amaan turned his head around, ashamed to have his friends see him weeping like a child.

Nathan put his hand on Amaan's shoulder and said, "It is good to cry, Amaan, a man must know compassion. You must weep for your mother. A man must first be a human being." Amaan bowed his head while fidgeting for his handkerchief.

After a moment, Amaan took his handkerchief and wiped his face. Looking at his friends, he said, "You know, I've never told this to anyone. Not even Amira. In fact, I thought I had forgotten all about it."

Nathan joined in, "How many things we hold, never told, forgotten secrets that live on – some even making us ill." Nathan looks away and Amaan notices something is amiss. "Nathan? What is it?"

"What is this, talk show therapy?"

"Not at all, Nathan. Tell us"

Adeep nods as Nathan takes a sip of his coffee then stirs only to delay talking.

"All right, but you must not tell anyone. I haven't even told Ruth or the children yet."

"Nothing leaves this circle of friends," says Amaan as Adeep nods in unison.

"Well, not to beat about the bush, it appears that the doctor is unable to heal himself."

"What? You're ill?"

Nathan clears his throat and adopts an objective professional attitude, "Prostate cancer. Stage 4. Stupidly, I let it go too long."

"But you're well enough to work as a surgeon."

"Yes, for now."

"Surely, there's some treatment? If not western, then Ayurvedic?" offers Adeep.

"Too late, I'm afraid." Then Nathan adds, in a lighter tone, "And, unfortunately, unlike you, Adeep, I do not believe in reincarnation. So, there is only this life to live."

Amaan, moved, "Oh, Nathan, I don't know what to say."

"There's nothing to say, but I confess that I'm glad that someone knows. You know what Woody Allen says? 'I'm not afraid of death. I just don't want to be there when it happens'."

Adeep tries to laugh but only manages a weak smile. Amaan sits as though struck dumb.

Adeep finally speaks, "I wish you could believe as I do, Nathan, for to me, death is simply walking from one room into another."

"Sadly, not for me, as I do not believe in either heaven or hell except the man-made variety."

Amaan adds, "The price of a good education. We can no longer believe in fairy tales. Nathan, is there anything we can do? Anything at all?"

"Well, stay my friends until the end?"

Both speak at once, "Yes, yes, of course."

Adeep adds, "I think you must tell Ruth, don't you?"

Nathan nods, fighting tears at the prospect of telling his wife that he may soon die.

Adeep, noticing that lunch is over and the waiters eager to clear the tables, says, 'What do you say we go downstairs for a cup of tea?"

Nathan adds, "Perhaps a walk in the gardens first?"

The three men walk out more slowly than they had entered. No one speaks. They enter the expansive Lodhi Gardens adjacent to the India International Center. The weather is clear though overly warm. Middle-class men are walking their dogs, some smoking. The friends pass by a circle of nine men, standing and laughing, all together, non-stop laughter.

Amaan stops and asks, "What on earth is this?"

Adeep laughs, "It's a new form of yoga. Laughter yoga. The group meets daily, forms a circle, and laughs for no reason at all. Supposed to be good for the health."

Amaan chimes in, "Well, now, I've seen it all."

Nathan adds, "It certainly does no harm to them or anyone else."

The walk approaches the Muslim tombs.

"There, aren't they splendid. Built in the 15th century for the Lodhi's dynasty.

Adeep, the historian, adds, "That's right, Amaan, they came from Afghanistan and ruled for seventy-five years, until the Mughals came. No matter how great, how powerful, nothing lasts.

Amaan smiles, "Thank you, Professor. Still these tombs look like palaces. They are something."

"Palaces for the dead." Nathan looks up solemnly at the great tomb, then continues, "Adeep is right. Nothing lasts forever." The friends walk on as a multitude of large black ravens fly over the ancient tomb.

Returning to the Centre, the friends sit outside on the veranda, and order tea and biscuits carried out efficiently by a waiter dressed in white. The gardeners scurry here and there so that when Diwali comes tomorrow, the gardens will be perfect.

Adeep, as any habitual professor is apt to do, expounds, "Four major religions were born here in India. Twenty-three major languages and probably twenty-two thousand dialects for one billion inhabitants. The largest and most diverse democracy in the world, yet still we are more separate than unified."

Amaan watches two sprightly young men jog past, "Now the young are the majority and we are but another minority. The hope is that they will take up the challenge that is India today, but will they?"

Nathan speaks, "I simply do not understand this fervor and pressure to conform, and to think one group is more special than another. Are we not all human beings?"

Adeep responds, "Still, it is the individual that changes the world. Look at Gandhi."

Amaan rises, "Don't be an innocent, Adeep. The caste system is alive and well. Partition is only more subtle today than in 1947."

Nathan adds, "I read in the paper last week that

there are now a hundred billionaires in India and over three hundred million still live in poverty.

Amaan says, "That's right, Nathan, and our government pays only 1% for public health. It only takes one life-threatening illness to destroy an entire family."

Adeep muses, "Thirty years ago, we thought we could change the world."

Amaan, "To change the world you must first change yourself."

Adeep corrects him gently, "I think Gandhi said, "You must be the change you wish to see in the world."

They sip their tea and watch a white egret land near them on the pristine lawn – its beauty an antithesis to their despondent thoughts. Time passes.

Nathan says, as if speaking to himself, "Sometimes the value of old friendships lives not in what we say or even what we do, but rather in the silences we share."

The sun begins to set as the workers retire for their tea and supper.

Adeep stands and stretches. "Tomorrow is Diwali. The lighting of the lamps is a form of puja to the gods: the prayer and promise of health, knowledge, prosperity, financial security, and peace in life. I guess we are all innocents in the long run, aren't we?"

Nathan says with affection, "Adeep, never change.

True, you are still an innocent in many ways, but you are good. Truly good in every way. Something rare in today's world."

Amaan nods in agreement while Adeep avoids their gaze. "I am not as you think I am."

Nathan responds, smiling, "I think we know you pretty damn well after more than thirty years."

Adeep sits down again, takes a moment, then reveals what lies heavily on his conscience.

"There is one thing you do not know. One thing that not even Bhavani or my parents know."

Amaan, with attempted humor, "What is this, true confessions?

Nathan silences him with a look, then turns to Adeep, waiting.

"As you may remember, my parents arranged a marriage for me before I left India to study in the United States.

"Indiana University."

"That is correct. But the point is I was married before leaving India, then I was in Indiana the next three years for the Ph.D."

"Nothing uncommon about that. The young Hindu wife waits for you to return as Bhavani did."

"Yes, Amaan, she did and she has been a first-class partner and mother to our children." Adeep paused as the others waited.

"But while … while at Indiana University, I met a girl, a wonderful girl, and we fell in love. I told her

I was married but she did not care, and eventually neither did I. The passion was too great, you see. And Margaret – that is her name – Margaret fell pregnant. It was during the final weeks of completing the doctorate, and I was soon to return to India. I told her I had made a promise to my wife and to my family and had to return. I had no choice. She insisted on having the child – a daughter as it happened. By the time she was born, I was back home, back to a new job, and my marriage – a good Hindu girl from a good family."

Nathan exclaims, "My God, I don't believe it. Not you."

Amaan, "Why not him? This only proves that he is a man, a human being, with desires."

Adeep responds, "Yes, and also a fraud."

Nathan struggles for words, "But … then…I mean, what of the American girl and your daughter?"

Adeep answers, "I send money and once a year Margaret sends me a photograph of our daughter. Jenny. She is called Jenny. I have never met her. Margaret eventually married a more responsible man, and had two more children with him. And that is that."

Nathan, still in shock, "And you never told Bhavani?"

"Why would I? Why hurt another?"

"How to live with that?" asks Amaan.

"With difficulty."

Amaan adds, "This makes me wonder if it is ever possible to completely know another human being."

Nathan wisely adds, "No one is just one thing, Amaan. One might as well ask 'is it ever possible to completely know one's own self'?"

The sun sets slowly as the darkness of the evening envelops the friends. There is the piercing sound of strolling peacocks calling for rain while a few hurried bats begin to dart here and there as if to say, "The night has come. The darkness belongs to us."

Nathan winces at the bats then says, "You know, the bar should be open by now.

Shall we?"

Adeep nods, "Yes, please. A Kingfisher beer would be most welcome. Amaan stands up, "A whiskey for me, if you please."

For a minute, Adeep stands with his friends as they grasp the moment in stillness, watching the night arrive. Standing firm and together, committed without words to support each other's weaknesses, a sense of sacredness prevails.

Adeep speaks softly, "Somewhere in the Puranas, a disciple asks, "When does the night end and the dawn begin? And the Sage answers, "When two travelers from opposite corners meet and embrace each other as brothers, knowing that they both sleep under the same sky, see the same stars, dream the same dreams. That is when the night ends and the dawn will begin."

~ 7 ~

# A Fulbright Folly

*There's no place like home.*

L Frank Baum, *The Wizard of Oz*

Amy was born in a small suburb near a large city in Texas. Her parents, upper- middle class, decent Americans, were proud of their daughter and hoped that she would marry well and settle down in Texas near them. But the very week after graduating from university, she flew away. Her dream was to be an actor in the theatre and for this, she knew that she must go to its mecca. New York City, the city of dreams, had seen many Amys arrive to pursue their dreams. Only a tiny few succeeded – most settled for marriage and a contented life somewhere in other suburbs.

Not Amy. She had an unshakeable, focused vision, and a determination to get what she wanted. After five challenging years, if not a star, she had become a respected actor earning her livelihood from her chosen vocation. Later on, surprising even herself, she began to write plays with strong female roles. Her first play won a prestigious prize that allowed her to live without having to earn a living for one year. Since an early age, Amy had also possessed a spiritual bent from an early age, leaving organized religion behind in a relentless quest for an alternative that would provide meaning to what was already a purposeful existence. Unfortunately, this sometimes made her prey to various charlatans who had gained popularity in the West, and who relied on those like Amy to create their own livelihoods.

First, a popular Indian guru who chanted Sanskrit verses and urged all to discover the blue pearl within. She sat for hours in this attempt only to fail - even when the guru passed by gently taping her on the head with a large peacock feather meant to awaken the seeker. Next came a yogi, dressed in a white dhoti and long, white kurta, of undetermined age from north India with long, limp, white hair and beard, and who smiled all the time. She took naturally to Hatha Yoga as though she had done it before and soon became a favorite pupil of the master. The old yogi made unwelcomed advances not long after, so she hurriedly left.

Despite these early experiences, her thirst for all that was India persisted. She read Hindu philosophy beginning with the *Upanishads* which she remembered had influenced Emerson in the nineteenth century when he began the transcendental movement in New England. She read the great epics, the *Ramayana* and the *Mahabharata* – the latter becoming her favorite, especially the chapters known as the *Bhagavad Gita*. She felt deeply that if one understood the *Gita,* this alone could become a firm foundation for life.

But though she read profusely and meditated daily, she felt intuitively that something was missing. As the scriptures said, a true, living Guru was needed: Guru and disciple are one, like a candle and its flame.

"If I am to discover what I seek, I must go to the source – and that is India."

Amy read of the Fulbright Scholarships and applied for a Research Grant to India. She had been asked to teach playwriting at a prestigious university in New York and had done this for the past two years. She hoped that the university affiliation might help her to win the Fulbright. Three months later, just after a new play of hers was successfully produced in New York, Amy received a letter announcing that she had indeed won the Fulbright Research Grant to India. She enthusiastically began to prepare for the adventure that she hoped would change her life. Perhaps this would tame the restless demon of never being content with who she was or where she was. The demon of feeling that there was something missing, that whatever was achieved or known was never enough.

Her actor friends thought her mad to leave a promising career as a playwright and asked, "What is this folly you are undertaking?" Amy simply laughed, tossed her long, dark hair, and responded, "A Fulbright Folly." She sublet her midtown high rise apartment to one of her older graduate students and after goodbyes to friends and family, headed east.

Arriving at Delhi Airport, Amy was confronted with the cacophony of sounds and smells that abruptly catapults the unaccustomed Westerner into the exotic chaos and confusion that is India. After two sleepless nights in the air, Amy was grateful that she was met and driven to her hotel.

The next day the eleven other Fulbrighters were introduced to her at breakfast. She learned that they came from all over the United States and were widely diversified in their chosen study topics from classical Carnatic music of south India to modern politics after India's Independence in 1947. She felt proud to be part of this brilliant effort to broaden the mind by studying far-flung places and varied cultures. Amy thought to herself, "This is how government money should be spent rather than bloody wars."

At a government party that evening, they were told that each year, a different scenic trip was scheduled for the Fulbrighters, and that last year it was the famed Taj Mahal. This year, they were to be flown to Bombay (Mumbai as it is called nowadays) then onto Aurangabad before being taken by bus to visit the amazing Ajanta Caves – one of the seven wonders of the world. That night. Amy tried in vain to quell her excitement and combat the inevitable jetlag in order to sleep. She dreamt of becoming lost among the hordes of people circulating in the Delhi airport. In the end, she managed a mere three hours of sleep, yet the next morning, her enthusiasm spirited her quickly into action. She had another plane to catch.

Seated next to an Indian civil servant on the plane to Bombay, Amy smiled thinking that if she were casting a spy in a play or film, she would definitely cast the man sitting next to her, dressed in dark suit and tie with close cut hair, and asking too many questions. After arriving in Aurangabad, a designated bus was waiting to carry the dozen Fulbrighters the next 165 miles to the famed Ajanta Caves.

Their guide, a young man in his mid-twenties who spoke excellent English – a legacy from two hundred years of British rule - stood at the front of the bus and tutored them enroute. "The thirty rock-cut Buddhist cave monuments date from the 2nd century BC to about 480 AD. The caves include colorful mural paintings as well as rock-cut sculptures that are among the finest surviving examples of ancient Indian art. They are very expressive showing the emotions through gesture, pose, and form."

"How and when were they discovered?", asked one of the more academic Fulbrighters.

"Yes, yes. Discovered in 1819, by a British soldier, Capt. John Smith, who was in a tiger hunting party near the caves. A local shepherd boy showed him where the entrance was and Smith asked the villagers to come to the site with axes, spears, and torches to cut down the tangled jungle growth that made entering the cave difficult. Once inside the caves, he vandalized a wall mural by scratching his name and the date over the painting of a bodhisattva.

"Bodhisattva?" another fellow American asked.

"Yes, a bodhisattva is any person who is on the path towards Buddhahood."

As Amy stood in the wilds of India, outside the entrance of the first cave and looked around at the multitude of open cave entrances, she keenly felt how far she had come from Times Square and the Broadway theatre district. Laughing out loud, she said, "We're not in Kansas anymore!" Tom, a Fulbright historian from San Francisco, overheard her and laughed in recognition of the well-known line by Dorothy in The *Wizard of Oz.*

"Well, Dorothy, shall we enter?"

"How wide and amazing the world is," she smiled, before stepping into the second- century caves.

After an exhilarating and breathless two hours, she entered Cave 4 and came upon a huge, overpowering rock-cut sculpture of the Buddha in teaching pose surrounded by bodhisattvas, his disciples on their way to Buddhahood. Tears filled her eyes, as she felt the deep desire to know the peace visible on their faces and to one day acquire the wisdom that years of turning inward might yield.

As she walked on as in a waking dream, exploring other caves, she visualized Capt. John Smith crudely scratching his name and date on one of the priceless murals in sharp contrast to the many anonymous artists who left no trace of who they were or even when they drew or carved their masterpieces. Amy was grateful to have visited the caves as she felt she had touched the ancient depth and wonder that is India.

From Mumbai, Amy said her goodbyes to her American companions and flew to south India, her chosen area for research. The research project she had submitted to Fulbright was titled *The Actor-Storyteller of South India* where story and drama had more than mere commercial appeal. In fact, she had chosen Kerala for her study of dance-drama and shamanic rituals as that state had been less influenced by the invasions of the Muslims as well as by British rule, thus better preserving the purity of the ancient traditional forms.

She sought the oldest known dramatic shamanic forms in India, more than five thousand years old, which were created by the indigenous Dravidians. Still performed, these pre-Hindu forms of dance and drama were slowly diminishing. She would study them and make sure there were film records. The dramatic forms had passed from father to son for thousands of years. Now, however, the younger men were more interested in becoming software engineers in Bangalore – India's Silicon Valley - and earning well which meant that these precious forms were in danger of decline – and even extinction.

Kerala is located at the southernmost tip of India – just across the sea from Sri Lanka (Ceylon). Amy had read a charming myth about the origin of Kerala, how it arose from the cosmos. Parashurama, an avatar of the god Vishnu, had performed severe penance to atone for his sin of killing his mother, so Indra, the main god, rewarded his devotee by reclaiming Kerala from the depths of the sea. Amy's heart and mind were well-primed to embrace her Oz. She would soon learn that myth and reality in India are so intertwined that one often becomes the other before you know it.

The luxury of having won a Fulbright Research grant was that the recipient could move freely and decide where and what to research, unlike the Student or Lecture grant which tied the recipient to one school. Amy decided to take a couple of days exploring on her own before contacting a professor she was told would assist her.

Arriving in Trivandrum, the capital and the largest city in Kerala, her first order of business was shopping for Indian clothes. She had been advised to go to the Emporium as the prices were fixed and fair. She decided that churidars or cotton pants with a long cotton kurta (shirt) that reached well below her knees were the most practical attire. And a young German woman at her hostel suggested she also try the new Fab India for the best clothes. Though more expensive, they were indeed much finer. She also purchased one sari in case of special events and found a local tailor to make the small gold-colored fitted blouse to go with the bright red cotton sari which had gold borders. With her dark hair and brown eyes inherited from her Welsh ancestors, Amy hoped that she would blend in and be taken for a north Indian rather than one more American tourist. She found at the Emporium a practical pair of sturdy leather sandals as well as a lovely grey, wool Kashmiri shawl with delicate pink and green embroidery, in case of cooler weather.

Amy was touched by the sweetness of the people who waited on her, and the slower pace of life which allowed room to breathe and simply be – unlike the hustle and bustle of New York City. And she loved the food! Delicate spicy curries and basmati rice or chapatis. Yet, most of all, she had the wonderful feeling that she was where she was meant to be at this time in her life.

She stayed up most of the night devouring two books on the history of Kerala that she had found in the Modern Book Centre. The following morning, after her porridge, she was eager to explore the city. After visiting the museum and Rajah's palace, she went to see the Sree Padmanabha Swamy Temple known as the richest temple in the world – with valuables more than one trillion dollars in its treasury. Its hoard of gold and precious jewels is believed to have accumulated in the temple over hundreds of years, donated to the Deity by various dynasties and Rajahs. Rumor has it that two enormous cobras protect the innermost hidden chamber, and anyone who dares to open the vault will meet with dire results. In 1908, two robbers broke in and found not two but hundreds of cobras encircling the treasures, and the terrified thieves ran for their lives, with nothing to show for their trouble.

The specific date of the temple's origin is vague, but was probably built some hundreds of years ago. Amy was discovering that as time is considered unreal, local people- unlike those in the West – are not bothered by exact historical dates. The great tower over the temple was later constructed by Rajah Varma in the eighteenth century. During the two equinoxes (Sept and March) one can see the rising sun pass through each of the ten floor openings at five- minute intervals in perfect alignment. "How clever they were – even then," thought Amy.

Amy was disappointed when told that only Hindus were allowed inside the sacred temple. But after she showed her Fulbright Guest of the Government card and made a small donation, an exception was made. She secretly delighted in the flexibility of India's bureaucrats.

Inside the temple, she was amazed at the eighteen-foot sculpture of Sri Padmanabha or Maha Vishnu reclining on a serpent. The serpent has five hoods facing inwards, signifying contemplation. The Lord's right hand was placed over a Shiva lingam. On either side of Vishnu, were his two full-breasted consorts, Sridevi, the Goddess of Prosperity and Bhudevi, the Goddess of Earth. Brahma emerges on a lotus flower, which emanates from the navel of the Lord. The deity rests on two platforms carved out of a single massive stone cut out of a rock measuring some twenty feet square which is two and a half feet. Amy stood there for several minutes to take in every single detail of the enthroned god who, in his divine majesty, lay in repose without fear or concern. She sighed, thinking, "Indians have no need to read mythology. They live it every day!"

After eating a light supper of lentils and chapatis at the International YWCA Youth Hostel, she wrote copious notes in her journal before going to bed. Tomorrow she would begin to make inquiries about shamanic or dramatic performances in the capitol. And, she probably should contact Professor Narendra Sharma who was to assist her in her research. Amy had done her homework and learned that Prof. Sharma was not only a respected professor at the University of Kerala but a professional theatre director as well. She would greet him as a colleague.

When they spoke on the phone, they agreed to meet at the university – not far from where Amy was staying. One of the largest buildings in the city, it was easy to find. She had read that it grew out of an earlier college established in 1834 and that its current name and form dated from 1937. Built from white granite stone, it would last for hundreds of years.

Upon meeting Professor Sharma in his office, she was struck by his kind yet enormous sad eyes. Though in his late forties or early fifties, he looked much older as his hair and short beard were speckled with many white hairs. Sharma was delighted to learn that Amy was a professional actor and playwright from New York.

Over coffee in a nearby café, Sharma told her that she was there at the best season for performances of Kathakali, the most famous dance-drama of Kerala, and Kutiyattam, a much earlier Sanskrit form dating from the tenth century. Amy smiled as she gently interrupted the professor.

"That sounds fine, Professor Sharma, but my research is for the indigenous Dravidian forms before the Aryans came."

"Oh, yes, yes, those, too, may be seen. Usually at the temples and villages not far from the city. In fact, there's a Theyyam performance. I could take you tomorrow at 5pm?"

"That's perfect. Oh, might I have a library pass for the university?"

This provided Amy with a full day to obtain some books at the university library and research before actually viewing the ritual dance. Amy learned that there are more than four hundred varieties of Theyyam. It is a ritual art form that predates Hinduism, going back over five thousand years to a time when the most common form of worship was tribal animism – worship of trees, serpents, and animals, with rituals sometimes involving blood sacrifices.

"What?" exclaimed Amy so loudly that others in the library looked up in wonder. Amy smiled apologetically. "Blood sacrifices?" she thought to herself, wondering what she had gotten herself into.

That night Amy wrote to Suzanne, a fellow actor and a close friend in New York.

Dear Suzanne,

India is a complex country so whatever you say about it, the opposite is also true.

India is a mirror that reflects what is within you

and then intensifies it. Perhaps this is why many Westerners are frightened or even repelled by this country as it forces you to face yourself. My demons are stirring. One moment I want to stay here forever and the next to run like hell.

New York seems so far away. Do send your news as I send my love, Amy.

Professor Sharma, as promised, collected Amy at 5pm in his black ambassador car and they headed north for her first experience of Theyyam. She learned that Sharma, never married, was devoted to his plays and his students. Apart from teaching, he was an active professional playwright and director in his own language, Malayalam. Amy noticed that whatever the hour, he always looked tired, not completely well.

"It will be a late night as the performances begin late and go until early morning."

"I don't mind, but I don't wish to impose on you."

"I enjoy it, but when you've had enough, just say the word and we can leave."

It was November, the best of the seven- month season for performances which are traditionally held outdoors. November and December provided the best climate, with less tropical heat. Unfortunately, the mosquitoes knew no particular season, continuously circling in clustered clouds, attacking at will.

Amy enjoyed a light supper with Professor Sharma, who then spread blankets on the ground, and procured water bottles for them. In a small, sandy ring, frenzied drummers began beating their drums in perfect synchronicity. Young priests lit palm frond torches, carelessly swishing embers off into the air. Older priests appeared in crisp white lungies then stood in line in front of the small temple, staring at the crowd as if to command their attention for the sacred moment soon to come.

As they waited, Amy liberally spread local anti-mosquito cream on her arms and neck while Sharma explained that these ritual dances can go on for hours, depending on how long it is before the god, Kutty, enters the trance, totally taking him over. The performer begins the day's events by singing and chanting stories in minimal costume. Only then, once painted and dressed in his most elaborate attire, is his transformation complete. Only then is he fully prepared to channel his god, Kutty.

Amy was about to say something when suddenly a collective breath was released from the crowd, and a sense of awe filled the void. The god had arrived. The Theyyam began.

The face paint was ornate: wide eyes sunken into black pits, while the rest of his face was a vivid orange. Red designs spread across his face as if a tiny lizard dipped in paint ran hither and thither, the lines so delicate that they were almost invisible. The overall effect was distinctly supernatural – which was precisely the point.

The dancer, now inhabited by the god, spins for what feels like ages. Sometimes he spins so quickly it's hard to focus in the low light. Other times, he spins slowly, as though dazed or drunk. Members of the crowd cautiously approach him bearing crumpled rupee notes, pressing them into the god's hands for a blessing as he continues to spin. Amy whispered aloud, "It's not only great theatre, it is sacred."

Finally, Kutty dashes to the front of the temple, walking back and forth several times before finally collapsing onto a seat before the priests. Young boys fan his sweating body with towels as the old priests bring him offerings of food and rice. As Kutty catches his breath, the crowd begins to disperse. Some move away to chat and compare photos with friends, while others move forward to whisper to the god, asking for advice and blessings.

Kutty then stands atop a wooden stool at the center of the ring. Two young priests hold his hands, steadying him as he circles in a tight, stomping dance to the drums. Bells and bangles clatter as he rattles his feet between rotations. He looms over the crowd, reminiscent of a giant serpent poised to make a kill. The drums halt and there is not a sound to be heard anywhere. And then, Kutty abruptly turns and exits. It is over. The god has vanished.

Amy was mesmerized and later could not remember how long he danced and twirled, spinning around and around as if carried by the increasing thunder of the drums. Time ceased to exist. In reality, what seemed a short time was several hours. Amy was surprised to witness the sun rising, for it was already the next day.

Driving back to Trivandrum, Amy could not speak for a long time. Sharma looked at her and smiled, understanding her mood. After almost an hour, Amy asked, "Professor Sharma, tell me about the men who perform these rituals."

"For over five thousand years, the young men have inherited from their fathers and grandfathers the calling to continue the tradition. A tradition handed down through family lines, the dancers begin preparing for their divine roles at a young age, often in their early teens. Years are spent learning the skills required for every part of the tradition, from how to make costumes from coconut husks to the delicate art of face painting."

"Say more."

"Well, let me see. When not performing, Theyyam dancers are mere mortals. The weeks leading up to a ritual demands of them, a life of purity. He consumes no meat or alcohol, nor does he lie or speak badly of others. He prays at the temple daily and cleanses himself before the dance."

"It is a sacred dance." Amy laughs out loud.

"What is funny?"

"I was just imagining what the Broadway critics would say about this performance."

They both laugh.

"Professor Sharma, if you don't mind my asking, why did you never marry?"

Shyly, he responds, "Well, the right girl said no, and I could not settle for less. You might say I married the theatre, and my students and fellow actors have become my family."

"Yes, I understand that. Theatre is a family – though sometimes dysfunctional."

She raised the possibility of having the dances and rituals filmed in order to preserve this extraordinary tradition. And Professor Sharma came up with an enticing proposition.

"Actually, some of my former students are filming the Theyyam and other early shamanic rituals, and donating them to the University in my name. So, we could make copies of them for you in exchange for a few acting classes, what do you say to that?"

"That's an offer I can't refuse."

He laughed, saying, "*The Godfather,* right?"

"That's right."

During the following weeks, a friendship emerged between them. Amy enjoyed teaching and even more so, experiencing more early rituals and dances. She respected how devoted Sharma was to his students and fellow actors, and touched by the growing affection she herself felt for the students and they for her. Over lunch one day, she asked Sharma, "What sustains you? I mean what makes it possible for you to get up every morning and keep on?"

"The belief and hope that things will improve. Also, the fact that there are a few who make life worthwhile, who balance the hundreds of others, and make me believe that some people are truly good at heart."

Amy smiled, "I suspect, Professor, that you have too much heart for this world."

Sharma chuckled, "That's what my doctor says."

Amy settled down into an enriching routine studying the ancient forms of storytelling blended with a deepening of her friendship with Sharma. As productive as he was with his students as well as his professional work in the theatre, he was a lonely man, a man who had known sorrow yet had persevered. He would often sit at the back during her acting classes and just smile and nod. This was just the break from New York that Amy needed in order to restore her faith in the work she did and would continue to do in the future.

The only setback was her health as the heat and humidity of tropical south India did not agree with her at all. Once back in New York, she knew she must attend to what was most likely some bug or other. But she refused to allow a weakening body to dampen her mission.

Some of the shamanic forms of early performance rituals were held in private homes. For instance, one lone performer enacted a ritual for fertility. Women who had trouble getting pregnant would sit in large circles surrounding the ritual while the lone performer drew them in with his intense movements and the inevitable loud drumming. Some of the women would swoon and cry out as in ecstasy. Great theatre, thought Amy, with good psychology thrown in! Before there were shrinks, there were shamans.

Another favorite Theyyam was a dancer on long high stilts making his god larger than life. Each dance was completely different in form and action. Amy knew that a dedicated researcher could spend an entire lifetime studying the four hundred forms of Theyyam, but she was happy to collect what she could so that this unique performance could be remembered. She and Sharma had discussed this often and she had pledged to donate the film material Sharma had given her to the university who had invited her to teach an introductory course on Indian culture and philosophy the following year. Sharma's trusting smile was a firm contract.

Amy stood near a Dravidian serpent shrine that stood just outside a Hindu temple that had been built centuries later. When the martial Aryans came from Siberia to India more than five thousand years ago, they conquered other parts of India by war. Yet in

Kerala, the Aryans seem to have taken over peacefully, respecting the Dravidian animist gods and shrines. So, the Aryans left them undisturbed and simply built their larger Hindu temples devoted to their pantheon of gods next to the modest indigenous shrines that can still be seen today.

This tolerance in Kerala is today seen in the Cochin Jews who have been here over two thousand years as well as in the Syrian Christians who began to follow Jesus Christ when doubting Thomas, one of the twelve disciples of Christ, came to Kerala. And, though there are fewer Sikhs. Jains, and Muslims than are found in north India, they, too, worship their own religion in peace.

At this spot, before the snake shrine, a special performance was scheduled. Sharma had warned her that this one might be unsettling. Amy watched in horror and fascination as a fiercely made-up Theyyam dancer with a coconut straw skirt and large headdress danced with a live chicken! The origin of this unique ritual dance was to summon the Kutty god to ward off the pox. After many frantic movements with fierce drumming building a tension that became almost unbearable, the drums and the dancer would suddenly stop. Then in eerie silence, the god, barring his teeth, bit off the live chicken's head as blood spurted everywhere. This was captured on film and would be later viewed by Amy's university students–much to their delight.

During her stay, Amy unexpectedly felt inspired to write a short play set in India with the theme of reincarnation. The main character is a young woman who others believe has gone mad as she mourns for a lost love. They were together in a past life and she is reincarnated only to discover that the one she loved had not yet been born again. Unable to bear the separation, she goes mad. Amy decided to say nothing about the play until it was finished. Later, she presented it to Sharma as a parting gift. Delighted after reading the play, he asked permission to translate it into Malayalam. and then to direct the play with his company the following season.

"I'd be honored if you would."

There came a moment when their friendship might have become something more, but Amy held back and Sharma was sensitive enough to understand. It was as if Amy transformed her feelings for Sharma into a new work of fiction, the play. In this way, she felt that she had given him the best part of herself.

Not long after, while she was absorbed in solitary research at the University in Trivandrum, she heard that Professor Sharma was in the hospital with a severe heart attack.

Stopping only to purchase some oranges at a local shop, she went directly to the hospital. The doctor had said he was not allowed any visitors as his life was hanging by a thread.

Amy gave the oranges to the ward nurse and looked through a glass window as she presented them to Sharma. Sitting in bed, Sharma opened the newspaper wrapped parcel and when he saw the fruit, looked up with his customary wide smile and drew his palms together in a namaste, raising his hands high above his head in respect.

Amy modestly returned the gesture, somehow sensing that this was a final goodbye. They held each other's gaze for a few moments until Sharma's strength ebbed and he had to lie back down. Amy left in tears.

The next morning, Ravi, Sharma's assistant, called to say that Professor Sharma had passed peacefully during the night. He had just turned sixty. After the cremation ceremony, Ravi informed her that before he died, Sharma had translated her play and it was to be performed three months later. Moved that Sharma had kept his promise in spite of his deteriorating health, Amy hesitated then said yes when Ravi offered to drive her to Trichur for an upcoming annual major festival. In this way, Amy was able to experience the Pooram Festival in Trichur with a parade with twenty ornately decorated elephants and the traditional fierce drumming.

Thoughts of Sharma penetrated her mind and heart as she watched the noisy pageant with the added chaos of chanting from hundreds of devout Hindus. She thought of her reincarnation play now translated and soon to be performed. Perhaps if Sharma waited a bit to return, they might meet again in another life, and have more time to know one another.

Saddened by the loss of her colleague and friend and now herself riddled with amoebic dysentery, Amy at last admitted that she was homesick for America. And though she wouldn't have traded the year in India for gold and would always be grateful for the profound experience of this vast and complex culture, she was more than ready to go home. In place of her usual restlessness was born a firm resolve to return home and create from the depths of her evolving self. She had learned that it was not where you were, but how you lived and gave back what you had found. In the end, in her attempt to embrace a foreign culture, she had faced herself – only to realize how American she was.

In truth, this was India's gift to her: to accept who she was. Dorothy was right after all. Though the land of Oz was wonderfully magical, "There's no place like home."

## ~ 8 ~
## Rukmini's God

*The two worlds, the divine and the human ...*
*are actually one. The realm of the gods is a*
*forgotten dimension of the world we know.*

Joseph Campbell

The caw-caw of countless crows ... the slow swish of coconut-stick brooms gracefully maneuvered by bent backs ... the tinny unhurried rattle of stainless-steel buckets full of sugared tea and coffee grown in the nearby Kerala hills ... village women at the river scolding children, slapping saris against an upturned flat rock. India awakes.

It is early morning in Kottayam. Who would believe the miracle that would soon come to this sleepy town. The land is brown, parched as always before the first monsoon. The open beak of the chakora – most auspicious of birds – is turned upward to the heavens. The ancient ones say that this is how one must thirst for God. However, most villagers settle for some rice paddy, lentils, green chilies, and, if Lakshmi smiles, a new piece of cloth at Onam Festival, when old King Mahabali fulfills his promise and descends from heaven to visit his people each year.

"Will the rains never come?" complains Meenakshi, stretching her fat arms over her head. "Look, there she is again. There, sleeping on the pavement. That new beggar girl. Humph. As if we had any food to spare."

"She's young, "observes Pachakaimal.

"And crazy," clucks Meenakshi, dismissing her with a motion of her hand, and turning her head to steer her husband's mind back to the shop. The floor swept, she begins to set out the glasses and pastries, chatting with her husband to pass the time. With her parents' dowry, she should have done better than to marry a tea shop owner – and a lazy one at that.

Suddenly a bell clangs as if heralding a royal visitor. Two white bullocks with patient eyes sway, pulling a heavy cart of ripe coconuts to morning market.

Rukmini stirs in her sleep as the bullocks pass by, but she refuses to awaken and leave dreaming behind.

Every night when she sleeps, Rukmini dreams the same dream of the lotus-eyed, blue-colored one, Gopala Krishna, the one who dances with the gopis. The gopis, as of course everyone knows, are great rishis reborn as cow maidens to be devotees of Lord Krishna. Why should Rukmini wake from such a divine dance to the life of a street beggar?

Pachakaimal turns his head to watch the sleeping girl with close-cropped hair and wonders aloud, "What is her name? Which village is she from? Is she a widow? How young she is."

Menakashi shatters his musing. "Enough. Come along now. Get the glasses so we can open shop. Go to now. We must work. Aio, are all men lazy?"

"Orange ... orange ... papaya ... mango ... orange ... orange," hawk the street vendors. Rukmini opens her eyes, causing her beautiful, blue-colored lord to vanish. Dust flies from the scurry of thronged feet and fills her eyes, which she wipes with the edge of a faded, torn sari. She stretches and rubs her taut stomach, trying to remember when she fed it last. Yesterday? The day before? Time has ceased to be a reality. She remembers walking away from her village, a distance of five or six days perhaps. How long she has lived on the streets now she no longer remembers, nor does she recollect the day her husband died – and her in-laws threw her out. One mouth too many to feed they reasoned. She was then childishly naïve, vulnerable to the drunken, frustrated males who harassed and used her. Now, in her mid-twenties, she has left that village for good and made her way to this larger town.

Rising unsteadily to her bare feet, Rukmini steps out onto the dusty road and is almost struck by a bicycle which rings and swerves just in time to avoid hitting her, the rider scolding her inattention. Almost deaf since birth, she cannot hear the bell or his scolding. Rukmini misses her dream.

Nearby, on a backstreet lives Aziz. With memory as blank as his unseeing eyes, the old Muslim spends his days begging, plucking the sleeves of indifferent passers-by with his grimy, gnarled fingers. Old, blind, and gaunt, Aziz has regressed into infancy, babbling incoherently. Pachakaimal says Aziz has been on the backstreets of Kottayam for the past twenty-five years, a red, tin bowl his only possession. No one remembers where he came from or if he had any family.

How it happened or what unspoken understanding passed between them, nobody knows. One day the old beggar was alone and uncared for, the next, there she was beside him on his patch of pavement. There they were: Rukmini, the crazy Hindu village girl in a soiled and tattered sari, and Aziz, a blind and wrinkled old Muslim, suddenly inseparable.

As dawn breaks over their corner of the world, Rukmini now wakes with purpose and wanders down to the local tea shop. A handful of coins jingles in her palm and Meenakshi notes she always pays without complaint for tea and bread. Carefully balancing the hot glass of tea and the slices of bread, Rukmini ignores the jeering comments of the crowd. With what clearly is devotion, she lifts the steaming glass of tea to the old man's lips, and smiles. She is now the mother to the child he has become. She washes away the grime from his face and sees that he never goes hungry, never feeding herself until he has been fed. The townspeople call her mad to sacrifice what little she has.

A crow swoops down and snatches a piece of bread from Aziz's hand just as he is about to eat it. Unable to see that it has disappeared, poor Aziz bites his finger, causing onlookers to laugh. Mirth soon turns to silence as the beggar girl places the hurt finger against her forehead and tenderly draws the old man to her breast. Another day, Meenakshi interpreting Rukmini's compassion as suggestive embraces, calls out, "Crazy, crazy girl. Why do you give yourself to an old beard that cannot even see?"

Weeks pass into months as the odd couple provides morbid amusement for the dull town. The beedi-smoking men jeer while the young boys, sometimes from boredom, throw stones. Mostly Rukmini ignores them or laughs back, but occasionally she breaks down and cries into the old man's lap. Then Aziz comforts her as a father.

At night they sleep amidst beedi-cigarette stubs and discarded trash, curled up on the darkened backstreet like contented kittens.

Sometimes Rukmini is lured into strange bedrooms, returning with a couple of rupees in payment. Then, disapproving, the old man refuses to speak to her. Often, he is heard to wail, "What will she do after I am gone? May Allah protect her." Both accept that only death will part them now.

In time, they learn to ignore the rude stares and lewd taunts and gestures – not because he is blind or she is deaf nor because he is old or she is young, or he a Muslim and she a Hindu, but because in the filth and stench of an Indian backstreet, they have transformed dark poverty into light. Aziz is mostly now a contented man, stroking his stubby, white beard, and listening for hours to the young girl's chatter. Her movements once hesitant, are sure and quick, and full of purpose. Her face shines like a maharaja's jewel. The village women who pass now avert their eyes, blinded by such brightness.

Rukmini has no need of dreams now. She smells the scent of white jasmine. Even Meenakshi leaves her alone for the most part, content to count her money and fight with Pachakaimal. Still, sometimes angry with her lazy husband, Meenakshi cruelly taunts the beggar girl. "Can't you see he's nothing but rotting flesh?" Rukmini looks up, smiles, and says, "I do not know what you mean, mother. He is my Gopala Krishna, my lord. He is my blue-colored One."

~ 9 ~

# Tea with Mrs. Gandhi

*The fault, dear Brutus,*
*is not in our stars, but in ourselves.*

William Shakespeare, *Julius Cesar*

Suzanne Bartlett was a proud woman who had enjoyed a distinguished career as an actor – both on stage and screen. She had studied at the Royal Academy of Dramatic Arts, then at the Actors Studio in New York with the well-known – if controversial – method teacher, Lee Strasberg, who referred to his classes as 'the work'. There were rumors that certain past luminaries such as James Dean, Monty Cliff, and Marilyn Monroe who had ended their lives too young, were influenced negatively by Strasberg.

Working with Lee was an intense, even a religious commitment – and one Suzanne took seriously. Though two marriage proposals had come her way, she had said no, as 'the work' came first. One of her rejected suitors had told her, "You're totally independent. The problem with you is that you really don't need anyone." Though surprised, she accepted that this was the *persona* others perceived. A *persona* perhaps created early on as a protective shield from real life.

She lived alone on the thirty-seventh floor of a modern high rise in New York City near the Broadway theatre district, with a view of the Empire State Building and the Twin Towers. Glancing below, she enjoyed the daily arrival of luxury liners departing and returning from exotic ports around the world that she hoped one day to visit. Her life was full with interesting friends and challenging roles. And yet, as time rushed on, she became more and more aware that something was missing. By withdrawing from her personal life to portray her diverse characters, she had begun to ask herself, "Had I neglected the very relationships that constitute life?"

It was 1983, Suzanne had just turned forty, and, for some time, she had felt the need for a change. So, when she received an invitation to visit India as a Distinguished Guest of the Indian government, she was tempted. Afterall, she was free for the moment, had no ties, and had never travelled to South Asia, so why not?

When she shared the news of the invitation with her friends, saying, "It would be an adventure," they were not so sure. They knew that she had just broken off a long affair with a Wall Street financier who had wanted to marry her and that she was between acting jobs as well, but wasn't an extended trip to India a bit extreme? Why not Palm Springs or even Hollywood? However, as her friends knew, once Suzanne made up her mind, there was no stopping her. Within two weeks, she flew east. Arriving in Delhi and securing her luggage, a long black car was waiting for her, and a uniformed chauffeur hustled her through the mob. The driver made sure that she was well settled in her luxury hotel room, telling her that someone would come for her the next morning.

The hotel was as luxurious as any 5-Star hotel anywhere. After a hot bath, she left a wake-up call for 8 A.M., and went to sleep almost immediately after the long flight.

The next morning, she dressed in a beige tailored pant suit, wine-colored silk shirt, and a colorful scarf that would suit all occasions. Ready for adventure, she left her room and ordered a continental breakfast in the downstairs dining room. Suzanne noticed that the other guests were mostly tourists from America, UK, or Europe, who remained aloof yet gazed with a lethargic curiosity at one another. Suzanne was pondering what had brought them to India when a nice looking Indian in his mid-30s approached her table. He was well-dressed in a suit and tie and introduced himself as Hari Mehta from the Indian Tourist Office. After finishing her tea, she was driven to the government building and introduced to the Head of Tourism who was a former princeling, son of a rajah from Kashmir. He told her that she could travel to any place of her choosing, and would have at her disposal, a car and driver. As two of her friends had recently visited Rajasthan, she suggested that she be taken there. The former rajah told her that after three days, she would return to Delhi and begin to meet various prominent people in the arts. She was also invited for tea with Prime Minister Indira Gandhi. Suzanne was suitably impressed and looked forward to meeting her.

Singh added that he would suggest his own home, Kashmir, but it was, unfortunately, not safe at this time due to civil strife – the control of Kashmir often being a flash point for violence between Muslims and Hindus. He continued, "Since India's independence in 1947 when the first Indo-Pakistani War was fought between the two independent states, the strife has continued."

"Did many die in the first conflict?"

"About one million lives were lost in the 1947-48 conflict."

"What a tragic waste," sighed Suzanne, "Perhaps one day I may visit Kashmir as I have been told how beautiful it is."

Later, Hari told her that they would leave for Jaipur the following morning, but that she was free to do whatever she wished that day, and that the car and driver were at her disposal. Her first thought was 'shopping.' Hari advised her to go to the Emporium as she might find everything she needed there. She bought three sets of pant suits, navy blue churidars with a blue and white print kurta, another in yellow, and a third outfit in rose color. The light cotton would be practical in the tropical heat and hopefully, she might fit in to some degree rather than being seen as another typical American tourist. The next morning after a quick shower, she dressed in the blue outfit as if donning a costume for one of her roles. In a way, this was apt. Room service had brought a light continental breakfast, and by 8 A.M., she was in the lobby, suitable costumed, and ready to step into a new experience.

The car was on time, and Hari efficiently saw to her luggage.

"It will take about five hours – depending on traffic – so we had best get started."

After an hour or so, still jet-lagged from her journey from New York, Suzanne lay down in the back seat and slept soundly. After touring for years in plays, she had the gift of being able to sleep anywhere at will.

The honking of horns abruptly awoke her, and Hari suggested a rest stop. A few minutes later, they stopped at a small roadside tea stall and relished tea and masala dosa – a crispy rice flour wrap, filled with lentils, potato, fenugreek, and curry leaves, served with chutney. Delicious. Suzanne watched in delight as a lean youth wearing a colorful lungi poured the hot tea, mixed with sugared milk, from one large stainless--steel container to another to cool it. It was a dance, and the youth never spilled a single drop. Suddenly, from nowhere, monkeys were everywhere, a startling sight. Hari smiled and said, "They won't hurt you. Just hungry." Then Hari clapped his hands and the monkeys, as if on cue, receded to a nearby tree.

"Oh, as you had requested, I found out the name of a well-known astrologer in Jaipur, and we can visit this afternoon if you like."

Suzanne learned that Hari had studied in the United States at the University of Pennsylvania and joined government service after his return eight years ago. He was unmarried, but his mother would soon find a suitable match.

"Marriages are still arranged?"

"Not always and it's not quite the same. We meet each other now and then decide for ourselves."

"Well, it's probably as good a chance for success

as in the States where more than 50% of marriages end in divorce."

"Perhaps better odds here in India. And the horoscopes are compared as well to see if it's a good match."

"Soon, the DNA will decide as well, no doubt."

They shared a quick laugh at this.

Hari hesitated then asked, "And you? Marriage? Children?"

"No and no. But no divorce either."

The driver was back in the car and they returned as well. They would be in Jaipur in two hours, and Suzanne longed for a hot bath and rest. After they had checked into the hotel and rested, Hari rang her from the lobby and they headed to her appointment with 'destiny' "This should be fun", thought Suzanne.

The modest cottage in which the astrologer lived was set back from the road and almost hidden by banana trees and flowering bushes. In his mid-sixties, he wore a sacred thread that high caste brahmans wore. He was bare-chested with a pristine white dhoti, balding with intelligent eyes that indicated great knowledge. He sat on the floor on a straw mat. In front of him was a small polished wooden table with short legs of an inch or two in length. On top of the table, he had spread many tiny white sea shells and used these to count. After being told Suzanne's birth date, time, and place, he began to calculate using the shells and referring to a tattered large book. He knew nothing about her except the birth info which Hari had given him earlier, but Hari had mentioned that astrologers also went by the date and time of when the client came to see them.

"It is said that a great astrologer would know who would come to him that day though no one had told him before."

As he moved the shells on the wooden board, Suzanne began to gaze at a tiny house lizard on the white wall behind the astrologer. It sat completely still, waiting, then quick as lightning, its long tongue targeted a small fly or mosquito. Suzanne thought to herself, "Predator and prey. Thus, the world is divided."

She looked back to see that the astrologer was patiently gazing at her and showing that he was ready to begin. He knew some English, but sometimes Hari would translate. Expecting only to be amused, Suzanne was taken aback at how accurate the old guy was.

"You will know much fame as a performer, but will not be happy. This is because of what happened in a previous life in south India. When you were very young, you were given to a temple to become a devadasi."

"What's that? I don't understand."

Hari explained, "Dasa means servant of God. The Devadasis were female dancers who worshipped the gods, and danced in the temple. Usually dedicated to the temple at an early age, seven or so, they returned to the temple to work after puberty.

"When was this?"

"Some say the tenth century. Others that it goes further back to the third Century BC."

"What was their work? Dancing?"

"Yes, but also sex work, and the money went to the temple."

"You mean prostitution?"

"No, not at all, with a devadasi, having sex with nobles or rajahs was considered a sacred duty. The tradition was for patrons – usually nobles – who supported their education and that of their children. It was an acceptable part of Indian culture."

"When did this practice end?"

"Well, it still continues but not in the same way. It is no longer the upper-class girls who are dedicated to the temple."

"But the sex work continues?"

"Hmm, but these are not ordinary girls walking the streets," Hari insisted.

"A sacred duty."

"Yes, at least, that is what it was for several hundred years."

"Hari, ask him what happened back then to make me unhappy?"

"You were very much in love with a rajah and had a son by him. The baby was taken away, and you were not allowed to see either the father or the son."

"I don't understand what all that has to do with now."

The astrologer rattled on in Hindi as Suzanne grew impatient. Finally, Hari translated, "He says that is why you will in this life avoid both marriage and children."

The astrologer kept talking and after a moment, Hari added, "But you will never lack for money and will become even more known as a performer in this life. Your fear of loss will guard you against forming any serious attachments."

"I think I'm ready to leave now. "

Hari paid the astrologer and he nodded his head from side to side as if to say, "Yes, that will do."

Suzanne was quiet as they drove back to the hotel, but her mind was not. 'Fear of loss,' he had said. She had recently lost a cat who had lived with her for eighteen years, and her friends could not understand why when Bianca died, she had adamantly refused to get another cat. She knew she could not experience another loss.

She thought, too, of Mark, her Wall Street boyfriend for the past three years and why she refused once again to marry. The old man was right about this continuous pattern in her life of refusing to marry and have children. She had convinced herself that it was because she was married to her work – 'the work' as her teacher, Lee Strasberg, called it. But what if there were other reasons, reasons carried over from a past life. Could this be?

They pulled into the hotel and Hari opened the car door. Lost in her thoughts, she turned to him, "Hari, India certainly forces one to turn inward and think about life and things we have tried hard not to think about."

"It is my observation that Westerners either are shocked and dislike India or they are in some way changed, usually for the better, by being here."

"Really. Well, let's hope in my case, it is the latter."

The next day she was taken to visit the Jaipur City Palace, built as the residence of the Maharajah in the early eighteenth century. She rode upon an elephant up the steep hill to the sprawling palace, then walked about, though seeing little as she kept remembering what the old astrologer had said. Suzanne had never considered herself cowardly, yet perhaps years in the theatre had served as a major barrier to facing real life. There she could become everyone while staying nobody. It seemed that India was a mirror held up to whatever lay unseen within, intensifying both the good and the bad which each individual harbors. The only cure she knew was work, for in her work she knew who she was, and from the beginning of her career, had always felt at home becoming someone else. She wondered now if all actors felt the same.

Suzanne was glad that they were returning to Delhi. She asked Hari for information about

Mrs. Gandhi whom she'd meet the following day. She had read that Indira Nehru had married a man from Gujerat named Gandhi, apparently a common surname there, and that she was no relation to Mahatma Gandhi. Her father was Jawaharlal Nehru, a devoted supporter of the Mahatma and the first Prime Minister of India. After her mother died, she became even closer to her father, staying by his side as he led India after independence in 1947. When Nehru died, Indira entered politics becoming, in only a few years, India's first female Prime Minister. To keep herself in power, following the Supreme Court decision to strike down her election on the grounds that she had spent more on the polls than was allowed, Mrs. Gandhi declared a National Emergency, which lasted from 1975 to 1977. She suspended civil liberties and censored the press; all dissenters were killed, imprisoned, or bribed into becoming supporters. After lifting the Emergency, she was trounced at the National Elections that followed. Later the disunited opposition parties which opposed her soon lost power and, in 1980, she returned to power as a result of free elections. Suzanne had done her homework but wanted to know more.

Suzanne raised the subject, "Her father was elected as the first Prime Minister of a free democracy and yet his daughter acted as a dictator."

"The Prime Minister had no choice in the circumstances. It was a last resort."

"And now?"

"Now, she is a strong leader for our country."

"What is she like in person?"

"She has great dignity and is totally committed to her father's legacy."

"Well, then I am honored to be invited for tea."

Suzanne fell quiet, grateful for the air-conditioned car, and contented to watch the now familiar monkeys scampering across the road as the vehicle passed village after village. Here was India with its endless population – the largest democracy in the world.

Suzanne decided to stay in the hotel and rest before meeting the Prime Minister. She retired early, watched the government-controlled Doordarshan television even though most programs were in Hindi, then fell into a deep sleep.

The next morning, she awoke early, having dreamed about monkeys and the large swaying elephant she rode in Rajasthan. Impulsively, she called her agent in New York and told him that she was ready to work again – as soon as possible. That decision settled, she booked an Ayurveda oil massage which made her so relaxed that she could barely walk back to her room. She wondered if she would ever manage to get the oil out of her hair yet admitted to herself that she felt more at peace than ever before. Then, after a long hot shower and two shampoos, she slept again.

Room service obliged by bringing a grilled cheese sandwich and lime soda. Then she considered what to wear to tea with Mrs. Gandhi. After much consideration, she decided to wear her western pantsuit. After all, she was an American and there was no point in trying to be anything else. She wore her hair in a small bun at the nape of her neck and the 22--carat gold earrings purchased in Rajasthan. She felt tired but reasoned that she was just more relaxed than usual and it just felt liked tiredness. The phone rang. Hari was waiting in the lobby to take her to Government House.

Suzanne was ushered into a pleasant – if austere – room with two chairs facing each other, separated by a small exquisitely carved wooden table. After a brief moment, Mrs. Gandhi came into the room and they both did namastes with palms touching. The Prime Minister wore a well- pressed beautiful light green silk sari that reminded Suzanne of the draped yet stiff statue of Athena, the Greek goddess. Mrs. Gandhi gestured for her guest to sit and then ordered tea. Suddenly, she turned and asked her assistant where her son was and the reply came in Hindi. She seemed heavily weighed down with concern.

Suzanne's impression was that the Prime Minister was charming yet calculating. Kind yet shrewd. Slow to trust, she lived in constant fear for herself and for her sons. An attendant poured the dark fragrant Indian tea laced with milk and sugar, then disappeared. They exchanged pleasantries, but Suzanne did not feel that there was an opening to discuss anything in depth. She had tried to meet Mrs. Gandhi's eyes to make some human contact as strangers often do when meeting for the first time. But this other woman met her inquiring gaze with dark, hooded eyes, barricaded with burden and distrust, a walled fortress, and her tight, perfunctory smile did little to warm the atmosphere. Suzanne sadly felt the weight of the Prime Minister's responsibility, guardedness, and distrust that prevented any genuine conversation between them and seemed to crush any latent humanness. She had heard that Mrs. Gandhi was not overly keen on Americans and wondered if this was true. Sensitive to the forced atmosphere, Suzanne struggled within to take a breath.

In the end, she put down her tea and said, "I'm grateful for the opportunity to visit your country. Everyone has been very kind.". Apart from the attendant, she noticed two tall Sikh bodyguards standing not far away and realized how much pressure and courage lay on this woman's shoulders - which she carried with a determined dignity.

In the next few days, Suzanne met several creative luminaries in Delhi, including the head of the National School of Drama, Ananya, an impressive woman who asked if Suzanne might one day return and teach an acting course at the school. She accepted though she wasn't sure when that might be, but she would very much enjoy working with the students.

Suzanne returned to New York feeling more herself than ever before. Within two weeks, she was in rehearsal for a new play by Edward Albee to open in Philadelphia before coming to Broadway. At home again, she was grateful for her sojourn in India which had helped her return to herself in a deeper way. Her worst trait, she reasoned was her pride – a quality regarded highly in the heroes and heroines in western literature and history. Whereas in the great Indian epics she had read, humility always marked the great ones. The emphasis was not on individuality but instead surrendering themselves to serve their dharma. Not Scarlett O'Hara but Sita. Not St. Joan but Draupadi. Not knights and heroes but saints and sages are the true archetypes of India. This had so taken root in Suzanne that when she returned to America, others at once noticed a change. Both friends and colleagues saw a more introspective Suzanne, one more considerate of others.

Now and then, she would hear from Ananya, the head of the National Drama School in Delhi, and intended to keep her promise to return and teach an acting class – though it would be seven years before Suzanne would fulfill this promise.

Much had happened since her journey to India in 1983. She had learned from keeping in touch with friends in Delhi that Prime Minister Gandhi had remained fearful. Apart from her trusted Sikh bodyguards, she would always have three extra persons with her both in Delhi and when she travelled: a doctor, a person with her blood type, and a food-taster. Mrs. Gandhi always feared being poisoned and the taster would take a small bite of every dish on her plate. Suzanne recalled how cautious and slow to trust Mrs. Gandhi had seemed when they had tea.

Then, the unexpected happened. Less than one year after their meeting in Delhi, her two Sikh bodyguards brutally assassinated her on 31 October 1984. There is forever a religious strife in that beautiful country, thought Suzanne when she heard of Mrs. Gandhi's tragic end. Later the same day his mother was assassinated, Rajiv Gandhi was appointed Prime Minister, becoming the youngest Prime Minister of India at age forty. In his first week in office, organized mobs of the Congress party supporters rioted against the Sikh community. Somewhere between eight thousand to seventeen thousand Sikhs were massacred in Delhi. And so, the son revenges the mother's death.

"It's like a Greek tragedy, *The Trojan War*." Suzanne said to a friend.

Seven years later while campaigning for the 1991 elections, Rajiv Gandhi was himself assassinated in Chennai in May of that year by a suicide bomber representing the Tamil dispute in Sri Lanka – another conflict over religion and territory.

Such is the complexity of India, a country known for its saints and sages, yet which, on occasion when aroused, displays a bestial brutality. Suzanne was saddened and moved by what was happening there. After much thought, Suzanne called her agent to say that she was intent on returning to India. As it happened, the very next day, she received a letter inviting her to be a delegate at the India International Film Festival in Delhi, and that the government would cover her expenses. Synchronicity! Delighted, Suzanne took this as a clear sign that her decision to return was meant to be. Was this part of her dharma? She informed Ananya that after the Film Festival, she would be happy to stay on for another week and teach the promised acting class at her school. In return, she asked only for lodging and per diem costs for meals and transportation. Ananya was delighted and made the necessary arrangements.

Less than three months after the death of Rajiv Gandhi, Suzanne arrived once again in Delhi, this time for the Aug 1991 International Film Festival. All the delegates were to be treated to a day trip to see the Taj Mahal in Agra.

The bus trip reminded Suzanne of high school field trips, a fun way to get to know her show biz colleagues from India and those across the world. Though she had, of course, seen film depictions and photographs of the Taj Mahal, they did not adequately prepare her for the sheer perfection of beauty that it was. The guide began to explain, "It is said to be one of the finest examples of Mughal art and architecture -that is, the architecture is a combination of Persian, Ottoman, Indian, and Islamic influences. The Taj Mahal has exemplified perfection for over three hundred and sixty years."

"All very interesting, "said Suzanne to herself, "But what is the story?"

As if hearing her, the guide continued as they entered the building.

"The Taj Mahal is a symbol of everlasting love. It was built because of the Mughal Emperor Shah Jahan's passionate love for his beloved wife, Arjumand Banu – also known as Mumtaz Mahal."

"But this isn't a palace and could never have been their home."

"Yes, what was to have been her palace became instead her final resting place."

Suzanne's eyes filled with tears seeing the ever-burning flame inside the tomb, symbolizing everlasting love. She thought, "I could play her but I could never be her." The old astrologer in Jaipur was right. I will not marry or have children, but I shall never want for anything and my success will continue – as it has. I may win awards, but no everlasting love will be mine.

Suzanne was quiet on the return trip to Delhi, looking back on her life and the countless times she had avoided intimacy – except on stage. Suddenly, she smiled, thinking, "Who knows, perhaps the next phase of my life will be different and, in the end, I will get it all. Mrs. Gandhi seemed to have it all: success, marriage, children – yet look what happened in the end to her. Perhaps it is better to accept what is and not worry about the future. At that moment, riding on an Indian bus back to Delhi, Suzanne realized that she had accepted her life, grateful for what she had, and without remorse or regret for what would not be.

The young guide approached her, "Madam, all is well?"

"Yes, very well, thank you. India is a great country, and each time I come, I learn more."

The International Film Festival, as most other film festivals, was both exhilarating and exhausting. Girish Karnad's realistic social films moved her. Suzanne knew he was one person she would like to meet, if possible.

The next morning as she entered the dining room, there he sat alone at a far table. Brazenly and like a true fan, Suzanne crossed the room and introduced herself as a fellow delegate. Over breakfast, she was struck and intrigued by his forthright and perceptive comments about India and the film business. Suzanne was impressed that Karnad, a former Rhodes Scholar at Oxford, was a celebrated actor, playwright, and film director. A handsome man with a good heart was her lasting impression of this cultural icon.

After the festival ended, Suzanne met with Ananya at the National School of Drama to discuss the upcoming five-day acting course with twenty selected students. Suzanne learned that they were in rehearsal for *Oedipus Rex*. Inspired, Suzanne was eager to meet the students and offer an alternative approach to their craft. She knew that the school, modeled on British drama methods – was poles apart from the Actors Studio and Lee Strasberg in New York - and that this would be a challenge for actors trained only from without. That is, training body and voice without consciously drawing from their own emotional past. Yes, it would be a challenge for them both. But then, Suzanne thrived on challenges.

The same afternoon, the twenty students gathered for an introductory talk by her. Suzanne began by saying, "As you know, I'm an American, and my approach to acting is in many ways quite different from that of England. You are probably well schooled in preparing your physical instruments – your body and voice. These, of course, are essential, but there is another training equally important, and that is a psychological, inner approach that makes the role uniquely your own. In this way, no one else could play the role as you would. Perhaps the best acting lies between NY and London, and if we could integrate these two approaches, well, it would be quite amazing. I should warn you though that it takes a certain courage to be open to use your own memories and feelings in this work. Are you prepared to do this?"

At first, no one spoke or even moved. Then one dark skinned young man slowly nodded then smiled. Suzanne asked his name, and he shyly said, "Raghu". She learned later that Raghu was a lower caste scholarship student from a small farming village. She had already noticed how despite Mahatma Gandhi's legacy, the caste system was alive and well in India. Change in any culture comes slowly as she had learned from Working for Civil Rights in America. But Indian culture was entirely held by centuries of the caste system despite reformers dating back to the 6th century BC – centuries before Gandhi.

Slowly the other students raised their hands until all had expressed their willingness to try something new. And so, 'the work' began. They met three hours a day for the next five days and focused on *Oedipus Rex*. At first, predictably, they moved well and spoke their lines in a formal diction learned at their school, but there was no 'life' in the acting.

Suzanne introduced a method exercise called "Emotional Memory" where the actor focuses not on the play's text but inwardly on a personal experience from the past, thus infusing the ancient text with a reality born in the moment and authentically felt by the actor. This was quite foreign to the students – except for Raghu who took to it at once.

It encouraged Suzanne to use Raghu to demonstrate the power of the exercise. Raghu cast as the messenger to Queen Jocasta, exclaims that a stranger has murdered her husband, the King. At first, Raghu recited the lines without feeling. Then Suzanne shocked the class by telling him, "I want you to forget the story of the play, but instead imagine you have just heard that Rajiv Gandhi has been assassinated and you are sent to tell his wife, the Queen, what has happened. You are to speak the lines of the play, but think and feel the story that happened here in India three months ago. Shall we try it?"

Suzanne again thought of her own meeting with Mrs.Gandhi and the two Sikh guards nearby. With determined discipline, Suzanne turned her attention to Raghu after her direction to think on the death of Rajiv Gandhi as he spoke of Oedipus.

Raghu started to shake while the silence in the room was deafening. Slowly, Raghu nodded then left the room to re-enter as the messenger to Queen Jocasta. After a long pause, Raghu the messenger entered running, out of breath, emotionally shaken. "The king ... the king ... is dead, my lady." He continued the speech - so alive that the rest of the class was in tears. When he finished the monologue, no one spoke. They knew they had witnessed something real, something current, something each one of them had experienced when their own former king, as it were, had been murdered.

Suzanne kept having flashbacks to her tea with Mrs. Gandhi seven years earlier and her obvious concern for her son and fear for herself as well. Did she know then what the future held?

Later that day, Ananya summoned Suzanne to the head office and told her that others were talking about what had happened in her class. Some of the staff felt it disrespectful to use the death of their former Prime Minister in an acting exercise. Suzanne only said in her defense, "It was a way to make the old play live today. And it worked."

The few days left in class were electric, yet some of the staff were reserved and not sure they trusted such new American methods. Suzanne felt fine, knowing that she had done her job and it was enough that the students had responded – or most of them.

The final evening of her stay, Suzanne was invited to the National Drama Festival at the Sri Rama Centre where all her students would be. It was an experimental retelling of the Rama-Sita epic, *Ramayana,* where the good king triumphs over an evil demon king. Suzanne could not help but think, "Would that it was always so in real life!"

Suzanne got up and started down the aisle at intermission when Raghu walked toward her with great emotion and leaned down and touched her feet. The audience looked on with confusion at this low caste Indian bowing to an American woman.

At first, embarrassed, Suzanne pleaded, "No, no, Raghu."

Raghu stood back up and with bowed head and folded palms did a namaste to his teacher, in gratitude. Suzanne was moved, and with folded palms returned the ritualized greeting which she had been told means, "The Self within me greets the Self in you."

It was a perfect ending to her trying week at the National School of Drama where she had challenged the acting methods of the British Raj. She wanted to tell the old astrologer in Jaipur that she had discovered what Shakespeare knew when he penned *Julius Cesar,* "The fault, dear Brutus, lies not in our stars, but in ourselves." Character creates our destiny, and she must own hers. Had Mrs. Gandhi owned hers as well? She must have done, for she had lived in fear of her destiny long before the fatal event.

Suzanne felt pleased that she had changed this young actor forever. She would learn later that Raghu went on to have a successful cinema career in Bollywood, able to support his whole family. Yes, she was pleased at the work in the class yet curiously, not proud. Somehow the pride she had carried for so many years was slowly transforming into a humility from having experienced the depth and breadth of India. A complex country, full of sweetness and brutality, and yet behind all 'the players on the stage' as the Bard would say, stands an unchanging, infinite, impersonal background called the Absolute. Such is the wonder that is India.

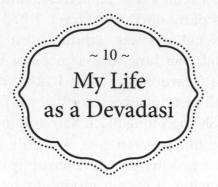

~ 10 ~

# My Life as a Devadasi

*The past is never dead. It's not even past.*

William Faulkner

*I*s it possible, do you think, to remember a life that existed before you were born? Some might think me mad to even consider such a thing, but it was not some random, wild thought. No, it was direct experience, indisputable and true. But I am getting ahead of my story.

It all began at a party in New York. I had recently come home from India where I had been the guest of the Indian government, and something had changed in me – something I had not yet assimilated. I had returned to my life: living in New York and earning my livelihood as an actress. And one night attending a party on E. 76<sup>th</sup> Street, I had just taken a glass of wine and was standing near the cheese table, considering how nice a piece of brie would be with the Chardonnay, when I noticed a strange woman with piercing eyes staring at me from across the room. She had long black hair and looked to be in her early fifties, green eyes, and pale white skin. When I returned her gaze, she abruptly crossed the room, and without even a moment's introduction, said, "You were a temple dancer in India before."

I laughed and thought this an unusual first greeting.

"Let's start again, shall we? I'm Suzanne Bartlett."

"Everyone knows who you are, Miss Bartlett. I'm Margaret Harwood."

I did not know then what a profound impact Margaret Harwood would have upon my life. As we found a quiet corner and began to talk, she repeated what she had first said, "It's true, you know. You were once a temple dancer in India."

"It's odd that you should say that. Just two weeks ago, I met a Vedic astrologer in Jaipur who told me the very same thing: that I was a temple dancer in India … in a past life."

"Would you like to know more about that life?"

"Yes, yes, I would."

"Not here. Let's meet next week and we can explore it together."

We exchanged phone numbers and agreed to meet again the following week. As often happens with free-lance actors, I was between shows so I had ample time to 'explore'. I called Margaret who invited me to her apartment for tea the following Thursday.

She lived on the upper west side in an old brownstone, some twenty blocks from my own more modern flat in midtown Manhattan, only a short bus ride away. As is my custom, I arrived promptly and rang the bell. Soon we were seated and having tea as I looked at those striking green eyes. I laughed from nervousness, and said, "You seemed to know me when we met."

"Yes, I know. I saw you in the Tennessee Williams play last season. You were wonderful as Maggie in *The Cat on the Hot Tin Roof.*"

"A theatre lover?"

"At times."

"Do you work as a psychic?"

"No, I work at Young and Rubicon, advertising. I guess you might say, the other is my avocation – if not my life. I serve as a psychic – but not for money."

"Have you been to India?"

"Not in this lifetime."

This began a long friendship and together we explored the past, from my life as a devadasi in India at some unknown and far away date. I had already done some research and learned that *devadasi* means 'a servant of God'. Young girls usually from upper class homes were sometimes dedicated to the temple to become devadasis. The usual age that those chosen would leave their homes to live in the temple was nine. It was considered a sacred calling and they were schooled in the arts – mostly music and dance. And the girls were highly regarded.

Margaret suggested she use hypnosis to take me back to my time in India, so we could reveal more specific details about my own story. She had been trained and licensed as a hypnotist and had done this many times before, assuring me that it was quite safe. She would record the sessions as most who are under hypnosis do not recall what comes through.

"Well, I'm not one to say no to new adventures. When do we begin?"

"Today the moon is void of course, so, I think, tomorrow morning, ten?

"I'll be here."

That night, I had an intense dream, but when I awoke, the details vanished - only a feeling of fear and excitement remained. Was this a good idea? Or was I opening Pandora's Box? After a strong cup of Earl Grey Tea and a pumpernickel bagel with cream cheese, courage returned, and I prepared for the next adventure.

Margaret suggested I lie down on her couch and she covered me with a light cotton blanket. Then we began.

"Let's start by breathing in through the nose and out from the mouth. Breathe in slowly for the count of five, hold for the count of four, then slowly breathe out for the count of seven." After repeating this three times, on the last breathing out, she continued, "Roll your eyes to the back of your head. Now breathe in again from your belly … from your knees … open your eyes, look up without blinking and stare at a point above. Your eyes are getting heavy, they may sting. Now, when it feels right, slowly close your eyes and breathe normally. In through the nose and out from the mouth. As you breathe out, say these words after me. Calm. Peaceful. Tranquil. Relax."

I learned only later what had occurred, yet thanks to the recording, I was able to listen to the entire session. Margaret told me to visualize going back into time … to India … to another life in India. Surprisingly, my voice on the tape recorder sounded like that of a little girl. I was with my grandmother on a bullock cart, going through a rice paddy field, and I was very frightened.

"Why are you frightened?" asked Margaret.

"I will be dedicated to the Big Temple today."

"Why is this/"

"Because that is what my mother and my grandmother did, so now it is my turn."

"What is your grandmother's name?"

"Aaya. I call her Aaya."

"What is your name?"

"Chandra."

"How old are you, Chandra?"

"Nine."

"Do you know where you are going?"

"Yes. To the Big Temple near Madraspatnam."

"Chandra, can you tell us when this was?"

"Long, long ago."

After the hypnosis, I began to cry as I listened to the recording. Hearing myself speaking in the voice of a child. In shock, I could not hear all that was said so I asked Margaret if we could listen to it again. This time I was more focused and clearly heard the whole session, determined to commit it to memory. The recording continued.

As the bullock cart pulled up outside the Big Temple, I remember seeing a great banyan tree with long hanging roots and near it a neem tree outside the temple. I heard the temple drums with cymbals, and priests chanting Sanskrit slokas as I was led inside the temple. I held on tightly to my grandmother's hand as she pulled me into the inner sanctum of the temple and sat me down. I asked and she stroked my head to calm me. Then a priest marked my left upper arm with a piece of charcoal. The drumming became louder and louder as well as the chanting and the clashing of cymbals. The priest held a silver instrument inscribed with a trident – Shiva's trident – and placed it into an iron pot of burning coals. After some time, he took it out and plunged it into a bowl of water which made it sizzle. The steam rose and was felt everywhere. It was then I began to tremble. But Aaya held me firm as the priest took the instrument and burned my upper arm with the mark of Shiva's trident. I bit my lip and tears rolled down my face. But I had promised I would not cry as this was my destiny. Then I heard the priest say:

Lord Shiva, take this girl to be your wife for
    all eternity;
She will be your faithful servant and vessel.

Then Aaya, my grandmother, applied cooling herbs wrapped in muslin to my arm which helped the pain, and the priest slowly stood up and bowed to me. I looked up at Aaya and she smiled and nodded her head, as if pleased that I had kept my promise and did not cry.

Then the priest placed a golden pendant around my neck, a golden pendant such as those given to girls when they marry. I was now married to Lord Shiva. That was my destiny.

Margaret switched off the recorder, and we sat in silence for a long time. After handing me a cup of chamomile tea, she said, "That was your initiation as a devadasi."

"A temple dancer."

"Yes."

"I'm exhausted, Margaret."

"Of course, you are, Suzanne. Go home and rest. Do absolutely nothing, then call me tomorrow and let me know if you want to know more."

"More? What more?"

"Well, Chandra was only nine. Don't you wonder what happened to her later on?"

"We can do that?"

"You can do that. Don't decide now. Just go home and rest, ok?"

"Yes. Rest. But, Margaret, I didn't imagine it, did I?"

"Oh, no. No. You lived it."

I walked home as in a waking dream. It was all so real and, at the same time, unbelievable. Dare I believe it? Arriving home, I ignored all messages on the answering machine, skipped dinner, took a long hot shower, then went early to bed. Again, there were troubling dreams, but they all vanished as I awoke the next morning after a sound sleep. My eyes opened with the full resolve to know more about my life as a devadasi.

It was Monday. Margaret had to work all day and every day until the following weekend. She suggested we wait until Friday evening, then could have the entire weekend if we needed more time.

I took the Fifth Avenue Bus to 42nd Street and Fifth Avenue to the New York Public Library and spent most of the day there, researching. I first looked up the name of the place of the Big Temple.

Madraspatnam. I discovered it later became known as Madras. I learned that an astrologer would consult the *Panchangam* for an auspicious date for the initiations of the young girls. The details my unconscious mind had recalled were accurate as to the initiation, including the symbol of Shiva's trident, permanently burned into the flesh of the young innocents.

I read on. In addition to taking care of the temple and preparing rituals, these young girls also learned and practiced classical Indian artistic traditions such as Bharatanatyam, Kuchipudi, and Odessa dances. Their social status was high as dance and music were an essential part of temple worship.

After puberty, they would also perform sex with men of a higher rank – even royalty – and the donations would go to the temple. No one knows how far back this practice goes. Still, a temple in Tamil Nadu, south India has the names and addresses of four hundred devadasis which were inscribed on its walls for the eleventh century inauguration of a Big Temple near Madras. However, some scholars believe the tradition of temple dancers goes much further back – probably to the third century.

I looked up from the stack of books and thought to myself, "Big Temple near Madras! Yes, Chandra called it Big Temple near Madras – now called Chennai." As one possessed, I could not stop reading. I learned that a law was enacted on 9

October 1947, just after India became independent from British rule. The Madras Devadasis Act which gave devadasis the legal right to marry and made it illegal to dedicate girls to Hindu temples. Yet, the practice continued into modern times, though not with upper class girls, and the prostitution was open to all sorts of men, the money still going to the temple. This was not only in the south but also in many states in India – and continuing to this day. Only recently has the Devadasi system begun to slowly disappear when it was formally outlawed throughout India in 1988.

I went home and tried to return some of the calls. Brent, my agent, had scheduled an audition and interview for Thursday and Mark Brockman had called twice. Brent confirmed the interview and audition without even asking what the play was. Then I called Mark, loyal Mark, who had waited more than seven years for me to marry him. I then recalled what the old astrologer in Jaipur had said.

"It is because of this past life that you will not marry and have children."

"But why?" I asked out loud though no one was there to hear. "How can a life hundreds of years before affect my life now?"

"Dinner tonight?"

"Yes, Mark, that's fine. Seven is fine."

"Trout Almondine and wild rice and asparagus. Chardonnay."

I ordered though was not really hungry. Meanwhile, I tried my best to have a normal conversation. I could not tell Mark what was happening to me. He'd think I'd gone mad. Mark is the kind of man my mother would wish me to marry. Wall Street solid, kind, charming, handsome, dependable, and from a good family.

"A dollar for your thoughts."

"They're not even worth a penny, Mark."

"I thought we might go away for the weekend. Connecticut, maybe?"

"I can't, Mark. I'm working with a therapist and we're doing an intensive."

Mark opened his mouth to protest.

"Please don't ask me to explain. It's something I'm trying to work out."

"You know, my dear, even since your trip to India, something has been bothering you, hasn't it?"

"How about the following weekend? That would be lovely."

"You know, you're very lucky that I'm a patient man."

"Yes, I know that."

Thursday came and the audition and interview for a new play called *Choices,* by an award-winning playwright, went well. I was asked to return the next week to read with the actor who would play the male lead. Brent was pleased as the play would perform first at the Long Wharf Theatre in New

Haven, Connecticut, before coming to Broadway in the fall. I liked the play and was relieved that due to years of discipline, nothing could affect 'the work' as Strasberg would say. Whatever troubles arose were usually dumped into my separate compartment called *personal life*.

At last, it was Friday, and I would go after dinner to Margaret for our second session.

I returned calls from friends though said 'no' to meeting or going to plays or parties. My focus had shifted away from the present to the past.

Arriving at Margaret's home, I noticed she had lit candles and there was the smell of sage in the room. Margaret held a lit bunch of sage which she used to smoke me up and down and front and back.

"Just to purify. I learned this when I studied with an old shaman in Arizona."

After the cup of chamomile tea, she again led me in the breathing technique as preparation for the hypnosis. There was no fear this time, only a sense of urgency to revisit the past and learn more.

Again, after the session, I had no idea whatsoever of what came through, but I felt less tired this time, more relaxed, more trusting of the process. Margaret was watching me carefully and with a sense of wonder. I waited for her to speak.

"Oh, my. I don't know where to start. Do you remember anything, Suzanne?"

"No, nothing. It's recorded though, right?"

"Oh, yes, it is. Prepare yourself for an extraordinary tale."

"Well, I love a good story."

I listened to the recording.

Chandra grew tall and strong, and was an apt pupil in both music and dance. She embraced her destiny totally as had her mother and grandmother before her. The priests were kind to her as were her teachers. Even as a child, Chandra was well respected. She acquired grace and technique and none could match her achievements. All passed well enough until her fourteenth birthday. She had come to puberty at thirteen but the temple priests kept her isolated for longer than usual.

As a response to having seen Chandra dance in the temple, a young Rajah had gifted her with a green parrot she called 'Joshi'. Delighted, Chandra would sing and talk to Joshi all day long and they soon became inseparable. Chandra, now fifteen, was happy and had grown to love her temple duties – especially the dancing.

The priests had noticed that the young Rajah, Vijaya Raja Sethupathi II would come every time that Chandra danced or sang. He was nineteen and handsome like his late father. As was custom, those that came to see the devadasis dance or sing were not allowed to meet them. The priests held a council to discuss the matter and quickly decided that Chandra was ready to embrace her other duty.

The next time Chandra danced the story of Krishna and Radha, Vijaya Rajah was overwhelmed and lingered long after the performance ended. An elder priest approached him, bowed, and asked if the Rajah would like to meet the dancer. Vijaya waited as requested, rubbing his hands nervously.

After some minutes, Chandra came with Joshi perched on her arm. Vijaya was happy to see that she had liked his gift of the green parrot and asked if she had named him.

"Oh, yes, his name is Joshi. Isn't he lovely?"

The old priest whispered in her ear that the parrot had been given to her by the Rajah.

"Oh, thank you, kind sir, for he is so very precious."

They walked in the back garden with the old priest following at a distance behind. Vijaya was well aware of the custom and that having a devadasi was his due yet seeing her pure innocence, would not rush. First, they would get to know and trust one another. There was no hurry.

In the coming weeks, after she danced or sang in the temple, Vijaya would walk with her in the garden and bring her sweets. How refreshing it was to see her spontaneity – so different from the usual palace concubines. No, Chandra was a delicate flower and one that must be nurtured before plucking.

Aaya would sometimes visit her granddaughter and had soon learned of the young Rajah's visits.

"Oh, Aaya, he is my friend and I have grown quite fond of him. Did you know that he gave me Joshi?"

Combing Chandra's thick black hair, Aaya softly said, "Yes, my dear, Aaya knows. Aaya knows that this young Rajah is part of your destiny as well. You must love him as he will you. The stars have written it."

Chandra drank her lime juice and said nothing as she pondered Aaya's words. Joshi fluttered his wings and squawked causing Chandra to laugh.

The following Monday I returned to the library with the intention of finding out who the young Rajah was and when he lived. After an hour, I discovered a list of the Rajahs of Tamil Nadu. Eureka! There he was. Vijaya Raja Sethupathi II, from the mid-eighteenth century. Impatiently, I waited until evening to call when I knew Margaret would be home after work.

"Really. Eighteenth century. What a clever girl you are to have discovered this."

"Oh, Margaret, it's not imagined. He lived and we were in love. Isn't it wonderful?"

"Well, we have yet to know the whole story."

"Oh, Margaret, don't spoil it for me, please. Falling in love with a king – that's awesome."

The following Friday, Margaret led me in our third session. Again, I had to wait until I listened to the recording to learn what had happened. As I had hoped, it got better and better – so much so that my modern life seemed to pale.

After three months of walking in the garden and after Vijaya had made a substantial contribution to the temple, he invited Chandra to visit his second palace. Aaya stood unseen as Chandra stepped into the ornate palace chariot and drove away. The grandmother had tears in her eyes as she turned away, not wanting the old priest to notice her.

Chandra was excited to see the palace and the lovely rooms so different from the austere rooms in the temple. She sat upon a silk-covered couch as Vijaya fed her ripe grapes and oranges. She loved the song birds in gold cages that sang nearby. Gently, the young Rajah touched her cheek as her eyes grew wide in wonder. Then he leaned over and kissed her gently on her forehead as she sat, still as the grave. She remembered Aaya's words, "It is your destiny to love him as he will you." So, Chandra surrendered to destiny as she had been schooled to do."

After listening to the recording, both of us were excited and would have begun another session, but Margaret advised waiting.

"Perhaps tomorrow, it's Saturday."

"Oh, darn, Margaret, I can't. I promised Mark that we would spend the weekend together. I had put him off for a week, you know."

"Then the following Friday?"

"For sure. Only …"

"Only what?"

"Only Mark is no match for the young Rajah, is he?"

"Well, Suzanne, he has one trait that the other doesn't."

"What is that?"

"He's still alive."

Mark had told me to pack summer clothes, a swim suit, and a passport, but wanted to surprise me about where we were going. As it was only for two days, it couldn't be far. We were driven to the airport by a driver in a luxury limo.

"Mark, what is all this? Tell, please."

"OK, a client, whom I invest for, has invited us to his place in the Bahamas. He's already there, but has sent his private plane for us. How's that for a surprise weekend?"

'I feel like Cinderella."

"Good. That's the idea."

As Mark kissed me in the backseat of the limo, I kept imagining the young Rajah. I told myself not to think of him this weekend. What a spoiler that would be!

"Isn't it great to live today? Just two hours and forty minutes and we're in another world." I could only smile as the plane landed in Nassau with Mark looking like the man who broke the bank at Monte Carlo. Yes, it is great to live today, but if Mark only knew that part of me was living another life, in another country, in another time.

I think I was born a nomad and adore seeing new places. One always learns so much about history and about people different from ourselves. That's why I always enjoyed touring shows. Each day, each week a different audience, a new venue.

"Mark, tell me about the Bahamas as I've never been here before. Fill me in."

"Well, since the eighteenth century, it was a British colony. Then, after the American Revolutionary War, the British Crown resettled thousands of the American Loyalists here in the Bahamas, and the Loyalists all took along their slaves to establish plantations here. Later in the 1930s, the slave trade was abolished in the Bahamas. So, this beautiful paradise also became a haven for freed African slaves. This is why from that time on - even today – the African-Americans make up 90% of the population.

"But it's not still a British colony, is it?"

"Nope, they gained independence in the early 1970s, but Queen Elizabeth remains their queen.

"I love it that you know so much about so many things and places."

"Did you know that the Bahamas is one of the richest countries in the Americas - after the United States and Canada?"

"Where does the money come from?"

"Tourism and offshore finance."

"Ah, and that's where a clever Wall Street financier comes in, right?"

"You are an apt pupil, my dear."

The following Friday, I invited Margaret for dinner at a swank restaurant not far from her home. After a good Chardonnay was brought, Margaret asked what she had been dying to know.

"So, how was the week-end with Mr. Wall Street?

"It was a weekend in paradise. We flew in a private jet to Nassau in the Bahamas. We swam in the ocean, had massages, ate fresh seafood, and cocktails. It was like acting in a Noel Coward play, and it felt just as unreal. I played it well, but it was not me. Mark is a considerate lover, and so kind and generous. If only I could love him as passionately as Chandra loved her prince charming. I sometimes think I am falling in love with the Rajah.

"But Mark is real. The Rajah is not."

"Isn't he? He is real to me."

I found myself waiting impatiently for my next session.

The third session had an even more profound effect on me. As if now by rote, I quickly surrendered to the breathing and holding my breath, opening both mind and heart to my earlier life as Chandra. And though, as usual, I remembered no details from the sessions, I would awake with stronger feelings each time. This time, however, was most unusual as when returning to consciousness, I noticed that my underwear was damp. Before tea and listening to the recording, I made my way to the bathroom only to discover that I had not urinated as thought, but had been sexually aroused and had *come* during the session. I took two sheets of toilet paper from the roll to place in my panties, saying nothing to Margaret when I returned to the living room. Composed, I sat and nodded for her to play the recording, recognizing at once the young voice of Chandra.

My prince would send for me and we would meet in his second palace three or four times a week, and these visits would become my entire focus. Between visits, he would send a messenger with sweet mangos and poems he had written for me.

The peacocks scream and the grey doves coo,
Little, green talkative parrots woo.
You were mine, from dusk until dawning light,
For the perfect whole of that bygone night
You belonged to me!

Unlike Chandra, Vijaya was already skilled in the sexual arts, having read the *Kama Sutra* and guided by artful palace concubines. Yet though his prowess was undeniable, Vijaya had never known love – until now. He had never before experienced its sweetness and tenderness and quiet passion. He had never realized how natural it could be to make love – not only enjoy the sensation of sex. For the next three months, Vijaya guided her into the many forms and techniques as described in the *Kama Sutra*. Chandra remembered the names of the various positions: Lotus, Doggy Style – this made her giggle when he told her –, Cowgirl's Helper, Magic Mountain, Dancer. After years of dance training, Chandra could easily adopt all the positions which pleased the young Rajah.

A few days later, the palace messenger came with sweet grapes and a longer poem.

Whether I love you? You do not ask,
Nor waste yourself on the thankless task.
You are wise, my love, and take what the
    gods have sent.
You ask no question, but rest content;
So, I am with you to take your kisses
And value you the more for this.
For this is wisdom: to love, to live
To take what Fate may give,
To ask no question, to make no prayer,
To kiss the lips and caress the hair,
Speed passion's ebb as you greet its flow –
To have, to hold, and – in time – let go!

One visit, Vijaya sat her down and quietly fed her the purple grapes she loved, placing one into her mouth at a time while watching her tenderly.

"There is something you must know, my love. And you must understand that I have no choice but to follow my dharma as a king."

Chandra could not imagine what he wanted her to know, so she waited for him to speak.

"It is time that I must marry and my queen has already been chosen by the pundits. I have no choice about this. Neither did my father nor my father's father. Do you understand, Chandra?"

Chandra lowered her eyes, "Then I will not see you anymore?"

Vijaya smiled and embraced her, "No, no, my jewel, nothing will change in that regard. We shall meet as often as ever. And you will be provided for – and your family."

They undressed in silence and Chandra learned two new positions to enhance sensual pleasure. She knew that it didn't matter what happened in the outer world, as long as she could come together like this with him.

Chandra continued to perform her devotional dances to Shiva and Vishnu and all noticed her devotion to God was extraordinary when she danced. People came from miles around to see her renditions of Krishna and Radha and would weep at their great love. Three years passed as her fame spread across the state. The priests were pleased, and the temple grew wealthier.

One morning Chandra awoke and felt sick at

her stomach and for several mornings she could not eat. The priests noticed this and sent for Aaya, her grandmother, to take care of their prized possession. It did not take Aaya long to discern what was what.

"You will have a child, my dear. And will it be fathered by the young Rajah?"

Chandra looked up in wonder, "Oh, Aaya, it could be no other."

"That is good. Not to worry. I must tell the priest though."

Chandra worried that Vijaya would no longer desire her when she grew fat – and she could not bear that. But it was not so, the young Rajah was pleased. Six months later, a male child was born. And the young parents were glad. The Rajah gave gifts to both Chandra and her family as well as a substantial offering to the Big Temple. All was well and, after a reasonable period, Chandra and Vijaya resumed their discoveries of love's pleasures.

In the palace though, there was sadness, for after three years of marriage, no offspring had come. Vijaya did his duty and lay with his queen though his heart was with another. The astrologer told him not to worry and assured him that his queen and he were both young and that a male heir would be theirs in time. The gods would decide.

Three more years passed. It was a time of peace and prosperity and the people were content. Vijaya was a just ruler and his queen knew her place. He continued to meet with Chandra three times a week, and enjoyed the young child they had created together. They called the boy, Bharat, the ancient name for India, and Joshi, the green parrot, looked after the child as if he were the father. Chandra continued to dance, and her maturity as a mother seemed to add a rich texture to her grace and movements. She danced no longer as a girl but as a fulfilled woman.

Margaret leaned over and touched me on the shoulder, "Awake. Awake."

Reluctantly, I opened my eyes, returning to the present.

Laughing, Margaret, said, "I don't think you wanted to leave the past."

"No, I did not. Oh, Margaret, what a life that must have been."

'I have a present for you," as Margaret rose and walked across the room, returning with a CD, and handed it to me.

I smiled and opened the case which read MS Subbulakshmi, then looked questionably at her friend.

"The celebrated singer and actress, MS Subbulakshmi, was born to a Devadasi mother. As a result, she received extensive musical training. She is a most famous classical Indian singer, known all over the world. The Sanskrit slokas she sings would have been sung in the eighteenth century – perhaps even earlier."

"Oh, thank you, Maggi, thank you. But I should be giving you gifts."

"Don't you understand that the work we do is a gift in itself."

The two friends hugged as Margaret looked at her watch and said, "Now, my sweet, I must say good bye, as I have a date."

"Oh -h, and is it the same young man I saw here last week?"

"Jeremy, yes. He has just been cast in *Love of Life*, a daytime drama on television.

"How old?"

"Young."

"Good. It's about time we had older women and younger men instead of the usual."

I went straight home and placed the new C.D. into the player. *Sri Venkatesa Suprabhatam Morning Shlokas* by M.S. Subbulakshmi. As the music played, I read on the back of CD, "It is believed that Lord Venkatesa will bestow prosperity in abundance to devotes who recite this shloka every morning."

"I hereby pledge to play these shlokas daily," I said aloud to myself.

The next day my agent called to say that the call back with the lead actor had gone well, and I had won the leading role in *Choices*. I laughed out loud, thinking, "And I only played the CD once!"

The phone rang and, of course, it was Mark. Somehow, I was not eager to see him right then, and was determined not to disclose why.

"Hi, Mark. No, just busy. I got the part. We start rehearsals next week so I'm afraid I'll have to put you off for a bit."

"What? Yes, I do have to eat. All right, dinner Thursday night then."

Come Thursday, all I could think of was, "At last, tomorrow is Friday, and the fourth session with Maggie." I made a decision telling myself that I am fond of Mark, but I must insist it be just dinner tonight and nothing else. I want to be well rested for the session tomorrow.

The next afternoon, I stopped and purchased a large white orchid plant in an oriental pot for Margaret. How do you adequately thank someone who has changed your life? Margaret loved the plant and placed it on her dining table. Then she poured the chamomile tea and we started.

This time, our fourth session, I awoke feeling heavy, sad, and no arousal at all. What had happened? Margaret looked all too serious and forgetting the tea, turned on the recorder.

Chandra was still breast-feeding Bharat who was now four years old – not uncommon in India. She would call to him, and he would come running, climb upon her lap, touch her cheek with his little hand, and begin to suck. This intimacy enhanced their closeness. Chandra had thought nothing could be more powerful than her love for Vijaya, but she was wrong. Being a mother seemed to crown all that had gone before. It was an unselfish love, unconditional, a love that cared only for the child.

Joshsi would perch close to Bharat just to keep a sharp eye on him, and the boy would giggle in delight. At one time, the old priest called her away and Aaya, who had come to visit, stayed with Bharat.

The old priest – the same who had first burned Shiva's trident into her arm when she was nine - had grown fond of his charge. He stood with her now, fingering his beads, trying to find the right words.

"What is it? What is wrong? Have I done something to make you frown so?"

"No, no, my child. You have not."

Chandra sat near the water tank and watched the floating pink lotus, dipping her hand into the cool water. She looked up at the neem tree and saw a flurry of fearless, black crows. Suddenly, there was a cry from inside.

"Bharat? Why does he cry?"

Chandra stood up and turned to go, but the old priest held her arm.

"My child, you must do nothing. It is written."

"What do you mean? My child is calling me." Chandra turned and ran, only to see Aaya dragging the little boy into the palace cart which carried her every week to the young Rajah.

"Bharat! Aaya! Aaya!", she shouted, as the cart and horses drove on, leaving only heated dust behind them.

Chandra turned to see the old priest slowly walking toward her. She waited for him to speak without taking her eyes off him.

"My child, the young Rajah has no children by his queen, and the Raj depends upon an heir. It is your honor and your duty to offer this boy. You will receive much benefit as will your family and the temple."

Chandra screamed, "No, no." and fainted, falling to the ground like a dying banana leaf. She did not stir from her bed or eat for four days. Aaya tried to comfort her granddaughter, but Chandra now saw her as the enemy – the one who had stolen her child.

Then Chandra slowly ate some rice gruel as was given to those who were ill. She heard nothing from Vijaya and gradually understood that he would never send for her again. He would do his duty to his people - but not to her. She did not dance for a year then slowly returned to perform her devotions to her god through music and dance. Joshi was always by her side and grieved the loss of young Bharat as keenly as the mother. When approached, Chandra resolutely refused to be with other men, threatening to shave her head as widows do and to cease to dance at all.

The priests called a council and as the Rajah had been more than generous with his offering for the child, they agreed that Chandra no longer had to do the other duties given to devadasis. So, from the age of twenty, Chandra would never love again nor bear any more children. She lived through her art and danced beautifully for many, many years demonstrating every known emotion that could be felt by a woman.

When I came out of the trance, I sat very still, unable to move or speak. Margaret poured a cup of tea and placed it in front of the couch. After some moments, Margaret gently asked, "Did you remember anything?"

"No, but I felt it. I still feel it. And I feel sad. Very sad."

"Perhaps you'd like to wait before hearing?"

"No, Maggie, play it, please."

The minutes passed as I listened, without moving, with hardly an expression on my face.

At the end of the tape, I rose to leave.

"Thank you, Maggie. We'll talk tomorrow."

Margaret moved to hug me, but I was already turning away to leave as quickly as possible.

I walked home as if still in a trance, and felt tears rolling down my cheeks. And then the thoughts came. "Is it possible to feel something so deeply that happened more than two hundred years ago? What would Mark say?"

I stayed home the next day and the next, thinking, writing in my journal. I tried to think back to my last visit to India, in Jaipur, and what the old astrologer had told me. What was it? Yes, I remembered. He told me that I would not marry or have children because of my past life as a devadasi. But that I would lack for nothing and have fame and fortune.

Of what use is fame or fortune without love? He was right about children as I am too old now to bear them. But, as God as my witness, I will not give up on love.

I called Mark, faithful, patient Mark, and we made a date for the following evening. I thanked him for his patience and asked his forgiveness for putting him off. Over dinner at our favorite restaurant, I again ordered trout almondine and chardonnay – this time sensuously enjoying every sip and bite. Mark was encouraged, seeing me relish the fine dinner, and over espresso, reached in his pocket and placed in front of me a small box.

For a moment, I simply stared at the unopened box, knowing well what it contained yet uncertain of what I truly wanted. Not wishing to wait, Mark opened the box and I saw the beautiful green emerald engagement ring, shining like a beacon to the future. I thought of the play I was rehearsing, a play called, *Choices*. A play about how a moment's choice can dictate an entire life.

The next day, I called Margaret, and arranged to meet with her as soon as possible.

"Well, I'm free for lunch if that works."

"One o'clock?

We fixed a restaurant near her office so that we could have longer to talk. I arrived early and hugged her before she sat down.

"What is it?"

"First, I want to thank you for the sessions. They changed my life, Maggie, and you are responsible for that."

"You did the hard work. You had the courage."

"Well, I need that courage because of what I called to tell you."

Margaret sat, waiting for the news.

"I'm going to marry Mark."

"Really?"

"Really, and I have the ring to prove it," as I stretched my left hand over the table for her to see. Margaret grasped my hand and squeezed it.

"I don't believe it. You said that being with Mark was like playing a role and not being you."

"Yes, I did say that, didn't I? How can I explain? These past weeks have been extraordinary, Maggie, and I am ever so grateful. It's as if Chandra has merged into me, and somehow made me more a whole person. Experiencing emotions that I could only pretend to live in the roles I play. The young Rajah is a dream, but Mark -- well, as you once said, Mark is real, isn't he? I have always lived a dream and played many roles, and for a long time now, the dream has been my only reality. But now, after experiencing Chandra's past life – my past life -, the dream is not enough. No, now I want a real life. I want a lasting love. And who knows, Margaret, if I'm lucky and the gods smile, we just might have a long run."

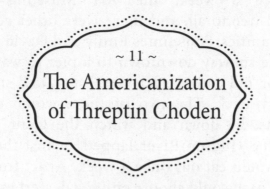

~ 11 ~

# The Americanization of Threptin Choden

*If you think you are too small to make a difference,*
*try sleeping with a mosquito.*

The 14th Dalai Lama

*E*mily lived in midtown Manhattan on the Westside with her son, David, who had just turned twelve. Divorced, Emily supported herself and her son, teaching at The New School University in downtown Greenwich Village. It was the 1980s and you didn't need to be wealthy to have a good life in New York City. As David was bright and scored high on exams, he was recently admitted to an exclusive and tuition-free school where he thrived.

Once a week, the Art Museums were opened free to all, and there were other cultural opportunities. Sometimes Emily and David would take the subway downtown to a pier to watch an outdoor old movie such as *Moby Dick* starring Gregory Peck. The two of them would spread blankets, lie down and watch the giant screen while the Hudson River lapped against the pier. They would eat out once a week. Apart from the entree, each could choose either a dessert or drink – but not both. It seemed like a game. Many years later, David would tell his mother, "You know, I never knew that we were poor then."

One morning, Emily read in the newspaper that the Dalai Lama was visiting New York and would speak at St. Patrick's Cathedral on Fifth Avenue. He would share the podium with a Roman Catholic bishop and a rabbi.

"This sounds both entertaining and educational. David, what do you say?"

"Sure, Mom. Tonight?"

"Yes. I think we should go early to get a seat."

Emily was right. The church was packed. Luckily, they got a good seat – tenth-row center. First, a Roman Catholic bishop spoke about the wonders of Christ. Following the bishop, the rabbi heralded his faith. Lastly, the 14th Dalai Lama began his talk. Unlike the rabbi and the bishop, the Tibetan spoke simply, modestly – speaking to each one in the congregation.

He did not try to convert anyone to his Buddhist faith. He spoke of tolerance and compassion and that we are all human beings.

"Our prime purpose in this life is to help
        others.
And if you can't help them, at least don't hurt
        them."

"If only every religion would adopt this one basic concept," thought Emily.

But the comment that stayed with Emily was when the Dalai Lama smiled and softly uttered, "Love is the absence of judgment." At the end of his talk, he pressed his palms together, smiled and bowed to one and all, and then humbly returned to his chair on the podium. What followed was silence – a rich silence, filled with a shared humanity.

It was a lovely and temperate evening. Mother and son, moved by what they had experienced, opted to walk home. David began to sing the John Lennon song, *Imagine,* and Emily heartily joined him.

Nothing to kill or die for
And no religion, too.
Yoo hoo -oo- oo

They were home in no time at all, and after a cup of hot chocolate, retired in utmost contentment.

The next morning, Emily called Marion Stein, a woman she had met recently through a mutual friend, who had mentioned doing volunteer work for the Tibetan cause. Marion had strong opinions and admittedly had her edges – often rubbing people the wrong way – but she had a warm heart and, unlike many *nice* people, had at least – in her own small way – set about the task of making the world a better place. Emily admired her while tolerating her sometimes acerbic personality. It turned out that Marion was having a party Saturday evening to raise funds for the Tibetans, and Emily responded that she would like to learn more about the cause.

Marion Stein was a New Yorker, born and bred, whose grandparents had fled Nazi-occupied Austria in time to live and prosper in America. Marion loved America and understood the necessity for freedom – and this inspired her to pour her heart into worthy causes.

Emily had been especially moved by a BBC television interview with the Dalai Lama when a journalist asked the Dalai Lama if he had been able to forgive the Chinese for their massacres of his people in Tibet and the senseless destruction of the Tibetan temples and monasteries. The Dalai Lama became very quiet, paused, smiled, and replied, "Almost." Emily later told her son it was the "Almost" that had won her heart.

"What can I do, Marion? You know, I am not rich but will give what I can."

"Can you give some time to help us?"

"Yes, yes, I can."

"First you need to do some homework. Here are some booklets that will help. Read them."

Marion thrust the material into her arms and barked the order, but Emily remembering the Dalai Lama's instruction not to judge, accepted her as she was.

Emily learned that the Dalai Lama was head of all the lamas. He had first been discovered living in a hamlet at the age of three and later, at the age of fifteen years on November 17,1959, was officially recognized as the reincarnation of the thirteenth Dalai Lama. In the same year, the Chinese communists brutally invaded Tibet. The situation worsened each year until the Tibetans, who are very religious people, could not abide by the ban on their worship, and revolted in 1959. As a result of the further atrocities by the Chinese, the young 14th Dalai Lama fled Lhasa along with one hundred thousand of his followers. Welcomed by India, they settled in the town of Dharamshala at the foothills of the Himalayas, where the Dalai Lama established a Tibetan Government in exile. The repression and near genocide of his people still living in Tibet continues, so the Dalai Lama travels the world speaking for freedom and non-violence.

Emily began to devote a few hours a week helping in whatever way she could. One morning, Marion called to ask if she would like to host a young monk who had recently arrived from Dharamshala. He already had a place to sleep, but said he would welcome a visit to a family to practice his English. He is very close to His Holiness, and this is his first time in America.

"When can we meet him?"

"That's the spirit., Emily. I'll bring him over to you tomorrow afternoon around four, if that works? Marion added, "Oh, and he likes Coke."

Emily expressed surprised, then Marion laughed, saying, "Not that kind – the soda. He likes Coca-Cola."

That evening over dinner, Emily told David that he was about to meet someone from India who happened to be a Tibetan Buddhist monk.

"Whatever," said David, the almost teenager, as if nothing surprised him anymore, as he nonchalantly finished his dinner.

The next afternoon, promptly at four, Marion arrived with her young charge. She introduced him as Threptin Choden from the Nechung Monastery and Dharamshala, adding that Choden was a representative of the Dalai Lama. Emily smiled and bowed as did the young man. He was strikingly handsome and about six feet tall, shy, with wide eyes full of wonder.

"Hi," said David, intrigued at the sight of his first Tibetan monk.

Choden wore the long maroon robe of a monk and had a close-shaven head. After a few minutes, Marion hastened away to return to her many duties.

"David, put the kettle on and we can have tea."

Seated at their round dinner table near the windows overlooking the skyscrapers, Choden looked out from their twenty-fifth floor, highly curious about all he saw. He had arrived only the day before from India and looked to be in his early twenties, though more innocent than boys that age in New York. Though he spoke softly and was quite shy, his English was much better than one might have thought. At one point, when Emily wasn't sure what to say, David asked, "Choden, want to see my room?" The young monk nodded and smiled as the two boys got up from the table and casually walked away. Emily cleared the table and washed the dishes, thinking, "That went rather well. They're just two youngsters."

It was agreed that Choden would come each day and the boys would explore the city and hang out together. First, the Natural History Museum where David showed Choden his favorite dinosaur, Anatosaurus, which David enjoyed explaining, means 'duck reptile'. That's because his mouth is shaped like a duck's bill. It can grow eighteen feet tall and thirty-feet long, and weighed as much as a huge elephant.

"Ah, yes, I know elephant," said Choden, trying to find something to relate to his years in India. "Are such animals still living in America?"

"No, man," continued David, "not for hundreds of years. The Anatoasaurus is a plant eater and to a hungry Tyannosaurus – see there he is – well, the plant eater is just the right size for his supper."

"This one is much bigger than the plant eater, yes?"

"Sure he is, and meaner. He could kill the Anatasaurus easily."

"Then it is good he no longer exists."

"I guess so, but it's neat to see them."

They moved on to the stuffed birds, and Choden seemed to enjoy them. He asked David, "Did you know that India has the largest variety of birds in the world?"

"Really?", David liked learning new things.

"Choden, are you a plant eater? asked David," I mean a vegetarian?"

"No, Tibetans rarely are, because Tibet has a very cold climate, and meat is necessary. Many Hindus in India are vegetarians – especially the brahmins."

Emily was impressed by how easily Choden adapted to wherever he was – especially because he had lived in a monastery since childhood. Perhaps, she mused, because he was at ease with himself, this made him at home everywhere. She noticed how he concentrated on everything he saw or heard and surmised that this must be due to his training as a monk.

The next day, when she discovered that Choden had never seen a movie, they decided to take him to one currently playing. It was called *The Black Stallion,* and an older Mickey Rooney played the trainer. It was showing at the Ziegfeld Theatre, which had the largest screen in the city. Emily sat on one side of Choden and David on the other. Several minutes into the film, the ship explodes, then sinks, and the only survivors are a small boy of twelve and a black Arabian stallion. The next half hour shows the boy and the horse surviving on a remote island in the middle of nowhere. Emily had seen the film earlier, and now became fascinated observing Choden watch the movie. He sat on the edge of his seat, totally focused on the screen, not moving for the length of the two-hour film. Later when Emily commented on his concentration, Choden remarked, "I could not shut my eyes." Choden explained that monks are taught to concentrate on the moment, and the movie didn't allow any gap between moments. So, Choden could not physically close his eyes. Such was his concentration.

Leaving the theatre, on the sidewalk, a rough-looking teenager pointed at Choden and yelled, "Hey, lady, nice dress!" David went ballistic and wanted to go after the boy, but Choden gently held his arm and said, "Do not let the behavior of others destroy your inner peace." David looked at Choden who was smiling – and became calm. Later, after Choden had left, over hot chocolate, Emily told her son, "You know, I think that it's not only Choden who is learning from us, but the other way around, too."

David nodded, "Yes, Mom. He's pretty cool, isn't he?"

The next week there was a meeting at Columbia University about a special event soon to take place at The Natural History Museum. A group of four Tibetan monks who were mandala sand painters was arriving from India. Excited, Choden began to tell them what would occur.

"Mandala is a Sanskrit word that means circle. A mandala is a square containing a circle with smaller circles within. Inside are geometric shapes and many ancient spiritual symbols. Once the mandalas were made of crushed jewels, but now Tibetans use plain white stones ground down and dyed with inks to achieve the same effect."

"They're coming to New York to make one?" piped David.

"Yes, my brother monks have been trained ever since they were children to do only mandalas. You will see, David. They make very beautiful art."

"How many artists make the mandala?" asked Emily.

"Four. They sit on the floor around a circle and the mandala in the middle. It takes many days – sometimes even weeks to complete."

David was impatient to see it, so Emily decided to accompany Choden to the opening ceremony the following week at the National History Museum – where they had seen the dinosaurs.

Just before the opening ceremony, the Dalai Lama appeared with several monks. After he was introduced to the museum hosts, he noticed Choden, and smiling, walked toward them. Choden immediately bowed low but the Dalai Lama grabbed him and gave him a brotherly hug. After a few words in Tibetan, Choden introduced Emily and David. The Dalai Lama took both of her hands and looked at Emily as if no one else was in the room except the two of them. Then he thanked them for hosting Choden.

"Our pleasure," said Emily.

Soon others claimed him, and he smiled, giving both mother and son a wave as he crossed the room. The ceremony was beginning. The monks chanted mantras and played flutes, drums, and cymbals. Then the four artist monks got down to work. First, they carefully measured and drew the outlines for the mandala with chalk or pencil, using rulers and compasses. Once the sketch was drawn, grains of colored sand slowly began to be laid into place. Emily later learned that some mandalas use millions of grains.

When they returned to the museum two weeks later, Choden spoke softly to explain what Emily and David were seeing. The colored sand is poured onto the mandala with a metal funnel called a 'chakpu' then is scraped by another metal rod to make vibration for the grains of sand to fall delicately into the right places. This takes great patience. Look, you see that they always create from the center outwards."

"What happens to the mandala when it is completed?"

"When the mandala is completed, the monks destroy it."

"What!" exclaimed David.

"Patiently, the monks who have created the mandala destroy it to symbolize that nothing lasts forever."

Emily asked, "How do they destroy it?"

Choden continued, "The sand is swept up and poured into a jar then wrapped in silk and carried to a river where it is given back to nature."

David frowned, "That's depressing, Choden, after all that work."

Choden laughed, teasingly, "David, choose to be optimistic. It feels better."

The days passed, and it seemed more and more natural to Emily to share their lives with Choden – as if the three of them had formed a kind of family.

One afternoon, David returned home, depressed because he had failed a test – something he almost never did. He was Mr. Glum – that is, until Choden arrived. When David told him that he had failed a test, Choden smiled and said, "Forget the failures. Keep the lessons." And presto! David was David again.

Later on, David asked Choden, "What if I fail again?"

Choden, as usual, had the right answer, "If it can be solved, there is no need to worry. And if it cannot be solved, worry is of no use. Can you solve the thing you are afraid of?"

"I guess."

"How?" asked Choden, never taking his eyes off David.

"Study more?"

"So, no need to worry. You know what to do."

Later that evening, after Choden left, over hot chocolate, David turned to Emily and

said quite seriously, "Mom, maybe I should become a monk."

Trying hard not to smile, Emily paused, then said, "I think there is plenty of time left to decide what you will be, don't you?"

It wasn't always David who sometimes needed the comforting words. Emily was confronted with a problem with her Dean at the university where she taught. A popular teacher, her class had grown too large to offer the students the individual attention she wished them to have. On the other hand, she didn't want to create a problem as she needed the job, so she wasn't sure what to do.

"So, I can do nothing but accept."

Choden to the rescue, again quoted the Dalai Lama, "There are only two days in the year where nothing can be done. One is called yesterday and the other is called tomorrow."

Upon hearing this, Emily immediately picked up her phone and made an appointment to see the Dean the following day. Before the appointment, she centered herself, as Choden had taught them to do while meditating. At the meeting, Emily explained her concern to the Dean. He thought for a moment, then agreed to cap the enrollment at twenty-five. Emily expressed her gratitude, and the Dean thanked her for thinking first of the students. A win-win.

Just when she thought she knew Choden well, an unusual and unexpected event occurred. He was asked to do something which meant traveling to Westport, Connecticut. He asked Emily if she would like to come with him. David would be in school, and Emily did not teach that day, so she said, "Of course."

Typically, Choden said nothing about what he was to do, as more than anyone she knew, he lived entirely in the present. So, they enjoyed the train ride and were mostly silent until they reached the Westport station where they were met by a chauffeur in a large black Lincoln. Choden entered the car with ease and sat in the luxury limo as if it were a daily occurrence.After a few minutes, the car turned into a large iron gate which the driver opened with his remote and they headed down a long driveway to a stately mansion probably built in the 1930s.

The hostess greeted Choden and told them to follow her into the garden room where tea would be served. She was a cultured woman, dressed stylishly in black, and appeared to be in her mid-fifties. Tea was served by a Hispanic maid, and the scones and pastries were delicious. At some point, Choden replaced his cup and looked at the woman, saying, "Shall we?" The woman nodded and stood up, expectantly. Emily followed her example, wondering why he was asked to come.

The woman guided them inside her home through a couple of large rooms until they came to a smaller room that seemed cozier than the rest of the mansion. On the mahogany wall, she pointed to a portrait of an older man, handsome and serious, whom Emily assumed was her husband.

"When did your husband pass over?"

The woman whom Emily now understood to be a widow replied, "Two weeks ago."

Choden, as simply as if he was unloading groceries, placed his cloth shoulder bag on a small table and took from it incense, an incense holder, lighter, and a small bell. He moved the small table to stand directly in front of the portrait and placed the incense in the holder and the bell next to it. Then lighting the incense, he closed his eyes and began to chant Tibetan slokas for the peaceful journey of the man who had died. It lasted only a few minutes then Choden lifted the small bell and rang it several times, uttering a final chant. Silence followed as the widow stood quietly by, a few tears streaming down her face. Choden, in a most simple manner, collected his tools and replaced them into his shoulder bag, before bowing to the woman in black, who was now smiling.

"I cannot thank you enough, Threptin Choden."

The chauffeur drove them back to the train station where they sat for a few minutes awaiting the next train to Manhattan. After several moments, Emily turned to Choden, saying, "I gather you have done this before?"

"Yes, when needed."

Emily laughed and said, "Choden, you never cease to amaze."

Choden blushed and laughed.

Time flew by as the three friends continued to enjoy each other's company while discovering the city anew. David had been influenced for the better, had good friends, and was now doing consistently well at his challenging school. Emily had begun to send out her resume to other universities on the chance of a higher position so that she could better support David when it was time for him to go to college.

Then, one day the most amazing news exploded upon the world. After years of traveling the globe, spreading his philosophy of peace and non-violence, in 1989, the Dalai Lama was awarded the Nobel Peace Prize. Emily collapsed on the couch and wept for joy. Several weeks later, she joined Choden and other monks with Marion Stein and other volunteers for Free Tibet, watching on television as the Dalai Lama stood in Stockholm to receive the prestigious award. He bowed and simply made his acceptance speech, from which Emily would forever remember these words:

'Your Majesty, Members of the Nobel Committee, Brothers and Sisters. I am very happy to be here with you today to receive the Nobel Prize for Peace. I feel honored, humbled, and deeply moved that you should give this important prize to a simple monk from Tibet. I am no one special. But I believe this prize is in recognition of the true value of altruism, love, compassion and non-violence."

In the hall, everyone stood and applauded – as did his many friends and followers in New York and elsewhere.

All too quickly from Emily's point of view, David graduated and left for university while she gained a tenured position at the University of Southern California in Los Angeles.

Though Emily never quite developed a taste for what Tibetans call 'tsampa' (barley tea) and never became a Buddhist, she felt that both she and her son had become better people from knowing Threptin Choden. David never became a monk but instead, after his first degree, opted for Harvard Law School. However, they both continued to take an active interest in the *Free Tibet* movement, and enjoyed many events supporting the worthy cause.

Even in sunny California, people can sometimes wake up in an odd mood. When that happened to Emily, she didn't feel like teaching. Yet soon would come, unbidden to her mind, something Choden would say, and then Emily imagined him saying to her, "Just one small positive thought in the morning can change your whole day." Remembering Choden was her one small, positive thought – and it, inevitably, did the trick.

However, as sometimes happens, even with the best of friends, they lost touch with the young monk. Still, they often thought of him as he had become a living presence in both of their lives.

Many years later, Emily was invited to New York for a conference and, while there, took some time off to explore SOHO galleries and look at contemporary art as she used to do when she lived in the city. As she wandered, it began to rain, so she ducked into the first shop she saw. It so happened to be a store with arts and crafts made by Tibetans. She began to browse when a young man, well-dressed in a dark blue Brooks Brother suit, approached her.

Emily was admiring an embroidered purse when the proprietor called out, "Emily? Is that you?" Surprised, she turned around and was amazed to see Choden.

"Choden? Is it possible?"

"Yes, it is." They hugged and laughed. Emily noticed that except for his attire, he did not look a day older than when they had last met.

Choden, delighted, set her down on a carved wooden chest and began to tell his story. He said that he had met a young woman from Oklahoma living in New York, and they had decided to marry. So, he left his life as a monk and became a citizen of America. His wife was the daughter of a rich man with many oil wells in Oklahoma. They had bought a beautiful home in Connecticut – not far from the widow we met so many years ago, remember?

Astonished, Emily nodded, waiting for him to continue his amazing tale.

"We have two daughters now and are very happy. This is my store, and I have two other Tibetan stores also in the city."

"What of the Dalai Lama? What did he say about all this?"

"His Holiness? He is very happy for me. I see him often, every time he comes to New York. And a percentage of what my stores make is sent to Dharamshala.

Noticing Emily's look of confusion, Choden

continued, "In Tibet, it is not unusual to pass from being a monk to being a householder. It is all the path of Lord Buddha, as long as one is true and follows the Eight-Fold path. Do you understand, Emily? Like the movies, it is a happy ending, yes?"

"Yes," laughed Emily. Then she told of David's success at getting into Harvard Law School and that she had a fine job in Los Angeles, teaching.

"You must come to Connecticut and meet my family, Emily."

"I would love to, but not this trip, as I'm due back to teach. Rain check?"

"Rain check?"

"It means another time."

"Yes, yes, for sure. Another time. Rain check."

The rain had stopped, and Emily had to get back uptown to her conference. They hugged., and Choden, with a bow to Emily, handed her a gift of the embroidered purse she had been admiring.

"Emily, I am always so grateful to you and David for making me feel at home. 'I was a stranger and you took me in' as it says in your Bible. You gave me so much."

"Choden, actually, I think it was the other way round. You gave us both so much."

They then parted until another time.

Later that evening, after the banquet at the conference, Emily lay awake looking back on the extraordinary meeting with Choden – as if by chance. And his transformation from monk's robes to Brooks Brothers suits! She thought, "I must call David tomorrow and tell him."

Just before Emily drifted off to sleep, for some strange reason, she remembered, when she was twelve, seeing Audrey Hepburn in *The Nun's Story*. Based upon a true story, the film portrayed Hepburn as a nun and nurse who went to Africa, saving people's lives. There, in time, she found her work more important than scheduled prayers, and a few years later, stopped being a nun. The movie ends with her removing her nun's dress and leaving the order. Emily thought to herself, "I like to think she married and had children, but I don't really know what happened after she stopped being a nun. Perhaps, like Choden, she, too, found a happy ending."

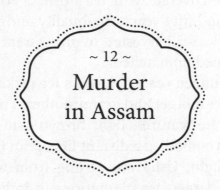

~ 12 ~
# Murder
# in Assam

*Everybody wants to go to heaven,*
*but nobody wants to die.*

Anonymous

Assam is a northeastern state of India, one hundred and sixty feet above sea level, located near the eastern Himalayas – with luscious valleys, rivers, creeks, and waterfalls. It became an ideal setting for the first known tea plantations in India when a Scottish adventurer, Robert Bruce, visited India in 1823 for trading purposes. While exploring Rangpur, he encountered wild tea bushes growing near the area. By the late 1970s, the estate spread across eighteen hundred acres of which a thousand acres were covered with tea bushes. For over one hundred and fifty years, the quality and rich aroma of the tea leaves harvested by the Assam Tea Estate has remained unmatched.

Usha, fifteen years old, was a tea picker in Assam – as was her mother and grandmother. Young, pretty with delicate features, light brown skin and green eyes, Usha embodied a distant lineage of British rule. Though slight, Usha was strong from working on one of the largest tea plantations in India since age ten. She lived with her mother, though only thirty-one seemed older, and with her grandmother, who was in her fifties yet seemed ageless. Neither spoke of her father or grandfather, and Usha understood enough not to ask.

Though the family that owned the tea plantation earned billions, the tea pickers barely had a minimum wage. Ninety-four rupees a day ($1.27) was not even enough to survive, which was designed to keep the indentured tea pickers there for years– even generations.

Usha was very close to her grandmother whom she called Nani. She loved it when after a long day of tea plucking, Nani would tell her stories and legends. Her favorite story, the one Nani repeated for her over and over again was about a great Asura king's daughter, Princess Usha – her namesake. One night Princess Usha dreamt of a handsome prince, and though it was only a dream, she fell madly in love with him. Her friend, Chitralekha, a talented artist, not only painted the prince but recognized him to be Aniruddha, the grandson of Lord Krishna, the ruler of Dwarka. Using her magical powers – for Chitralekha was also a witch – she spirited the young prince away to Usha's boudoir where the two married each other according to Gandharva rites. The ancient marriage tradition based on mutual attraction has no rituals, witnesses, or family participation. Unfortunately, this also meant that the marriage took place without the knowledge of her father, the king. When he learned of the romance, the king imprisoned Aniruddha. At this, Lord Krishna came at once to rescue his grandson. A fierce battle followed, bathing the entire city in blood. Tezpur got the name 'the city of blood'. Yet the eternal love between Usha and Aniruddha lives on to this day.

"Oh, Nani, tell it again."

Ma, Usha's mother, who thought such stories a waste of time, shouted, "Time to sleep. Dawn will not wait for silly stories."

So, Usha would close her eyes, and dream of the day her own prince would come.

It was Nani who taught Usha to read. Usha loved history. Knowing that the stories were true made them all the more precious. One evening after chapattis and green gram, she laid down near the fire with her head on Nani's lap, and listened in awe to another true story.

"After the Mughal invasion, Nani said, "the British took Assam into the British Empire. But the people in Assam did not like it. They wanted to be free, so they joined the Civil Disobedience Movement. At this time, before you were born, Mahatma Gandhi visited Tezpur. Later it was called the *Quit India Movement* and banners proclaimed "Do or Die." Toward the end of this movement, during the second great world war, a young village girl – about your age – led a procession of unarmed villagers under the Indian Congress flag. Her name was Kanaklata Barua. As soon as Kanaklata unfurled the flag, she and her friend, Mukunda Kakati, were gunned down by armed police.

"That's why, Usha, we do not trust the police. The police are for the masters – not for the poor, not for us. Remember this. On the same day the Police killed Kanaklata, the Police gunned down eleven unarmed villagers, just for trying to raise the flag – and three of them were teenaged girls – just like you. So, don't trust the police."

"But Nani, it's different now. The British no longer rule us, right?"

"After years of struggle and many deaths, on 14 August 1947 at midnight, India finally gained her Independence."

Ma turned off the kerosene lamp and turned over to sleep.

"Nani, even girls like me helped to free India, isn't that right?"

"Shhh," hissed Ma, "We must rise early to work."

The morning came too soon and after some left over roti and vegetable curry, it was time for work. For the next eight hours Usha with her large straw basket hung over her shoulders plucked the bright green leaves that would become black tea. She tried to imagine homes in England and America where far-away families enjoyed tea with the rich aroma of Assam.

Ma would tell her true stories sometimes, but they were never happy ones. They were told to frighten or warn Usha so that she didn't end up in a bad situation like some tea pickers.

One such story was of Somila, a cousin of theirs. Like Usha, Somila was a tea picker from childhood. When she was sixteen, a man from Delhi told her he needed suitable girls to work in Delhi for better jobs, better pay. The opportunity seemed so promising that Somila went away with the Delhi man, and was never seen again. Ma told Usha that Somila was one of hundreds of young girls who left and never returned. "Who can say what happened to these poor girls lured far away to the big cities. only to disappear?" Usha did not wish to hear this story again and again, but she never forgot it.

Clive was the English overlord in charge of the female pickers, working in the tea estate as his father before him. Though British, he had never been to England, and was the third generation of his family to work in Assam. At fifty, he had a failed marriage, no children, and had remained single for the past twenty or more years. Ma had taught Usha not to look him in the eye, and to always look down and keep working. As he was not very much to look at, Usha found it easy to ignore him. Clive liked to chew betel nut and leaves, and would spit the juice anywhere and everywhere.

One day, he spat the chewed betel leaves so close to her, that she felt the droplets on her cheek. She looked up to see Clive smiling at her. Taking the edge of her cotton sari, Usha wiped her face and kept on working. After this, more and more, Clive would watch her. He liked to come up behind her as she was bent over plucking the tea leaves, all the while, chewing, chewing, chewing. One morning as she bent over to work, Clive placed his hand on her backside and squeezed, as if Usha were a mango fruit he was testing for ripeness.

Usha wondered if she should tell Nani. She knew her Ma would only get angry. So that evening, rather than ask for a story, Usha whispered to Nani about what Clive had done. Nani looked very serious, and for a moment did not speak. Washing the dishes, she did not look at Usha for some time. Later, drying her hands on her old sari, Nani whispered to her granddaughter, "Don't do anything. Be careful. Never be alone with him – no matter what."

A few days passed before Clive made his move. He told Usha to go to the shed and bring back some shears to cut the vines. As soon as Usha found them, she turned to leave and there was Clive, smiling, and shutting the door of the shed. He took the shears from her and replaced them on the shelf. Then he walked toward the girl, speaking softly.

"Just be quiet and do what I say, you'll be fine."

The overlord unbuttoned his khaki pants, backing the frightened girl into a corner. He pushed her down on some sacks of tea, and when she resisted, he struck her hard on the face til she went limp. He forced a cotton handkerchief into her mouth as he roughly lifted her sari in order to gratify himself. Usha struggled briefly, then surrendered to the inevitable. She noticed a glimmer of light shining in the darkness of the shed, a small window where she could see a slither of sky. She held her gaze on the shimmering light until the Englishman groaned, sighed, and got up from her bruised body.

"Say nothing or it will harm your family. They will starve," he warned.

Still in pain and shock, Usha looked at the man who had brutalized her, unable to speak. Clive hurriedly left, buttoning his pants as he walked quickly away, not noticing that the girl's mother had seen him. Ma understood at once what had happened when she found Usha bleeding in the shed, where Clive had left her. She immediately darts out of the shed after him, just as he was finishing buttoning his pants. He tried to turn away from her when she cried out, "You monster, don't you realize who she is? She's yours." Clive, at first surprised, abruptly turned his back on the shouting woman, and angrily shaking his head, trudged off.

Back at home, the women wept. Nani cried softly, saying, "Once again, I weep my pain. That is all we women know, that is all we have. We live the pain. Pain is what life is for the poor."

In contrast to Nani's pain and Usha's trauma, Ma's anger grows more and more until her face turned red with rage. She chops the raw cabbage for the evening meal as if attacking an enemy. Then when the oil was boiling, pours in the chopped cabbage mixed with cumin and mustard seed. As it sizzled, she stared at the iron pan as though reading the future of what is to come. Noticing her daughter, Nani, says, "No, my child, be still. There is nothing we can do. Nothing. It is our duty to survive for Usha. That is our dharma." Nani crawls over, sitting near her disturbed daughter who turns away preferring her anger to Nani's prudence. Instead, Nani strokes her granddaughter's head, mourning for the beloved innocent she once was.

The following days at work, the three women stayed close to one another, never letting Usha out of their sight. One day, watching her like a hawk, Clive noticed where Usha went into the brush to relieve herself.

It had been a week since the rape. As an exotic fruit once tasted, Clive knew that he must have Usha again. He approached her unawares, causing her to hastily rise up and adjust her sari. Holding her arm tightly, Clive hoarsely demanded she must meet him in the shed or her mother and grandmother would pay the price.

"They will lose their jobs. They will starve if you do not come to the shed tonight. "

Usha understood that she had no choice. She must protect her mother and grandmother. So late that evening when her family was sleeping, Usha stealthily left their shack and made her way to the tea gardens. The moon was round and bright. "Even the gods are watching," thought Usha. Clive was smoking a beedi, impatiently waiting at the shed when she arrived. He opened the door, looked around, then closed it after they were both inside. She looked even more beautiful in the moonlight. Her green eyes shone, as if mirroring his own. Knowing what to expect, she did not resist this time, and let him have his way with her. She was still in pain from his first assault, only this time she did not bleed. He finished and stood up, nodded to her and left. Then Usha slowly made her way home.

Ma heard her come in, and must have guessed what happened. Saying nothing, she pretended to sleep. Nani was in a deep slumber, and Usha was grateful she did not have to face either woman with her shame. Usha soon fell asleep, and did not notice that her mother had left.

The next morning while plucking the ripe leaves, there was a buzz among the women in the fields.

"Did you know?"

"Have you heard?"

It was some minutes before news reached their area.

"The overlord is dead."

"His throat was slit like a slaughtered pig."

"Killed in his own bed, he was."

Nani first looked at her granddaughter who looked back, obviously with as much surprise as the other women. Then she looked across the tea bushes at her daughter who, avoiding her mother's gaze, spoke out, "Who will miss him? None will weep for this man."

"Ay. A man like him would have many enemies," added another tea picker.

The police came and all the women pickers told the same story: that there had been thieves in the village and perhaps one attacked the overlord. After a brief investigation, the police were satisfied that the Englishman's death was as the women said. The matter was settled, the police left them alone, and no one mentioned him again. As Ma had said, "Who will miss him? None will weep for this man."

Life returned to normal for the three women as they continued to pluck leaves and, at home, their lives encircled each other even more tightly. After some time, Nani began again to tell Usha stories after supper. Even Ma seemed less angry with her daughter.

Time passed uneventfully, that is, until a few months later when Nani noticed that Usha was getting a round belly. The older women knew what that meant, and though Nani was sympathetic, Ma again grew angry.

"What to do? It cannot be helped, daughter. It is not her fault."

Usha continued to work in the fields until her time came, and then Nani assisted her with the difficult birth. She was now sixteen, and the child was a boy.

Late one night, Usha woke to find Ma with a small blanket heading toward the sleeping baby. At first, Usha was puzzled for Ma usually had nothing to do with the care of the child. To her horror, she suddenly realized her mother wanted to smother the baby.

"No, Ma, no!"

Usha jumped up and grabbed her baby.

"Nani. Nani. Wake up! Help me."

"It must be done. Give him to me."

"No, Ma, no," Usha pleaded, "No."

Ma collapsed in tears, and Ma rarely wept.

Nani was awake now. "Daughter, you cannot do this thing. It is no fault of the child."

"But it is a man child, Amma, I could bear it if it were a girl like our Usha, but not a man child," as Ma continued to weep as never before, crying out, "Oh, Amma, it never stops. It never stops."

Nani consoled her daughter, and Ma, for the first time in many years, allowed herself to be touched and comforted by her own mother. They never told Usha the truth of who her biological father – now dead – was. Or who was responsible for his murder. Usha knew only that the overlord was the father of her child, and this was a secret she would carry to her grave.

And so, Usha raised and cared for her son and, though the child would never know his British father, he would grow up to look just like him.

## ~ 13 ~
# The Ashram

*The soul, like the pigeon, has a homing instinct.*
*This, if heeded, will guide you to return to the Self.*

ℐ am in my hometown in America in what seems at first to be The Water Store on Main Street. Instead, as I enter, it is a huge, cavernous empty space with nothing and no one there. I hear someone calling my name, but it is far away, and I cannot discern who it is. Feeling uneasy, I decide to leave as quickly as possible. But then the person calling me becomes louder, and I recognize the voice as my mother's. "Kayla! Kayla! Wake up." I look around, but cannot see her. I wait, but though she is not there, I am keenly aware of her unseen presence.

I wake from this disturbing dream and notice that it is late. Since my mother always comes and wakes me when I oversleep, I wonder where she is. After a brief moment, uninvited reality intrudes, and I remember. Mother is dead and has been so for seven years. How slow the mind can sometimes be to accept what is true.

A year had passed since that dream. I'd graduated with honors, but yet again, found myself drifting, dreaming other strange dreams. At twenty-two, I did not fit in with the American way of life. Any ambition which may have once been there had silently fallen away, and, in its place, reigned a fervent search to find God – or Truth. Friends and family could not understand, who could blame them? What did I want? I knew only what I did not want. I did not want a committed relationship, a career – or even a job. And I certainly did not want any more disturbing dreams. I began to cry for no reason at all, and wrote in my journal:

I touched a star and kicked a clod
Then grew old within a year.

Yes, that is exactly how I felt. Old. Old at twenty-two.

A friend from university, during his travels in India, had met a sage, and suggested that I might find what I sought there, at the ashram. As the disciplined student I had once been, the first thing I did was to look up the meaning of 'ashram', to discover that an ashram is 'a hermitage, monastic community, or religious retreat'. And so, India.

Impulsively, I booked a flight to India for a two-week stay. Impatiently, I wait for the visa. I begin to wonder if it would come in time. Was this a sign that my impulsiveness was foolish? A sign that I should not travel to India? Then the day before my scheduled flight, the visa arrived. I packed, and the next afternoon, left for the airport. The trip was long yet full of expectation.

Life is relationship. Yet this may not always mean another person. It could be one's work, a pet – or even a place. Though this was my first trip to India, after changing planes in Delhi, the moment the plane touched down in Varanasi, I felt that I had come home.

Viewing the chaos at the airport, I think how worried Mother would have been – were she still here. Oddly, I have no fear – only fatigue. So, I decide to stay in Varanasi for a day or two before heading to the ashram.

Varanasi – or Benares as it was once called – is an ancient and amazing city. Where Hindu pilgrims come to die, and have their ashes scattered in the sacred Ganga.

Varanasi. A universe, layers behind layers confusedly blended into One. Contradictions abound: the smell of incense and urine; sadhus and cow dung; pigeons and vultures; the mythic purity of the Sacred Ganga River and the corruption where street beggars mutilate their own children — blinding them or cutting off a hand — to increase their revenue from begging. Here were not beautiful faces, but rather ones of holy resignation, a surrender to their individual and collective fates. Even the sacred cows seem evolved souls as I perceived past ages of India in their accepting eyes. Unchanged for centuries, ancient India was strong in the air.

At dusk, I engaged a small boat and boatman. Passing the holy Ghats, I observed nightly bodies laid on stacks of wood, burning on a pyre – taking them to the afterlife. According to the boatman, after the pyre is lit, the family stands in silence for three or more hours as ashes are returned to ashes. In the sheer silence of a centuries-old ritual, rested the poignant and overpowering impact of it all. Suddenly an explosion! The boatman casually explained that before lighting the pyre, someone had forgotten to crack the skull in order to prevent the head exploding. This final reminder of life's fragility. Then he pointed to a large, impressive house near the Ghats, "The largest house there is owned by the seller of firewood." Words fail to explain this contradictory, holy city. I felt that it would take me years to absorb all that I had experienced here in just one day. Intuitively, I knew that to comprehend

Varanasi is to understand the rich complexity that is India.

Later, as I walked through the darkening streets, the sounds of temple drums, cymbals, and chanting of Sanskrit slokas mingled with the smell of lit camphor, incense, and spices sold in the crowded markets. Near the Ghats where people bathed in the holy Ganga, purifying their souls, I noticed colorful graffiti murals on the walls: Shiva, standing on the demon of ignorance, dancing the dance of life and death, and another large, overpowering mural of a naked sadhu (one who has renounced worldly life) standing, holding a skull in his hands, with raised arms reaching to heaven. Another reminder that death comes to us all.

Overwhelmed by these first impressions and jet lagged, I purchased some marigolds and tossed them into the Ganges, bidding my deceased mother a blessed journey. Then I sat near the River Ganges as the humid night embraced me – and wept.

It was time to leave the ancient city and find the ashram. My friend had told me that the ashram was located about forty minutes north of Varanasi, so it seemed sensible to return to the hostel, book a car for the next morning, and retire early. Hopefully, answers would await once I reached the end of my pilgrimage. Truth, God, Purpose – and all that.

As I dried my tears and rose, and about a hundred feet away, I saw a young man in a white dhoti, bare chested, with a burning torch in his hand. With this flaming stick, he mumbled some words I could not hear, then lit the pyre of stacked logs, on top of which lay a dead body tightly bound in pristine, white cloth. Friends and family stood nearby, silently, solemnly, as the departed was burning on the banks of the holy Ganges. No sermon or eulogy, not even a hymn – only silence accompanied this timeless ritual of ashes to ashes. Death.

Unprepared for the humid heat of India, I tossed and turned that night, yet, finally two hours later, managed to fall asleep. I slept long and hard, relieved that I would soon be leaving this ancient city which had both amazed and terrified.

Well rested, I ate a solid breakfast of roti and potato curry with hot coffee mixed with buffalo milk and sugar. At breakfast, I met Margaret, an older woman in her mid-thirties who had just come from London. She was a small, slender woman who, when standing, only reached to my shoulder. She seemed frail, yet I would soon discover that Margaret possessed a strong will, and once decided on something, nothing could shake her. By the time, breakfast was over, we discovered to our mutual delight that we were both headed to the same destination. We agreed to leave directly and share the taxi.

During the dusty ride past paddy fields, bullock carts, endless people walking – some with baskets on their heads as they strolled with gentle purpose,

I listened as Margaret told me her sad story. British, she had married a Frenchman whom she loved very much. Six months earlier, she and her husband had been on holiday in the south of France, near Grasse. He had gone for a swim in a nearby river while Margaret stayed in the hotel to nap.

"And that was the last time I saw my husband. The villagers said he must have drowned. But his body was never discovered. How can I accept that he is dead when there is no body?"

"I'm so sorry, Margaret. Is this what made you come to India?"

"In a way. I have always searched for answers, and when I learned of the ashram, I thought perhaps I might find those answers."

"Yes, similar to my own reasons. Answers matter more to me than anything else."

"One day I will return and look for my husband - if only to know for certain that he is truly gone."

I could not find anything to say, so remained quiet. Then on a more casual note, I told Margaret that I had noticed that she had brought many parcels.

"Oh, yes, I had heard that it is difficult to find things one needs there, as the ashram is in the middle of nowhere. So, I thought I might open a make-shift shop for soap, toothpaste, and other sundries. What do you think, Kayla? Good idea?"

Taken by surprised, "Why, yes, of course. Consider me your first customer."

Margaret smiled, and we turned our attention to the endless paddy fields surrounding us.

We passed several tall poplar and neem trees with lively monkeys perching on their branches or screeching and bustling about. I told Margaret that neem trees have medicinal properties and are often used in shampoo and toothpaste – probably in those she had purchased for her store.

The taxi had turned down an unpaved, dirt road with several bumps, which took our attention. After some minutes, the car stopped in front of a large white-washed building with a red tiled roof probably built during the British Raj. Other smaller structures were scattered about encircling the larger building. Nearby, a tributary river flowed, making it altogether a serene scene.

A tall, slightly stout Englishman who looked to be in his mid-fifties, approached, welcoming us to the ashram.

"Good morning and welcome to the ashram. My name is David, and I have been asked to show you to your lodging. If we hustle, you will be able to meet Master for *Satsang* in about half an hour."

"I am Kayla from America, and this is Margaret from London."

"A fellow Brit," smiled David, as Margaret nodded in response and began hurriedly to collect her things.

A thin, energetic young Indian in his late teens,

ran up and began to appropriate our luggage while we paid the driver.

"This is Gopala, and he will make sure your things are taken to your rooms."

Following David, Margaret asked, "How long have you been here, David?"

"Five years now. It is home."

"No family?"

"Only a wife, but I could no longer live with her… so I became a celibate. Life is much less complicated now. Ah, here are your rooms. They are next to one another. The bathroom is shared."

"Thank you, David. Where is the meeting?" I asked as I bundled my things together.

"Oh, my dear girl, you can't miss it. It's the big building in the center. Just enter, leaving your shoes at the door. See you in half an hour then."

Eager to meet the Master, Margaret and I separated into our respective rooms and began to organize, then quickly changed into fresh clothes. Fortunately, yesterday we had both thought to buy some Indian clothes at the Emporium in Varanasi, cotton churidars and kurtas which seemed the most practical for the climate. And sturdy, leather sandals.

Twenty minutes later, Margaret and I left the rooms, locked the doors, and placed the key in a pocket while the more practical Margaret had pinned it to her kurta with a safety pin. We walked to the large building, the center of the property.

Two peacocks pranced about, sometimes uttering a piercing cry. Upon entering, we left our sandals with several other sandals, and respectfully entered a large room with mats spread on the floor before a small, raised platform where presumably the Master would sit.

There were about nine other Westerners and a few Indians, ranging in age from twenties to fifties, mostly women, and some men, sitting expectantly cross-legged on mats, made from coconut shell fiber called coir, in a respectful and meditative silence. No one spoke.

I was simply grateful to be out of the bumpy taxi, having arrived safely. A persistent mosquito buzzed around my neck, and I realized I had forgotten to bring any pesticide. Then I remembered Margaret and wondered if she had stocked up on that in her makeshift store.

During my mundane thoughts, all abruptly rose and, with palm- to- palm greetings, bowed to the Master who had just appeared. He looked to be in his late fifties, but he might have been any age. He was dressed in a floor length white cotton cloth wrapped around his waist and a lighter white cotton Indian long shirt. His hair was cut short and there was a small beard growth on his chin. Yet it was the eyes that drew attention. Luminous, kind, and when turned toward you, they seemed to pierce to your very depth. He quickly and modestly did a namaste with palms touching and sat cross legged upon a small, red cushion resting on the coir mat. He closed his eyes as did everyone else, and meditation began, lasting for about five minutes. Only then, did the Master look up and out at those sitting before him.

He rapidly scanned the gathering and appeared to wait for someone to speak.

After what seemed a goodly while, a young man spoke, "Sir, yesterday you told us that the mind creates the world and all its variety."

"Yes, that is correct. Just like in a good play you have all sorts of characters and situations, so you need a little of everything to make a world.

The young man countered, "But no one suffers in a play."

"Suffering is man-made. It is caused by the false identification of the perceiver with the perceived. In this way, desire is born, and with desire, blind action, unmindful of the results. Just look at the world today and you will see that suffering is man-made."

"But how not to suffer in this world, regardless of how it is created?"

"Don't identify yourself with the world and you will not suffer. Consider the play. The actor plays his part, then goes home. He doesn't take the role home with him."

A woman in her early forties, whom I would later learn was Adele from Paris, asked a question, "Master, isn't it important to love others?"

The Master smiled, leaned forward, and gently answered, "There are no others. There is only Self. One Self. Similarly, there is no time. You connect the dots, the minutes, yet there is only one dot, one moment, and that is now."

"There are no others?" responded a baffled Adele.

The young man again, "But what is the practice? Shouldn't we be doing hours of yoga daily? Or something?"

The Master chuckled, "When I lived near a wide river and was practicing my sadhana, a young sannyasi and yogi, approached me. I noticed he walked with a great opinion of himself so that his approach was so noisy, he need not have spoken."

Some laughed at this. After a moment, the Master continued, "The young yogi bowed and announced that he had practiced yoga asanas in a cave for six years in the Himalayas, and now could walk on water." He then turned and went to the river. I watched as he walked across the river and then back again. Then he proudly approached me once again, and stood – as if waiting for me to congratulate him.

"It took you six years to master this siddhi?"

"Yes, only six years."

Then I took out of my pocket, two annas, and told the young man, "Your ability to cross the river cost you six years. For two annas, I can pay the ferryman to take me across the river."

"The young man was disappointed with my response to his great power, and soon left me to my meditations. So, you wish to practice? For how long? For what purpose?"

"To know the Truth. To know the Self."

"All you are asked to do here is to see. That is all. There is nothing to practice. Just see who you are. Let your true nature emerge. Don't seek anything. Simply, see."

The room fell silent. The Master's presence was strong. Several closed their eyes and others smiled, looking devotedly at the Master. After several minutes, as quietly as he came, he rose and left the room. I looked across at Margaret who was also smiling. A mosquito buzzed in my ear, which reminded me to ask if she had brought anything for the bugs.

I walked by the river remembering the story told about the two annas. Adele came by, having seen a stray cat. She collected the stray and stroking it, said to me,

"Hello, I'm Adele. You just came?"

"Yes. Kayla from America."

"Isn't he sweet?" as she continued to stroke the cat, "Human beings are not worth one small cat. Cats are God's creatures. They are affectionate and caring, and they know what love is. I will protect and care for them as long as I live."

"You're French?"

"I live in Paris, but come from Switzerland. Geneva, the French speaking part. Welcome to heaven, Kayla. I must go and find some milk for this little guy."

I returned to find Margaret setting up her makeshift store of sundries. Luckily, she did bring a cream called *Odomos* for the mosquitoes. The smell was abhorrent but it worked well.

"You're my first customer, Kayla."

"You were right, Margaret. This is a good idea."

"Sleep well?"

"Yes, and no weird dreams either."

"Me, too. Guess we came to the right place."

"Look over there. No, higher up the cashew tree."

"It's beautiful, Margaret. What is it?"

"A kingfisher. All those colors. Did you know that India has the greatest variety of birds in the world?"

"No, I didn't."

We stood admiring the bronze-chested kingfisher with its bright turquoise head and wings. And a long black beak useful for catching fish in the river. I never thought to bring binoculars.

Dinner was vegetarian, tasty though not overly spicy – no doubt a concession for Western tongues. Porridge at breakfast, parboiled rice with various vegetable curries at lunch followed by raita – freshly made yogurt with diced cucumber. Supper was late, around 9 pm, and light – usually chapattis and green gram or masala dolsa. As meals were communal, it was an opportunity to meet other seekers. David came by to inform me that there was a dhobi to wash clothes.

"Just leave what you want washed outside your door, and Nanu – that is, the dhobi – will return them the following day. Only a few rupees."

"Oh, is there a washing machine?"

Others at the table laughed. David smiled and said, "Nanu is the washing machine. He washes the clothes on a flattened rock at the river."

I nodded, wondering what century I had stepped into.

"Oh, Kayla, do you see Shanta over there. She's serving the food. She will sweep your room every other day." I looked over and saw the smiling Shanta, a well-developed young girl of about eighteen.

Then, David introduced me to Claire and her young son, Tom – who looked to be about five years old. Claire was from Savannah, Georgia. She was lovely though pale with dark, black hair and light blue eyes. Her son probably resembled more the father as he was fair, though with his mother's eyes. Claire seemed to dwell in her own world so that young Tom had become used to being on his own.

In time, Claire would share with me her experiences before coming to India. Since her early teens, she would fall into mystical trance states where she heard voices, and sometimes would talk in unknown tongues. She explained that her church and others became interested in her voices and recorded them. They showed the recordings to scholars at the university who claimed they were old languages from Palestine and other early Coptic sites. Her husband had left, as he thought her mad when she preferred mystical orgasms to physical ones. Claire went on to share that Master had told her that she must transcend the psychic manifestations even though they are real. She must reach a state beyond manifestations.

I was grateful that it was time to attend the Master's talk since I could not find anything to respond to Claire's experiences. I had questions for him, which now seemed boring compared to Claire's mystical manifestations.

This time I sat on the second row, closer to the Master. And when meditating, found that it was easier to still the mind and become open to what was here. I had also used Margaret's cream so that the mosquitos were no longer a distraction.

Claire asked the first question, "What about good and evil?"

"Even what you call evil is the servant of the good and therefore necessary – like boils and fevers that clear the body of impurities.

"How can evil be good?" asked Hanna, a middle-aged Polish woman.

"Remember the story of Rama and Ravana. Rama, an avatar of Vishnu, manifested to demonstrate to the world a model of what is a good king – one steeped in the spiritual. And where there is good there must be the opposite, for one cannot exist without the other. So, Shiva asked Ravana while still in his previous life, "You have a choice for your next incarnation. If you return as a sattvic, good person, you will still have ten more lives to live before liberation. But if you return as Ravana, the evil king of Sri Lanka, a monster with ten heads, you will battle King Rama, and upon your death at his hand, will be liberated forever." As the *Ramayana* tells the story, Ravana chose to return for one more life in order to hasten his liberation, and remained Shiva's most devoted devotee."

Without realizing it, I heard my own voice, "Then there must be evil in order for the good to be realized?"

The Master turned and looked at me, and with gentleness said, "Yes, at least until you realize that neither exist."

Hanna, visibly upset, "Master, how can you say that there is good in Hitler? Are then the Jews the boils to be removed?"

"In Pure Consciousness, nothing ever happens."

"But it did happen. Millions of my people died."

"When?"

"When? During World War II. That's when."

Firmly, the Master spoke, "Life is only now. There is no past or future – these exist only in your mind."

At once, Hanna became silent, closed her eyes, and breathed slowly, more at peace.

After the morning talk, I walked about and found Hanna under the banyan tree, crying softly. I hesitantly approached.

"Hanna, are you alright?"

Hanna did not speak for several moments then smiled and said, "Kayla, I am a Polish Jew and as a small child, my parents sent me to England, and I was saved. Later, all my family perished in Poland. All of them. Many years later, I flew to Warsaw, and when I stepped out of the plane, though it made no sense at all, the very first thing I did was stand and look at all the faces in the crowd meeting the plane. Don't you see? I was looking for my parents – even though I knew that they had been killed by the Nazis. Still, I was searching for their faces. In a way, I am still searching for their faces."

I held her as she softly wept. Then she smiled, nodded, and added, "I know that Master is right. I feel it so, but it is still hard for me. So hard..I feel in order to honor the dead, I must remember them. I must not forget."

When I returned to my room, I saw Shanta leaving with her broom made of coconut palm sticks. I noticed that my journal was not where I had left it.

"Shanta, have you seen my journal. My book?"

She disappeared and after a few minutes, as I continued to search the room, Gopala knocked on my door, and handed me my journal. Angry at first, I chided him for taking it. He pointed to the journal as if telling me to open it. When I did, I saw on the back of the front cover a most beautiful drawing of Gopala Krishna, the avatar of Vishnu, all done with colored pencils.

"You drew this, Gopala?"

The boy nodded and smiled. "I, too, am called Gopala."

The next day, I asked Margaret to find me a new journal without lines and colored pencils which I later gave to Gopala. Shanta, seeing this, giggled, and the two hastened away. I noticed Gopal and Shanta meeting secretly more and more – their attraction to one another was obvious and as much a part of nature as the kingfisher or the ravenous crows.

Two weeks had come and gone. I had cancelled my flight home, leaving it open as to when I would return. The weeks passed quickly, turning into passing months, and I found myself going deeper and deeper within – as the outer world receded. "Perhaps this is the real world – the world within," I told myself. Daily, I would walk by the river and end up at the ancient banyan tree. David had told me that this tree was over three hundred years old. Sitting among the sprawling roots that had in time become young trees themselves, I felt their wisdom. If only trees could talk. Perhaps they do, and I must find a way to hear them. To understand the language of trees. Claire could probably understand them.

I had told Margaret that the dreams about my mother had stopped. She replied, "That means that she has gone on. If only my poor husband could do the same."

Two weeks later a terrible tragedy occurred. Gopala was attacked by a cobra and carried to the porch of the Talk Room. I tried to convince David to take him to the Clinic not half an hour away.

"There's no time, Kayla."

I watched in horror as this young Indian, in his early twenties, suffered terribly, and then suddenly raised up his head and made a circular motion as if he himself had become a swaying cobra. After this, he lay back and was gone. Shanta became hysterical, and ran away, weeping.

That evening after the talk, David explained what the Master had told him.

"Next to the temple in the village, there is a snake shrine. Such shrines are built as a haven for the serpents in the area and are blessed by the priests. In this way, the people are safe. They also warn the villagers never to enter the snake shrine as it belongs exclusively to the serpents."

"I don't understand what that has to do with Gopala's death."

"The boy and Shanta one night sneaked into the shrine and lay together. This was considered a sacrilege. And the cobra took his revenge."

"That's positively medieval, David."

"That's India, Kayla."

Late one afternoon, I bathed in the river and watched the cormorants and kingfishers diving for their supper. The sudden plunges that their splashes caused seemed to awaken me. As if a protective shell I had worn all my life was cracking and little by little, was falling away. This caused me to see without defense or rational thought, but to see as if for the first time.

Though I had never really spoken to her, I had noticed the lovely Prema, a young woman in her mid-twenties from south India. Prema was beautiful with large brown eyes and thick black hair worn in a single braid. She had a lovely voice and, after a brass lamp with oil and lit cotton wicks was placed in the doorway of the Talk Room at sunset, would sing kirtans (devotional songs). The Master had called this time, *Sandhya* - twilight, between night and day - symbolizing the space between darkness and light or the space between two thoughts, where the Absolute shines. I would attend nightly, sitting nearby outside, and anyone could tell that the music came from her heart. I knew from reading the *Upanishads* that her very name, Prema, meant the highest form of unconditional love. Unlike English, India has many names for different levels of love.

One afternoon, I had come a bit late for tea and noticed Prema sitting alone at the dining table. I asked if I might join her, and she nodded with a shy smile.

"I've been wanting to tell you how much I enjoy your singing. Did you study music?"

"Yes, my grandmother sent me to a Carnatic singer in Kerala and she taught me."

"Carnatic?"

"Yes, it's the southern classical form of music."

As we continued to talk, Prema told me she had lived at the ashram now for three years and was very happy here.

"I would have thought you'd be married by now."

"My family wished me to marry a suitable boy, but I refused. My family will never be able to understand why I refuse to marry."

"Because you want a spiritual love more?"

Prema paused, sipped her tea, looking at me as if to decide if she could trust me. I waited patiently and slowly she began to tell me her story.

"I loved once, Kayla. He was my uncle, my mother's brother. No one knew, but he would softly come into my room at night and showed me what love is. Between a man and woman. After a year, he left and married a suitable girl arranged by his parents, and moved far away. My family will never know why I refuse to marry, but I shall never love another. Never."

"Does it help to be here?"

"Oh, yes. When I sing, I know that Krishna hears

me, and I can feel his love. And it is a peaceful love."

"I am glad of it, Prema."

"It is time for Master's talk. We should go," said Prema, as she gracefully rose to leave.

Margaret now sat on the front row and was totally devoted as were the others – most of whom I had come to know in the last months. Later she shared with me that the night before, she had dreamed of her husband. He came to her and told her not to worry.

Eight months had passed when Margaret surprised us all by telling us that a telegram had come from France, stating that after all this time, her husband's body had been found. Identification was certain due to his dental records.

"I must go back now," said Margaret, as she hugged me, handing me a package of sandalwood soap which she knew I loved. She departed the following morning, and I could see that knowing the truth about her husband had, in some way, freed her.

Strange how when people came and went from the ashram, there was no empty space. It was as if they had never been there – as if awakening to a new day after a dream.

More and more, Claire withdrew into herself, leaving young Tom to fend for himself. After a few months, I was returning to my room when I noticed the young boy sitting on a stump, totally still, with blank eyes, staring at nothing.

"Tom? Tom? You all right there?"

No reply, and then to my horror, I saw from within his mouth, tiny white worms crawling outside through his lips."

"Oh, my God!" I rushed to find his mother, and when I told her, she smiled at me, saying, "No need to worry. Master is looking after us. Master is looking after all of us."

Furious and immune to such magical thinking, I called for a taxi and took the boy to the nearest clinic some twenty minutes away. Fortunately, David had told me about a Christian doctor's clinic. I arrived and Dr. Thomas immediately took the boy inside. I waited impatiently on the porch. After half an hour, Dr. Thomas returned.

"The boy will live."

"What is it?"

"Hookworms. They usually enter the body through bare feet. The boy will live, but if you had waited until the next day, it may have been too late. As it is, I'm afraid that his mind may be affected."

Tears in my eyes, I thanked the good doctor, heartened that, to a Christian doctor, the world was still very real. I promised myself then and there, sitting on the Clinic's outer porch, that I would never, never let go of my humanity no matter how deeply I pursued the spiritual.

Dr. Thomas invited me for lunch with his family come Sunday. So, in three days, I was seated at a comfortable home furnished in western fashion – not a half-hour drive from the ashram that had remained unchanged since the British first arrived in India. I learned from Dr. Thomas that he and his wife were originally from Kerala, the southernmost state in India. Over two-thousand years ago, Thomas or Doubting Thomas as he is sometimes called, one of the twelve disciples of Christ, came to Kerala, bringing Christianity after its founder had died on the cross. Later Thomas was martyred in Madras – now Chennai. Those who became Christians as a result of Thomas's preaching – and the descendants of those people – are called 'Syrian Christians'. Though I had myself left organized religion behind, and was drawn more to an agnostic spirituality, I valued the goodness and humanity that Christianity often brings. His wife, Aleena, showed me a small bottle of water taken from the Sea of Galilee when, two years before, they had visited the Holy Land. I thanked these good people for their hospitality and the lovely fish dinner.

Returning to the ashram that afternoon, I had much to contemplate. Walking by the river, I spied the colorful kingfisher diving for his dinner. First, he would hover in the air, then like a dive bomber, plunge forcefully into the river, returning with a small fish. Life always includes some form of violence. I secretly envied the bird, as I had missed having fish for my dinners!

The following morning, I sat on the third row, needing some distance from the Master, lest he read my conflicting thoughts. Perhaps as Doubting Thomas, I, too, entertained doubts – especially after what had happened to young Tom.

Suddenly I felt the Master's eyes on me, plunging so deep into me that I knew he saw my doubt. I heard myself ask a question.

"I still feel a huge gap between us. How to close the gap?"

The Master kept his gaze on me as he responded, "You yourself create the gap by imagining yourself to be separate. Give up the idea of being what you think yourself to be, and there will be no gap. There is no myself, no yourself, only the Self, the only Self of all. Misled by the diversity of names and shapes, minds and bodies, you imagine multiple selves. This talk of personal self and universal self is only the beginning. Go beyond, don't be stuck in duality."

"But I do perceive others, I perceive a world of suffering."

"Words create words. Reality is silent. Be silent, and see. I can only direct your attention to the sky. Seeing the star is your own work. Meditating means giving attention, awareness. That is all."

I keenly felt the presence of the sage and the power of his words, yet still, I clung to my doubt as if drowning. The Master continued to speak – without taking his eyes from me.

"The work, as I know you understand, is inner and silent. One thought is not connected to the next thought, any more than time or space. When you connect them, it becomes two. Duality is created. There is no yesterday, no tomorrow, only now. Not two, but one Pure Consciousness. One. One. One.

I began to cry and could not stop. And then, as if dissolving into that One, I was immersed in a deep-rooted peace and light. To cry or to laugh seemed the same. I experienced a bliss never before known. I left the Talk Room, unable to speak.

As if in a trance, I found myself at the banyan tree and sat there in a samadhi state for hours. When I opened my eyes, it was almost dark. I could hear Prema singing.

Returning to my room, I saw Nanu, the dhobi, folding the washed clothes he had spread upon the ground to dry. It seemed that though something in me had died, the world continued. Huge black crows screeched and flew higher into the neem tree not far from the Talk Room. I saw Adele with her easel and paints, drawing one of her rescued cats. Later she would paint the sketch and show them to us. My perceptions were crystal clear only with one distinct difference: I was no longer involved in any of it.

The next day, I sat on the second row and spoke to no one. I felt as though I saw the Master for the first time and felt bathed in his light as he looked at me. I felt in such a state that I did not hear all of what the Master said that day, but one story firmly stuck in my mind. He was responding to something Prema had asked. I don't recall her question as I was still in such a state. But I did hear his answer.

"It's like the story about the deer who ran from the hunter and entered the hut of a sage for safety. This sage was pledged to always speak the truth, so when the hunter knocked on his door and asked, "Have you seen the deer?" the sage hesitated before answering. The sage was silent for some time, then said, 'He who speaks has not seen. He who sees cannot speak'."

Then the Master turned his head, and looked directly at me, "All that happens in the universe happens not to you, but to the silent witness."

I could no longer see the Master, for what was once there was now only Light, shining Light. I had at long last experienced 'the silent witness' and would remember always the words of the Master, "The Witness is not a person."

That night, I opened my journal and smiled sadly seeing Gopala's rendition of Krishna, then turning the pages, I wrote, "I walk through life inward-turning. Once I believed the world to be the enemy only to discover in the end that it is only myself."

The next morning, I felt a lightness and freedom never before known. It was a freedom not from the world, but from myself – or my mistaken view of who I was.

During the talk, the Master quoted a sage called Swami Satchidananda, who once stated, "Do not expect to see a world where everyone is enlightened. When that happens, there is no world."

I laughed out loud, hearing this. "Of course," I thought, "In that transcendental state there is no outer world. And yet, we must have some people to keep the world going. People like the good Dr. Thomas."

The last thing that Master said at this talk, he said while looking directly at me, "To understand the Truth is to live it."

Later the same day, while sitting at the banyan tree, I experienced a waking vision where I saw for the first time a guardian angel of sorts, standing beside me, a shining white light. I knew at once that she was my intuitive heart. I named her LO for Love. She was a spiritual warrior complete with a protective shield. I invited her to return and stay within. Tears of gratitude came as I knew beyond doubt that after a long absence, I was returning to myself. LO dissolved into my heart, leaving this message: "Remain always aware of the reality within and the rest will come to Light. You will always know what you need to know, when you need to know it. In its own time, not yours."

Somehow, at that last Talk, the Master knew – even before I did – that I would be leaving the ashram. I had come to India for two weeks. Now, two years later, I knew from within that it was time to return home. Though India would remain my spiritual home, it was not home.

I said good-bye to my fellow pilgrims. Adele presented me with a painting of one of her feral cats sitting near the banyan tree. Prema had made a tape of her singing. Young Tom brought me a flowering lotus blossom. David gave me a small book of the *Bhagavad Gita.*

The next morning as I took leave, standing on the porch outside the Talk Room, the Master spoke to me for the last time, "The experience of being empty, uncluttered by memories or expectations, is like the happiness of open spaces. Once you are well-established in the now, there is nowhere else to go. Happiness is understanding that. Be the silent witness. Like a bird on its wings, leave no footprints."

As a peacock lifted its beak and screamed to the sky, I bowed to the sage, and left – without leaving. There were no sentimental goodbyes, the impersonal veil of Truth stood firm, and I was the beneficiary. My relationship with India would forever be imprinted on the geography of my heart. Persistent striving may sometimes be necessary, yet I understood now that realization of the Self is not a destination as once thought, but rather a moment-to-moment awareness of awakening to Truth.

I strove toward God,
And stumbled upon myself.
St. Anselm, 11th c.

~ 14 ~

# Lakshmi's Treasure

*God could not be everywhere
and therefore, He made mothers.*

Anonymous

$\mathcal{P}$unjab is situated between Pakistan on the west, Kashmir on the north, and Rajasthan on the south. Hinduism in the Punjab dates from ancient times when India's great epic, the *Mahabharata* was composed two thousand and five hundred years ago, or possibly even earlier. In 1947, when India won her independence from British rule, Punjab Province was partitioned along religious lines, West Punjab going to Pakistan and East Punjab going to India. Huge numbers of people were displaced, and there was much intercommunal violence resulting in around one million being killed. Following independence, and due to the ensuing communal violence and fear, most of the Sikhs and Punjabi Hindus who found themselves left in Pakistan migrated to India.

Punjab is the third largest agricultural producing state in India, but due to the increasing laws favoring multi-national corporations, the small farmers are amassing great debt and, all too often, losing their farms.

Lakshmi's husband, a farmer in the Punjab, had died, leaving her a widow with their five-year old son, Ravi. Lakshmi's mother had also died, so Lakshmi lived with her father who struggled to earn a living on his small, inherited farm. After centuries using their own indigenous seeds, farmers now were required to buy GMO seeds from corporate companies and grow wheat, selling at lower prices. The corporate pesticides they were forced to use were not working, only creating bigger and stronger pests, and often causing sickness and death among the farm workers themselves.

As with many other farmers, Lakshmi's father struggled in order to support his widowed daughter and her young son. Lakshmi's late husband had been accidentally crushed to death in Delhi when thousands of farmers had gathered in protest against the corporate control of their farms, seeking a return to planting their own seeds as their fathers and grandfathers and great-grandfathers had always done.

One evening, after a simple meal of chapatti and dahl and after Ravi had gone to sleep, Lakshmi was washing the tiffin. Her father, exhausted and not well, looked at his daughter, and said, "Lakshmi, I have been thinking."

"Yes, Papa?"

"About you and Ravi."

"Yes, Papa?"

"For your sakes, my child, you must leave this place. Go to a town or city, and find work."

"Papa? Leave home?"

"Yes, daughter, to survive, you must leave. There is no hope here."

Lakshmi looked down and tried not to weep. After collecting herself, she said, "No, Papa, I won't leave you. I cannot."

Her father shook his head then went to his bedding on the floor, and lay down to sleep.

The next morning, Lakshmi made rice gruel, and all ate in silence before her father went to the fields. When rolling up the bedding, Lakshmi noticed that her father had forgotten to take his pocket watch. His own father had given him the watch, and though only silver plated, he valued it highly. She laid it aside, planning to give it to him that evening when he returned from the fields.

After Ravi bathed and was dressed, as every

morning, they sat, and Lakshmi taught him his letters. Ravi was bright like his good father. She would make sure that he would study well to have a better life.

Ravi enjoyed learning and knew that it pleased his mother. What love can compare with a mother's love? Lakshmi gently smoothed Ravi's sometime unruly hair.

"You are my treasure, did you know that?

Ravi, smiling and shy, bobbed his head from side to side indicating 'yes'.

The darkness came. June had already ended and still no rain. The fields were thirsty, yet the monsoon was late again this year. She could see that Ravi was hungry, but they would wait for Papa. After two hours passed, she decided to go ahead and feed her son, and then she would wait for her father.

Another hour passed, Ravi was now asleep, and Lakshmi was worried. She peered outside their small house, searching for some sign of her father's return. Suddenly, a young man was running toward her, calling her name. It was Arman, a farmer her own age who lived not far from them.

"Arman? Arman? What is it?"

Arman stopped running and stood silent before her, not knowing what to say.

"What is it? Where is my father? Have you seen him?"

Arman bowed his head and nodded, still silent.

Lakshmi poured a cup of fresh water she had recently pulled from the well.

"Here, Arman. Drink. Drink."

The young man clumsily drank, then coughed as he handed the cup back to her.

Lakshmi waited, after a moment, Arman blurted out, "He is dead."

"No, you must be mistaken. Perhaps he is hurt. Where is he? We must find him."

"No, no. He is dead."

In late evening, two men from their village carried the farmer home, and Lakshmi learned the truth. Last week, he had not been able to pay his debt, and their farm was lost. He was ashamed to tell her, so as hundreds of other indebted farmers had done, he had eaten the pesticide, vomited, and died. He had known that now she would have to leave with Ravi, and go to town for work.

Lakshmi shed no tears as she prepared her father for the pyre. Due to the extreme heat, he would be cremated early the next day. The men who had carried him home from the fields would return with firewood and build the pyre near their home. Arman stayed behind, asking if he could do anything for them. He had known Lakshmi all his life.

"No, Arman, I will prepare him. Just come tomorrow."

Reluctantly, he turned and left the widow and her young son.

When her son was asleep and her work was done, Lakshmi sat next to her father who had been laid on the ground near his bedding. Lakshmi understood now that her father's death would force her to leave their village for town.

"Oh, Appa, why? If only you had told me. We could have all left for town. We could all have found other work. If only you had told me."

Alone, Lakshmi wept quietly, for fear of waking her son. She held the edge of her worn sari to dry her silent tears.

It was early July, and still the rains had not come. The men came in their stiff suits to tell her that she must leave the farm, as it no longer belonged to her family.

"Why are you packing everything, Amma?"

"We are leaving. Going to a big town. It will be an adventure."

"I am leaving, too?"

"Of course. Would I leave without my treasure?"

Arman came by with his wagon and bullock to drive them to the bus stop some miles away. She would take the bus to Chandigarh, the capital city of Punjab. The trip would be over fifty miles.

Lakshmi knew that this was where her father wanted her to go. They drove in silence along the bumpy dirt road.

"You will be far away."

"Yes, Arman."

"I wish I could come with you. But my mother and sister depend upon me."

"I know, Arman."

"Life is different in the city. It may not be safe."

"We will find work, and Ravi will soon be old enough to go to school. His grandfather would want that. Then he will have choices."

"Yes, that is a good thing."

Arman carried their small bags to the bus stop and waited for the bus with them.

"Arman, you must go now. You have work."

"I don't like to leave you."

"Please. Go. We will be fine. I will write to you."

"Yes?"

"Yes."

Arman turned the bullock cart around and headed home, looking back one last time.

In another hour, mother and child were on the bus headed to Chandigarh.

"Ravi, shall I tell you about Chandigarh? India's first Prime Minister, Nehru, arranged for the whole city to be built. That was the year we became an independent country, 1947. And it took more than 10 years to build, yes, as long as you have been alive. So, it is a modern city and very big. There is an ancient temple there called Chandhi Madir, a temple devoted to Chandi. Some people call her Parvati, the wife of Lord Shiva. But our people just pray to Chandi-ma."

"Will we see the old temple, Amma?"

"Oh, yes, we will go to puja there and ask Chandi-ma's blessing for our new life in Chandigarh. Is that a good idea?"

"Yes, Amma," yawned Ravi, who was very tired. Lakshmi put Ravi's head on her lap and had him stretch out his legs so he could sleep. Then she softly hummed a hymn to Chandi and watched the wheat fields and rice paddies of her early life fade into whatever their future would bring. Lakshmi learned from a village woman about an inexpensive hostel in Chandigarh where the bus would stop. They arrived after dark and she secured a room. They went to sleep right away in order to wake early.

The next day on the street, Lakshmi bought some hot tea, milk, and chapattis. Then, as promised, she took Ravi to Chandi Mandir to attend the Parvati Puja. First, they saw a giant statue depicting Lord Shiva with his trident, and nearby stood Shiva's consort, Parvati, the Divine Mother. The priest was in the middle of performing the puja and Lakshmi, covered her head respectfully with her cotton sari, and stood among the crowd with bowed head. Ravi, with wide eyes, watched the puja. He loved seeing the priest hold the flame and causing it to go round and round the Divine Mother. At the end, all were offered vibhuti to place on their foreheads.

Walking through the temple, Ravi spied a large statue of a young man with the head of an elephant. "Amma, who is that?"

"That is Ganesha. He is the son of Shiva and Parvati."

"But his head is an elephant!"

Lakshmi laughed, "Yes, that is so. Shall I tell you how it came to be?"

Ravi, "Yes, please, Amma."

They seated themselves against a wall and stared at the statue of Ganesha, as Lakshmi told the story.

"Well, when Lord Shiva saw that his son was no ordinary boy, he decided he would have to fight him, and in his divine fury, he cut off the boy's head with his trident, killing him instantly."

"Oh, no, Amma. How could he kill his own son?"

"It is only a story, my treasure. Listen to what happened next."

Ravi nodded, impatiently.

"Well, when Parvati learned what had happened, she became very angry. So angry that she was going to destroy the whole of creation. So that this would not happen, the angels or devas saw an elephant with one tusk, and asking his permission, they removed his head and carried it to Lord Shiva. Then, guess what? Lord Shiva placed the elephant's head on his son's lifeless body and breathed life into him."

"Truly, Amma?"

"Well, he was a god."

"And the boy lived?"

"Oh, yes, Ganesha, too, is a god, though he would always have the head of an elephant.

"Tell me more, Amma."

"There is another story I remember that my father told me once when I was very young – like you. Ganesh had a brother called Kartikeya. Parvati, Lord Shiva's wife, once told her two sons to go around the world in a race. Kartikeya set off at once, and as he was stronger than his brother, was confident that he would win the race. Ganesh first rested, then took a few steps around his mother and sat down again. Parvati reminded him that he was to circle the world.

"But you are my world," her son said, "So I have gone around you."

Ravi, his eyes shining, said, "Did Ganesh win the race, Amma?"

"Yes," my son, "Ganesh won the race."

Ravi jumped up and ran around Lakshmi, saying, "I win, too."

Laughing, Lakshmi embraced her son, saying, "Yes, my son. And did you know that when you pray to Ganesha, he can remove any trouble?"

"Truly, Amma? Then can we ask Ganesh to help us?"

"Yes, my treasure. We can."

Lakshmi, took Ravi by the hand, and stood in front of Ganesh, chanting:

"Om, I invoke the name of Ganesha
Bringer of peace over all troubles
Om, I invoke the name of Ganesha."

In less than a week, Lakshmi found work cleaning offices near the hostel where they stayed. She told Ravi that he must remain in the room each day until she returned after work, then they could go out and walk in the park to buy their supper from the street vendors.

She discovered that when her son turned six in only two more months, he could attend a free school a short bus ride away. After receiving her first pay, she wrote a postcard to Arman to tell him the good news and their address in Chandigarh. It felt good to have some connection to the village – the only home she had ever known.

On Ravi's sixth birthday in September, when the rains were less frequent, they travelled on the bus to The Parrot Bird Sanctuary on the other side of Chandigarh, and it was a happy day. Ravi loved seeing hundreds of parrots of all colors and sizes, and eating ice cream for the first time. On the way home, they purchased pencils, eraser, and a lined journal for school. In two days, he would go to school and meet other children. Chandi and Ganesha had smiled upon them, and they were happy.

As Lakshmi had to work, she taught Ravi how to get to school during the week with his school pass on the bus, and how to return. He felt proud to show his mother this new independence. She had bought for him a small brass pendant of Ganesh on a leather strap, and on his first day of school, she put it around his neck.

Lakshmi said, "Now, remember, Ravi –"

"I know, Amma, if ever in trouble, I ask for help, right? Lord Ganesh will protect me."

"That's right, my treasure, if ever you're frightened or in trouble, just ask Lord Ganesha for his help. He will remove any obstacle." Ravi climbed onto the bus and waved goodbye as Lakshmi stood outside, trying not to cry.

Lakshmi's employer was satisfied with her work and, in time, promoted her to oversee other women workers. This meant a raise in salary and fewer hours, so only two years after they had arrived in Chandigarh, Lakshmi was able to leave the hostel and find a small two-room flat near her work – not far from Ravi's school. It was no surprise to her that Ravi was doing well in school – and had made friends, too.

For the next few years, their lives settled into a comfortable rhythm, spending each Sunday going to a large park or sometimes to the cinema. Ravi, now ten, was used to the city, and quite easily took himself on the bus to school and back. Though he never removed his pendant of Lord Ganesha, he rarely asked for help. He loved reading, and Lakshmi had found a Public Reading Room where they could take out books on loan as long as they were returned on time.

Her father was right about moving to the city – if only he could have come with them. This thought sometimes made her sad.

A letter came from Arman that his mother had died, and that his sister was now engaged to marry. At the end of the letter, he mentioned that he would like to come and see Lakshmi.

She had enjoyed their correspondence and wondered why he wanted to come to visit. She wrote back suggesting that he come on Ravi's tenth birthday, in two weeks' time.

When asked what he wanted to do on his birthday, Ravi had no hesitation.

"Could we go to the Wildlife Sanctuary and see all the animals?"

"Is it far?"

"Only one hour by bus."

"Well, I think that is possible, but it will have to be Sunday."

"That's fine, Amma, it's still the week of my birthday, isn't it?"

"Yes, my treasure. It is indeed."

"Hopefully, Arman can join us," Lakshmi thought to herself. "It would be nice to see him after so many years, and to hear the news of our village."

In a few days, Arman wrote that unfortunately, he could not come next Sunday due to work, but he would definitely come the following week. He added a happy birthday to Ravi.

Lakshmi, as usual, worked hard in supervising the staff of workers she had hired to clean offices. She was delighted when her boss gave her a bonus for her son's tenth birthday. She shared that they would be going to the Wildlife Sanctuary come Sunday, and this bonus would provide an extra treat.

Before long, it was Sunday, and Lakshmi packed a picnic of roti, paneer cheese, and pickle. She added a Cadbury Fruit and Nut Chocolate bar as this was Ravi's favorite.

It was a fine day, and they sat at the back of the bus, opening the window, to let the fresh air blow on them.

"What's that, Amma? Those funny little boxes."

Lakshmi smiled, "Oh, those are for the bees to make honey. We should try and buy a jar at the Sanctuary, to take home with us."

They watched the water buffaloes graze around the banks of the river as they sped by.

Upon arrival, they paid their admission fees, and were given a brochure about what to look for. Lakshmi handed the brochure to Ravi who read quickly, "Here are the species you may see: otter, wild boar, wildcat, fruit bat, hog deer, flying fox, squirrel, and mongoose."

Ravi laughed, "Flying fox! That would be so cool, Amma."

"Yes, but we must be careful. I don't wish to be run over by a wild boar."

"I'll protect you. No worry."

"My treasure," said his mother.

Sometimes Ravi got so excited that he ran off, and Lakshmi couldn't see where he was.

"Ravi? Ravi?"

After a few minutes, though, she would find him and remind him not to get lost.

They watched a fearful sight of a cobra and a mongoose fighting. Fortunately, the creatures were in an enclosed area, but still, it was both exciting and fearful to watch. Of course, the mongoose would win every time.

All the excitement and walking made them hungry, so they found a lovely shaded spot by a large neem tree and spread a bedcover for their picnic. After eating, Lakshmi presented the Cadbury bar and enjoyed the big smile on her son's face.

One older boy came by and told Ravi that he was going to see the flying fox. Would he like to come?

Ravi, excited, asked his mother, "Amma, could I? Then you could rest and I'd come back soon."

"Well, if you promise not to stay long?"

"I promise," as he jumped up and joined the older boy who led the way.

Lakshmi felt the sun on her face and drowsily, closed her eyes, taking a short nap, listening to the sound of crows chattering. After twenty minutes or so, she awoke and looked around. Then she stood up and called, "Ravi? Ravi?" No answer was forthcoming.

She hastily gathered their belongings and walked quickly to the station gate.

"Sir, can you help me? My little boy is lost."

The station ranger smiled and said, "Don't worry, madam, this happens often.

How old is your son?"

"Ten years old. His name is Ravi. He was going with an older boy to see the flying fox."

"Then we'll look there first, shall we?"

"Yes, thank you, sir."

When they reached the large cage that held the flying fox, there was no one there.

After ten minutes, the ranger said, "Come, we will make an announcement over the PA system."

They returned to the main station gate, and the ranger turned on the machine and said in a loud voice, "Will Ravi please come to the main station gate where his mother is waiting for him?" Then he repeated this three times.

Lakshmi, still worried, found a nearby bench, and sat, thinking to herself, "He will come once he hears that. I am sure of it."

One hour passed, and no sign of Ravi. Distraught, Lakshmi assured the ranger that her son was a good boy and would never go off like that. Never.

After another half hour passed, the ranger said that he would call the police. Lakshmi again sat and waited, looking in every direction in case her son could be seen. As it was Sunday, the sanctuary was very crowded, and a few times she mistakenly thought she saw him only to realize that it was some other boy about the same age.

It was time for the sanctuary to close, but Lakshmi did not want to leave.

"What if he got lost? I must be here when he comes looking for me."

The policeman told her that they had all the particulars and would let her know as soon as the boy was found. Still, even after they closed the gate, Lakshmi waited just outside for another hour – until a police woman approached and told her that she must go home and trust that they would bring the child as soon as he was found.

With the greatest reluctance, Lakshmi got up and went to the bus stop. She purposely missed two buses just in case Ravi found his way. Then with a great heaviness, in the dark of night, she took the last bus back to the city.

Monday morning, she called the ranger station in case they had found her son. Then she called the police and was told to go to the nearest police station and lodge a missing person report. She called her boss to say she would be late for work due to an emergency then walked to the nearest station. Lakshmi waited impatiently in line until someone helped her file the report.

"What can be done? He is only ten years old."

The policeman routinely answered, "We must wait."

Three days had passed and Lakshmi was frantic. She went daily to the police station until the man at the front desk would sigh and look away, not meeting her eyes.

She wrote to Arman and hoped that he still planned to come this week. Thankfully, he did, and, upon seeing him, she collapsed into tears, telling him what had occurred. Arman was silent for a long time, then said, "We shall find him, Lakshmi. We shall find him together."

Arman accompanied her to the station and insisted on seeing a Captain in charge of missing children. They were ushered into a private room and seated across from the authority.

After he listened to the details of the case, and was given the report filed five days earlier, he paused, considering what to say to the mother. Arman spoke to him, breaking the silence.

"Sir, Ravi is a good boy. He would never just disappear on his own. It's not possible."

"I wish I could say something encouraging. I hope there is another explanation, but it is possible that he has been nabbed."

"Nabbed? What does he mean, Arman?"

Arman looked at the police captain, "Sir, do you mean someone may have kidnapped the boy?"

"That is what I mean. Hundreds of children,

even thousands now, are taken and sold, and are transported far from their homes."

"Thousands?" cried Lakshmi, "But why? Taken? Taken where?"

"Mumbai or even further to Thailand or other places."

"For adoption?" asks Lakshmi.

"Not exactly, madam."

"Then...."

"Trafficked."

Arman stood up abruptly," Sir, you mean sex trafficking?"

"I'm afraid so. I could be wrong. The boy just might turn up on his own, but as it's been about a week since he disappeared ...."

In a whisper, Lakshmi uttered, "But he is only ten."

"That's about the age it happens. They are more easily taken and trained."

"Trained?", she replied, her throat dry.

"Look, madam, I will personally look into this case. I know how to reach you, so go home, and know that I will let you know if we find any leads."

Lakshmi couldn't move. Arman gently took her arm, and guided her out the door.

Arman, angry now, "If only I had been there with you, this would never have happened."

Lakshmi looked at her old friend, "No, Arman, it is not your fault. It is mine. I should never have let him go off with that older boy to see the flying fox."

"If it's anyone's fault, Lakshmi, it is the sick people who do such things to children."

Lakshmi told Arman, "Maybe if we go back to the sanctuary, and look for the older boy, and maybe if we could find him, he could tell us where Ravi is?"

"Let's first give a description of that boy to the police and let them try."

And so, they did just that. Arman decided to stay in Chandigarh, and find work and a place near Lakshmi.

"But what of your farm?"

"I had decided to sell it and move to Chandigarh, in any case. There is no hope for small farmers anymore. The big corporations have won."

"That is wise, Arman. I wish my father had done the same. I wouldn't want what happened to him to –" she said, as tears overtook her.

"Don't, don't cry. You are not alone now."

Lakshmi spoke with her boss, who soon found work for Arman, driving the cleaning workers from place to place. His hours were the same as Lakshmi's and Arman would have dinner nightly with the distraught mother.

One year passed and then another, until one night, Arman promised Lakshmi that they would never give up and that one day, Ravi would return. He then went on to say more, taking her hand in his, Arman said, "I think that we should marry,

Lakshmi. You know I have always cared for you, and that if I had not my mother and sister to support, I would have –"

"I know, Arman. But all I can think of is Ravi. What they are doing to him. I cannot bear it."

"Come, let us bear it together, as man and wife."

"I will think on it, Arman. I would like this Sunday to go to the Parvati Puja at the temple." Lakshmi added, "And I would like to go alone."

Arman slowly nodded and reluctantly withdrew his hand.

"I will meditate on this, and next week you shall have my answer."

"That is good," the young man said.

The following Sunday, Lakshmi took the bus to the Chandi Temple and attended the Parvati Puja. She brought fruit and flowers as an offering to the Divine Mother. After the puja, the young priest, returned to her a banana as a prasad (offering), after which she bowed, and then hungrily ate the banana.

She then sat near Ganesha and after the puja to Parvati's son with the head of an elephant, she sat against the wall. Lakshmi remembered telling Ravi how Ganesh had died and been brought back to life again by Lord Shiva. She meditated for an hour with the prayer to find her son again. Seeing a young couple just married in front of Parvati, she accepted this as a sign to marry Arman – especially knowing that he, like her, would never give up looking for Ravi.

Two weeks later, at the Chandi Temple, they were wed. After the puja and blessings from the priests, they returned to Lakshmi's flat, Arman having given up his rented room. It felt natural to have Arman with her. Afterall, she had known him all of her life, and it made her feel more confident that together they would somehow – with the blessing of the Divine Mother – find her son.

Two years now had passed since her son's disappearance, and still Lakshmi would pray nightly to Chandi to find her son. Once a month on Sunday, she would go with Arman to the Chandi Temple and make offerings to both Chandi and to Ganesha for Ravi's return.

And though there remained a hole in her heart, Lakshmi was a good wife to Arman, and she knew she could depend on him. Though sometimes at night, Arman would hear her cry, and even in her sleep, she would whisper, "Where is my treasure? Where is my treasure?"

It was the week of what would have been Ravi's thirteenth birthday, and as she did every year, Lakshmi did a special prayer and puja for her missing son. She was now pregnant with Arman's child, and though they were pleased, nothing could replace her treasure.

It was later than usual when Lakshmi finished washing the tiffin dishes. Feeling the heat, she stepped out for some air and to look up at the sky. Standing there alone, she prayed again to Chandi, the Divine Mother:

"Mother, you know above all others, what it feels like to lose a son. I beg you, Divine Mother of us all, bring him back to me."

The breeze stirred the nearby eucalyptus tree, causing its aroma to fill the air. Lakshmi breathed in the sweet smell and felt the breeze swirl in her long hair. When she opened her eyes, she saw a beggar down the road and thought she would turn and go inside, but something stopped her. She strained her eyes to see more clearly, but the moon was only half full and the darkness reigned. She stood still, gazing at the beggar approaching, then heard the word she had dreamed of hearing for the past three years, "Amma? Amma."

"Could it be possible?" She thought.

"Amma."

"Ravi? Ravi? Is it you?"

Now the one she had thought a beggar stood before her, a ragged, thin boy with a small gold earring in his left ear. Though she was puzzled by the gold earring he wore, she knew beyond doubt that this was her son.

As he stood before her, taller and looking much older than his thirteen years, Lakshmi noticed he still wore the Ganesh pendant she had given him on his first day of school.

"Ravi. Ravi. It is you," as Lakshmi embraced her

son. Ravi, at first drew back, then collapsed into his mother's arms.

Ravi touched the pendant, saying, "I knew that Lord Ganesh would one day help me escape and find my way home. I knew because you always told me that He would answer my prayers."

Lakshmi held her son, and laughing with tears, cried out, "Arman. Arman, come quickly. He has come home. My treasure has come home."

~ 15 ~

# East & West

*It is returning,*
*at last it is coming home to me – my own Self*
*And those parts of it that have long been abroad*
*And scattered among all things and accidents.*

Nietzsche, *Thus Spoke Zarathustra*

"Wake up, Arjun. Brother, wake up," laughed Minoo, who at fifteen, sparkled like an evening star. No wonder her parents named her 'heaven'. Minoo always did what she was told -unlike her older brother, Arjun, who was seventeen. Arjun was a great challenge to his parents – especially to his father, Krishna – as he had begun to question their long-held traditions.

Dr. Krishna Sharma, was a distinguished brahmin whose lineage reached back hundreds of years to a great Sanskrit scholar and sage. Though now a learned professor of history, Krishna was first and last a brahmin, a devoted Vaishnavite – that is, those who consider Vishnu the Supreme Lord as well as his incarnations, the avatars Lord Rama and Lord Krishna.

For countless generations, the family had lived in Mysore in south India. Their habits were regular. Sheela Sharma, wife and mother, would rise early each morning at 6 AM, bathe and dress, then go into the courtyard to pick a few leaves from the sacred tulsi (basil leaf) plant to be used in her daily puja (devotions). Arjun would daily hear his mother singing kirtans to Lord Krishna. After puja, she would make sure that the servant had prepared a breakfast of hot idlily (made from steaming fermented black lentils and rice) with coconut chutney, and steaming hot coffee, at exactly 8 AM. All the family would be present as Sheela served the breakfast. Then Krishna would leave for college, and Arjun and Minoo for their respective schools. Sheela was content in the insulated world of her home which honored the traditions of her parents and grandparents. Yet when she left home and entered the busy, changing world of the twenty-first century, she always felt a certain unease. Things were moving too fast, and if that were not bad enough, they were changing as well – even

her own family. Like her daughter, Minoo, Sheela
had always listened to her parents and knew that they
could be trusted to do what was right and true. They
had arranged her marriage to a suitable brahmin boy,
and the marriage was successful in every way. Before
long, Krishna and she would do the same for Arjun
and later on, Minoo. And the world would turn as it
was meant to do. Still, Sheela was concerned about
Arjun and how he daily challenged his father.

At age fourteen, moving with the times, he had
changed his name from Arjuna to Arjun. At the
same time, in a symbolic act, Arjun stopped wearing
the traditional lungi at home and donned white
trousers. These two demonstrations were the first
of many debates between father and son, and where
once harmony reigned in the Sharma household,
now something Sheela could not understand was
intruding upon their peace. At age sixteen, Arjun
began to question their religious beliefs and practices.
This hurt her husband, and she feared for his health
as the breach between them grew. Despite having a
father who was both a distinguished Sanskrit scholar
as well as a professor of history, Arjun preferred
reading graphic books from America like the *One
Hundred Demons* or *It's a Good Life If You Don't
Weaken.* Arjun would wear jeans and T-shirts he
had ordered online from America – most were in
the same fashion as the ones from the *Hell Boy II*
movies. Arjun was a clever lad and had written and

illustrated his own graphic novel by time he was sixteen. Enamored of all things American, he called it *East and West*. To his delight, it was published in New York and sold well. His father was amazed and even embarrassed that Arjun's first check was more than he earned for six months teaching at the university in Mysore.

Though Arjun was a top student and excelled in science, his passion was not for books but for computer science – a new field for a new age. He had applied to IIT, India's top university for science – both in Delhi and in Hyderabad. Though Hyderabad was considerably nearer to Mysore, Arjun had his heart set on IIT in New Delhi. If he didn't get in to Delhi, Hyderabad would be a backup – but, this he did not tell his parents.

While his parents clung tightly to India's past, Arjun embraced the future as India became more and more westernized. Progress – not tradition – was his calling. Knowledge – not religion – was what he would pursue. Though Arjun loved and admired his father, he knew only that he would not be like him.

Arjun returned home to find Minoo in the garden on the swing. The swing was a replica of ancient swings made of teak wood and hung from the ceiling in the palaces of the rajahs. Often brother and sister would sit and swing together before dinner which provided a special time for them to talk and smell the sweet jasmine vines.

"Brother, why do you always fight with Father?"

"I don't fight with him, Minoo, I sometimes debate, that's all."

"Is it usual to debate with raised voices?"

Arjun looked down and kept swinging.

"Our parents are sad when you fight, Arjun."

"Soon I will be away at college, so they can be happy then."

"Oh, Arjun, that is not what I meant. You know it is not."

Supper awaited, and punctuality was a family virtue. Silence reigned as the family of four enjoyed the tasty dishes. Once they had sat on the floor to eat, but several years earlier, they had begun sitting at a large round table which physically brought the family closer together.

"So, Minoo, what did you learn today at school?" asked Krishna, looking up from his bhindi (okra) and rice and dahl.

"We are studying the Chola period and the great art of the temples."

Krishna smiled, "Good. Good. One of the longest-ruling dynasties in the world's history. There are inscriptions about the Cholas from the 3rd century BC by King Ashoka referring to the Cholas, yet the dynasty may go even further back. A great era in south India."

Krishna turned to his son, "Arjun, what about you? What did you learn today?"

Arjun hesitantly replied, "A new language for computers called Python."

"And of what use is this?"

"Well, sir, it's a programming language for computers. A set of instructions that produce various outputs such as implanting algorithms."

"Python, eh?"

"Yes, sir. Python."

"Be careful it doesn't swallow you up," laughed Krishna.

"It's the future, Father."

"Ah, the future."

As a diversion, Sheela rang the bell for ice cream to be brought. The servant hurried in with it.

Minoo chimed in, "Oh, good. Pistachio! My favorite. And yours, too, right, Arjun?"

Arjun tried to smile, "Yes."

Friday evening was the time to attend the temple puja, and it was a family occasion. This time, however, Arjun, declined to go. His parents looked at him, expectantly, waiting for some explanation. They knew that it was nearing Arjun's graduation, but the final exams were over, and he had done well, remaining at the top of his class. "I am asked to give a speech at the ceremony. And I'm not up to scratch. So, I need to stay and work on the speech."

Krishna turned away, calling, "Come, Minoo, time for temple."

Arjun watched them leave and felt a pain in his chest as though an invisible cord bound him to those three walking away from him. He went to his room and sat at his desk, looking out of the window at the tulsi plant in the center of the courtyard. In India, religion, he thought to himself, is always at the center of everything. And it has been so with this family for centuries. He took out his legal-sized yellow pad, and struggled with what he would say for his valedictorian speech. His theme would be "India's Future".

Introduced as the final speaker, valedictorian Arjun Bhattacharya saw his proud parents and Minoo in the audience. Nervously, Arjun approached the dais and arranged his speech in front of him on the podium. After clearing his throat and pushing back his thick black hair from his eyes, he shyly looked out at the crowd.

"Valedictorian is an Anglicized derivation of the Latin vale *dicere* that means 'to say farewell'. So, what is it that we are saying farewell to – and what are we going forward to? As young Indians in the twenty-first century, perhaps it is time to say farewell to the past and to embrace the future. To progress and not remain in antiquated traditions that can only hold us back. The *Dharma shastras,* written between 300 BC and 200 A.D., are about dharma, the law of our existence, and practices. But even at that time, they were not written as dogma, but rather as practices that would change with time and place. They did not deny humanity its future. Nor must we."

Krishna did not hear what came after this. The father bowed his head, ashamed of his son's words. He fell silent, and did not speak for hours. Sheela was frightened and, at the same time, angry with her son for his hurtful words.

Over supper that evening, no one spoke. A few days later, Arjun opened two letters that would change his life. He had been accepted into the IITs in Hyderabad as well as in New Delhi. The decision was easy: Delhi.

First, Arjun felt he must apologize to his father. He found him in his study, preparing for his next class. For two consecutive years, Krishna had received the teaching excellence award – voted by his students. His father's dharma was to teach and he was good at it. Arjun knew that now he must discover his own dharma and hold firm to whatever that would be.

"Come in."

Arjun took a deep breath then entered the sanctuary of his father's study. The entire room was lined with shelves of books, mostly of history and sacred Hindu texts in Sanskrit as well as various translations – some by his father. But Krishna was not reading any of those. Arjun was surprised to see that his father was reading *Jeeves* by P.G. Wodehouse, a favorite English author and the one author that never failed to make his father laugh.

"*Jeeves*," smiled Arjun, seeing the tattered copy.

"My guilty pleasure. P.G. Wodehouse, the funniest man who ever lived," replied Krishna.

Krishna put his book down, carefully marking the place. He looked up at his son, waiting for him to speak.

"Poppa, I wanted to apologize for the speech. I know it must have upset you, and I am sorry."

"Hundreds of years of wisdom leading to a brahmin denouncing his own religion. Then announcing it to the world. And now you apologize."

"Yes. But I don't retract what I said as it is what I believe."

Krishna shook his head in sadness.

"Father, even the *Dharma Shastras* support me in this."

"What are you saying, Arjuna?"

"Arjun. My name is Arjun. To quote the *Yaksha Prasha*, sloka 114, in the *Dharma Shastras*:

A profusion of arguments! The Smritis differ
    among themselves.
No one's opinion is final or conclusive.
The essence of dharma is hidden and elusive.
The right path is the path followed by great
    men."

"So, you have read the shastras?"

"Of course. They say that 'No one's opinion is

final or conclusive'.".

A slow smile crept across Krishna's face, "Two blind men touching different parts of an elephant and each describes the elephant in a different way."

"Exactly, Appa. Anything one says about Hindu philosophy, the opposite is also true."

"What is it that you actually believe, my son?"

"Appa, it's the twenty-first century."

"What is it that you actually believe?"

"I believe, sir, that we are born to question. That each must find his own path."

"Must you create a new path when you were born to this one?"

"Father, I did not come to argue. I have received a letter from IIT. I am accepted to begin my studies there in computer science."

"Computer Science? The python wins then."

"I must go my own way, Father."

"Well, at least, you will be near home in Hyderabad."

"No sir, I will be in New Delhi."

"Hyderabad turned you down? I don't believe it."

"No sir, both schools accepted me, but …."

"But you choose to go as far away as possible from your family."

"Delhi is a better school. I choose the best because I want to learn."

Krishna tiredly waved his hand, implying for his

son to leave, "You had better tell your mother."

"I am sorry, Appa."

"So, the python wins," repeated Krishna, with a defeated sigh.

Arjun started to speak then thought better of it, and left the room.

The summer seemed long as the silence between father and son expanded like the ocean's horizon. Krishna lost himself in his history books and his translations of sacred Sanskrit texts. Sheela prayed longer each day, asking her god to intercede. Even young Minoo withdrew and smiled less and less. Finally, as the summer ended, all four seemed relieved when it was time for Arjun to depart for Delhi.

The next five years at IIT Delhi confirmed that Arjun had made the right decision for his future. Though some of the students dated in what was now a co-educational institution, Arjun kept his focus entirely on learning. His professors recognized his talent right away for creating new platforms and codes, and with their encouragement, by the time he graduated, there were multiple offers waiting. One offer came from MIT in Cambridge, Massachusetts which excited the boy who had loved all things American since he was twelve. The only thing Arjun dreaded was going home and telling his father and mother that he would be leaving again, and this time to a farther shore.

Krishna had aged these last five years, and though the children did not know, his heart was not as strong as before. He had forbidden his wife to say anything to Arjun and she had reluctantly agreed. A suitable boy had been found for Minoo and, after her graduation the following year, they would wed.

Sheela planned to raise the issue of marriage with her son even though her husband thought it would do no good. She already knew of two suitable brahmin girls and would arrange a tea when he came.

Arjun arrived and, to his family's surprise, was totally changed. He wore black jeans and a black T-shirt with Einstein's image and *E-mc2* imprinted on it.

Minoo laughed and ran up to her brother, "Arjun, you look like an American!"

"And you look all grown up," Arjun affectionately replied to his sister.

Arjun did namaste to his parents, who had waited outside the train station. Though nothing was said, Krishna noted this further departure from tradition. Arjun had decided to wait some days before sharing his news about America. However, on the second day when he discovered that his mother had arranged a tea for him to meet a 'suitable brahmin girl', he decided to break the news earlier.

"America?" whispered his mother.

"Isn't Cambridge in England?" offered Minoo.

"No, Minoo, I mean yes, but this is another Cambridge, in America. Massachusetts."

"America is very costly. How will you manage?" said his father, trying to be practical.

"They have offered me a very generous scholarship, Father. And MIT is the best school for what I want to do."

"And that is?"

"Still computer science, but at a more advanced level. I want to create things that have only been dreamed of before now."

His mother spoke, "Won't you just meet this girl, Arjun? She is very nice."

"There's no point, Mother. I won't be thinking of marriage until I complete my studies."

"And after you do, then what?" queried his father.

"That's at least four years or more away. I can't really say."

"Brother, you will return for my wedding, yes?"

"I shall try, Minoo. I promise."

"Arjun, tomorrow is Friday, will you come to the temple with us, just this time?"

"Yes, Mother. Of course, I will."

Arjun and Krishna took a walk as evening began. At first, no one spoke. Then as the sun set, the father, without looking at him, spoke.

"What is it you believe now? Are you an atheist?"

"No, Poppa. I guess I might be called an agnostic. I do believe that there is a great Force – but no gods."

"I know what an agnostic is, Arjun."

They walked on in silence and said little in the two weeks remaining.

On the last morning, after Sheela had said her prayers, she came to her son's room, politely knocking before entering. She stood as if to ask a favor, and in her hand, she held the sacred ash from her puja to Lord Krishna. After a short pause, Arjun approached her and bowed, allowing his mother to spread the ash on his forehead. Her eyes filled with tears, as did those of her son.

"Time for breakfast. Idlily and coconut chutney still your favorite?"

"Yes, Mother, always will be."

At the airport, his father handed him a new copy of *Jeeves* and also a small hard back copy of the *Bhagavad Gita*.

"*Jeeves* so you won't forget to laugh and the *Gita* because even for an agnostic, it is a wise book."

"Thank you, Father. I promise to read both, often."

Krishna uncharacteristically took his son's head in both hands and placed his own forehead on Arjun's. The women were much moved, yet said nothing. After a long moment, the men looked at one another and saw that love was there.

Minoo hugged her brother, admonishing him, "Don't forget to write. Tell me everything."

"I will."

A final call was heard to board Indian Airlines to Mumbai. Air India then would take him to Boston – on the other side of the world. Arjun looked at his mother who simply placed her hand as a blessing upon his head. Fighting tears, Arjun turned to board the plane. He walked on without lookiing back.

America, at last! Boston, Massachusetts. It was the beginning of the Fall semester, 2012. Arjun was surprised to discover that some of his fellow American students knew about his graphic novel, *East and West* – still selling well in the West. The royalties came in handy, too, as America was very expensive. In the classes, Arjun was in his element. He liked his professors and the work was challenging – yet within his range. One attitude in his favor was that most Indians who immigrated to study or live in America, were well educated. So, there was the assumption that you were clever and bright if you were from India. Already, many brilliant Indians had excelled in Silicon Valley. Outside of his classes, however, was a different story.

Being Indian, he was less assertive than his American peers. Not pushy. Instead, Indians learn to adapt, asking themselves, "Where is the opportunity?" whereas Americans would ask, "What do I want?" then proceed to grab it.

Also, the American guys were dating – something he was ill equipped to do. Even in the twenty-first century, in south India, choosing a bride was mainly left to the parents, and brahmin boys never learned how to court a woman. Arjun decided that he didn't want the distraction anyway – if he wanted to do well. No dating – just learning. He would show his father what he was capable of in his chosen field.

He decided to stay on campus for the December holiday, and his professor permitted him to use the computer labs for research. This proved an excellent opportunity. By his first spring semester, he was in his stride, and the professors that mattered began to notice.

Arjun took up jogging to keep fit, which helped to balance the long hours of sitting at a computer. His roommate, Mike, encouraged him to sign up for the Boston Marathon in April. This meant they must begin now to prep for it. Each morning, he and Mike would jog for an hour before class. In time, Arjun became used to the colder weather, and it made the running even better. He would run to stay warm.

Mike was from Oregon and loved anything outdoors. He was intrigued to watch his roommate do hatha yoga asanas, stretching each morning before running. They got along well, though Mike could not persuade Arjun to date. Being the stronger runner, Mike would always be far ahead of Arjun, but that only meant Arjun had a good marker to improve himself.

Though increasingly challenging, his classes continued to go well, and Arjun knew he had chosen the right field. Before they knew it, it was towards the end of the spring semester, April, and what would be the 117th Boston Marathon was not far ahead. Mike teased Arjun that, on the day, he would wait for him at the finish line. The night before the race, the two young men lay in their separate beds, and talked. Mike invited Arjun to visit Oregon the following summer and go camping. "It's the only way to see Oregon at its best." Arjun reminded his friend that he had to fly to India for his sister's wedding in June. Maybe he could return early and visit Mike before school began in September.

"That's a good plan. I'm counting on it," countered Mike, before both drifted off to sleep.

The next morning, the boys decided wisely not to jog but to wait until the long run facing them. Mike told Arjun that it was the oldest marathon in the world.

"We're making history, Arjun."

They left together as Sean, a security policeman waved them good luck, saying forlornly that he would have to be on duty today of all days. The roommates arrived early in Hopkinton, Massachusetts to settle in and be ready for the marathon where they would run the twenty-six miles to the Back Bay section of Boston. They were like thoroughbreds at the race track, waiting restlessly for the starting gun. "Oh, Arjun, ...."

"Yeah, I know, Mike, you'll wait for me at the finish line."

They laughed as they stretched their legs. "It's good to be young and strong," thought Arjun. He tried to imagine what his parents would think if they saw him now, about to run the Boston Marathon. There was something about America: this feeling that anything is possible.

Three thousand runners – men and women – poised themselves, waiting for the gun to start the race. BANG! And they were off – one huge collective mass. The sun shone despite some light rain, and people cheered as they watched from the sidelines. Time passed swiftly.

Near the finish line, people had already started gathering to watch. Among the crowd were two brothers, originally from the Soviet Union. Both were Muslims. One was twenty-six, and the younger brother, nineteen. The younger brother had recently become an American citizen while his elder brother possessed a green card. They wore large backpacks and walked with purpose, not smiling.

Mike ran like a champion and began to smile as he neared the line. He ran hard and was among the first ten to cross the finish line while Arjun trailed two miles behind. Out of nowhere, amidst the cheers and shouts of the crowd, a huge explosion erupted. Then screams were heard. Then a second explosion. Pandemonium was everywhere. Arjun kept running towards the finish, not knowing what it meant. However, one by one, the runners stopped. They all began to walk. By the time, Arjun reached the finish line, he heard sirens and saw the crowd dispersing in a panic. He stood stark still, wondering what to do. As he looked around, he saw many people lying on the ground, crying for help, some not moving. A policeman herded him away and told him to wait. Another person handed him a bottle of water, and numbly, he drank the water as his head cleared. It was then that he turned back and saw three bodies on the ground. He walked over in case he could help. Standing over a young man with running shorts and a number on his back, Arjun froze. It was Mike's number. It was Mike and he was not moving. A medic tried to pull him away, saying, "He's gone, mate. There's nothing you can do."

Arjun stood firm, looking down at his friend. He spoke aloud to no one in particular, "He said he'd wait for me at the finish line. And, you know, Mike always kept his promise."

Hours later, Arjun was sitting with other students, in the lobby of their dormitory, watching the television news. He had called Oregon, bursting into tears as he informed Mike's parents. Now he mutely listened to the television, trying to fathom what had happened and why.

From the news, Arjun learned that there were three dead, and two hundred and sixty wounded.

Two Russian Muslims, brothers, had set the bombs at the Marathon's finish line in retaliation for wars America had waged upon Muslim countries.

"Why is it always religion?" said Arjun, not caring who heard. Two guys nearby nodded in agreement. The newscaster went on, "A police officer was found dead on the Cambridge campus. Then the Tsarnaev brothers attempted to steal his service weapon. The officer's name is Sean Collins. He was twenty-seven years old."

"Sean?", said Arjun, as he stood up, shocked.

Over the next day, the news went on and on. Both brothers had learned how to build the bomb from the internet. Both brothers had been shot by the police. As one lay wounded, the other brother had mistakenly run over him while trying to drive away. Later that brother was also found dead, having bled to death from his gun wounds.

Arjun returned to his empty room, sat on his bed, and stared at Mike's bed across the room. He sat and stared for hours, not moving. Unaware of how much time had passed, Arjun went to a phone and called his parents in India. He fought the tears, telling them that his friend, Mike, was dead.

"Come home, son," said his father, "Come home."

Arjun said, "Appa, I will call back tomorrow. I must see Mike's parents. They are flying here from Oregon."

After spending time with Mike's parents, he jogged as he had for months before in preparation for the race – only this time, he ran alone.

After breakfast, he called his father to say that as the term would be completed by the end of next month, he would finish the term before returning to India. As promised, Arjun returned, for Minoo's wedding in June, but he was not the same man who had left India only one year before.

Arjun noticed that his father seemed frail and that his shoulders hunched. Krishna had made Sheela promise again not to say anything to the children, so Arjun did not know that his father's heart was rapidly failing. In all other ways, Krishna was the same. It was his last year to teach – before retiring. He went to temple puja every Friday and took his daily walks. One thing had changed though – there were no arguments between father and son. As Minoo and her husband would be living near the parents, Arjun felt it was easier for him to return to Boston and complete his studies. This time, there were no objections.

Come September, Arjun had a new roommate called Stan, from Rhode Island. He was pleasant enough, but Arjun was reluctant to become friends. Mainly, he focused on his work and had been appointed to assist a favorite professor. The professor had told him that he would recommend him both to MIT and to Silicon Valley if he wanted to stay in America.

The year passed and, to no one's surprise, Arjun graduated with honors, and the offers came rolling in. Silicon Valley tempted him, but he liked teaching. MIT offered him a scholarship where he could be an assistant professor and study for his Ph.D. at the same time. What could be better? It was an offer he could not refuse. Meanwhile, he would take the summer off and spend it with his family.

Before leaving for India, he awoke early, jogged for two miles, and thought about Mike. Arjun thought long and hard about the terrible shadow side of modern America that he experienced first-hand. Mass shootings were increasing throughout the States. In fact, the very year of the 2013 Boston Marathon bombing, there were seven other mass killings. And the following year, another seven mass shootings in various corners of America. "With such freedom and prosperity, why so much violence?" Arjun asked himself – and found no answers.

India seemed changed after his two-year absence. Much, of course, was the same as it had been for thousands of years, but westernization was becoming more and more apparent in various ways. Television had invaded and in less than three years, had become widespread permeating the culture. It would soon add Hollywood films and Hollywood television series graphically offering sex and violence in a country that had not even seen actors kiss on the screen before. Videos and DVDs would make it possible to have your own cinema world at home. And the internet that had taught the Muslim brothers to build the bomb that killed and wounded so many in Boston, had spread across the world like a new virus. Of course, there was good in the advancing progress as well – outsourcing provided jobs and income for India, and technology brought other conveniences as well.

Arjun had stopped in Delhi on his way home to visit his friend, Kapil, who was now working at IIT in the computer science department. They had been undergraduates together and it was good to reconnect. Kapil tried to convince Arjun to join the staff at IIT but Arjun confessed that he had already accepted the offer at MIT and would be returning in September to Boston. That said, the two friends had a pleasant evening together reminiscing. Kapil had married and a child was on its way. "Life has a way of pushing forward," thought Arjun.

When he arrived in Mysore, the parents were waiting to greet him, as always. Arjun noticed at once that his father had become even more frail than his last visit, and his mother seemed to have grown older, too, in just the past year. He bowed respectfully to both parents with palms touching.

"Hi, Poppa."

Moved, Krishna nodded, then patted his son's shoulder.

"Where's Minoo?" asked Arjun.

Sheela smiled, "She's expecting – any day now."

Arjun slept more in a week than he had all year. He also ate better thanks to his doting mother and their wonderful brahmin cook. He surprised his parents by joining them for the Friday temple pujas. Arjun seemed now to take comfort in the rituals of his childhood. He visited a very pregnant Minoo, liked her husband, and knew they would make good parents.

Arjun returned home to find the household in tears.

"What is it? What has happened?" He found his mother, head bowed, crying softly, and his father at his desk very still, head back, eyes closed – to open no more.

"No. No, Amma. How is it possible? He's barely sixty."

His mother raised her head and looked at her son through her tears, "I'm sorry, Arjun, he made me promise not to tell you. His heart … not good for a long time. I think he waited for you to come home."

Arjun sank into a chair near the door. 'Why? Why not tell me?"

"He did not want you to worry. He wanted you to focus on your studies. That's what your father wanted."

Arjun put his head in his hands and wept like a small boy.

Minoo, her time due any day now, needed her

mother. As the eldest son – the only son -, it was Arjun's duty to honor his father's wish. Like many devout Hindus, after cremation, Krishna wanted his ashes carried to Varanasi and placed into the sacred River Ganga. Arjun knew that his father faithfully believed that this carried the promise of *moksha* – liberation from the endless cycle of death and rebirth.

Within two days, Arjun was on a plane to Varanasi, carrying his father's ashes. The following day, at dusk, after bathing and clothed in loose-fitting, white Indian traditional attire, Arjun arrived at the Holy Ghats, holding his father's remains. He stood by the river for some while then opened the box, and handful after handful dropped the ashes into the Holy Ganges, reciting the Gayathri mantra in English:

> "OM. O God! Thou art the Giver of Life,
> Remover of pain and sorrow,
> The Bestower of happiness,
> O' Creator of the Universe,
> May we receive thy supreme light,
> May Thou guide our intellect in the right
>     direction.
> OM. OM. OM."

The sun had gone to rest, as had his good father. Arjun sat near the water watching the Ganges serene, changeless, eternal flow. Not far away, a bright-colored kingfisher perched, alert, confident to secure his dinner from the sacred river. Even in this place of death, life could be found and the promise of a future.

He bowed to the river, with palms touching, saying, "Forgive me, Father. I always thought the conflict was between you and me. It wasn't. It was about identity between East and West. Yes, it was about identity. Who was I? Who am I? Indian or westerner? I had felt that India was yesterday – and that America stood for the future. I could not have been more wrong, Poppa. I am not one or the other – but both. Perhaps the real challenge is not in choosing East or West. We must discover how to integrate – not the worst – but the best of both worlds. Then will East be West, and West be East. Then our beliefs shall meet, for then the world will be One."

There exists an ancient link maintained
   through many lives.
You know everything, but you do not
   know yourself.

                          Sri Nisargadatta

# Author's Note

During the pandemic and lockdown, unable to travel to my spiritual home, writing this book of stories brought India to me – every day. I am first grateful to my good friend, Muzaffar Chishti, who introduced me via email to his friend in England, Prabhu Guptara, the publisher of Pippa Rann Books & Media. I am grateful as well to both the publisher and his editors for their editorial suggestions. It takes a village to make a book.

Special thanks to my longtime first readers, Dr. Betty Sue Flowers and Dr. Dianne Skafte for their continued support and invaluable suggestions.

More than anything, I am grateful to my years in India and its life-changing imprint. No matter where I roam, no matter where I live, India remains the inner core.

# Pippa Rann Books & Media

*and*

# Global Resilience Publishing

*imprints of*

# Salt Desert Media Group Ltd., U.K.

*Working in collaboration with international distributors from the whole of the English-speaking world.*

. . . . . . . . . . . . . . . . . . . . . . . . . . . . . . . . . . . . . . . . . .

**Salt Desert Media Group Ltd.** (est. 2019) is a member of the Independent Publishers Guild. At present, the company has two imprints, **Global Resilience Publishing and Pippa Rann Books & Media (PRBM).**

**PRBM** was launched on August the 17th, 2020, with the first title published in Autumn 2020 – Avay Shukla's *PolyTicks, DeMocKrazy & MumboJumbo: Babus, Mantris and Netas (Un)Making Our Nation.* Since then, we have published:

- Sudhakar Menon's *Seeking God, Seeking Moksha*;
- Sudeep Sen's *Anthropocene: Climate Change, Contagion, Consolation* (joint-winner of the Rabindranath Tagore Literature Prize 2021-22);
- Brijraj Singh's *In Arden: A Memoir of Four Years in Shillong, 1974 to 1978*;

- Valson Thampu's *Beyond Religion: Imaging a New Humanity*;
- *Mantras for Positive Ageing*, edited by Padma Shri Dr V. Mohini Giri and Meera Khanna, with a Foreword by H. H. The Dalai Lama.
- *Business Storytelling From Hype to Hack*, by Jyoti Guptara, which has already become an Amazon bestseller,
- *Converse*, an anthology of Indian poetry in English, especially chosen by the international prize-winning poet, Sudeep Sen, which was commissioned by PRBMfor the 75th anniversary of India's independence,
- *The Village Maestro and 100 Other Stories* by Varghese Mathai
- *An Unfinished Search* by Rashmi Narzary

and now, of course,

- *East or West: Stories of India* by Catherine Ann Jones – another book especially commissioned for the 75th anniversary of India's independence.

If there is no further significant disruption by pandemics and wars, PRBM plans to release, in the near future, Anthony P. Stone's *Hindu Astrology: Myths, Symbols and Realities*, as well as the 25th anniversary edition of Vishal Mangalwadi's *India: The Grand Experiment*.

We are always open to winning ideas for books, provided complete manuscripts can be turned in on time.

Please note that Pippa Rann Books & Media focuses entirely and exclusively on publishing material that nurtures, among Indians as well as among others who love India, the values of democracy, justice, liberty, equality, and fraternity.

That means we publish:

- Books and media by **authors of Indian origin**, on any subject that broadly serves the purpose mentioned above.
- Books and media **by non-Indians** on any subject connected with India or with the Indian diaspora, which serves the purpose mentioned above –again, broadly interpreted.

\* \* \*

**By contrast with PRBM, Global Resilience Publishing** began operations in Autumn 2021, with the first publications being released from Summer 2022. As the name suggests, the imprint focuses on subjects such as:

- Climate Change
- The Global Financial System

- Multilateral Governance (e.g., the United Nations)
- Public-Private Partnership
- Leadership around the World
- International System Change
- International Corporate Governance
- Family Firms around the World
- Global Values
- Global Philanthropy
- Commercial Sponsorship
- New Technologies, including AI

Two things make GRP unique as an imprint:

1. Our books take a global perspective (not the perspective of a particular nation);
2. GRP focuses exclusively on such global challenges.

* * *

**Global Resilience Publishing and Pippa Rann Books & Media** are only two of several imprints that are conceived of, and will be launched, God willing, by Salt Desert Media Group Ltd., U. K. The imprints will cover different regions of the globe, different themes, and so on. And if you have an idea for a new imprint that you would like to establish, please get in touch.

Prabhu Guptara, the Publisher of Salt Desert Media Group, says, "For all our imprints, and for the attainment of our incredibly high vision, we need your support. Whatever your gifts and abilities, you are welcome to support us with the most precious gift of your time. The seva you do is not for us but is for the sake of our nation, and for the world as a whole. Please email me with your email, location, and phone contact details on *publisher@pipparannbooks.com*, letting me know what you feel you can do. Could you be an organiser or greeter at our events? Could you ring people on our behalf? Write to people? Write guest blogs or articles? Write a regular column? Do interviews? Help with electronic media, social media, or general marketing? Connect us with people you know who might be willing to help in some way or other?"

He adds, "I am one man, so I do not and cannot keep up with everything that is happening in India, let alone in the world. There are many challenges and numerous opportunities – help me to understand what these are. Pass information on to me that could be useful to me. Put your ideas to me. Any and all insights from you are most welcome, as they will multiply our joint effectiveness. It is only as we work together that we can contribute effectively to changing our nation and our world for the better".

\* \* \*

Join our mailing list to discover books which will inform you on a wide range of topics, and inspire you as well as equip you.

**www.pipparannbooks.com**